The Caging of a Well-Padded Scotswoman

THE BIG
BLUE
JOBBIE

BY YVONNE VINCENT

THE INTRODUCTION

On the 16th March 2020 the Prime Minister advised against non-essential contact. I called my lovely boss to say 'see you when I see you', popped my laptop in my handbag and buggered off to work from home. Soon afterwards, the country went into lockdown.

Towards the end of March, the NHS wrote to say I should spend the next 12 weeks shielding. This meant living in a separate room and social distancing from my family. Some would say that getting rid of old McSnorey to the spare room was a good thing. As I write this intro, it is now June and I actually miss having someone to elbow in the ribs at 3am.

Since 2018, I've written a Facebook blog, Growing Old Disgracefully, keeping people entertained with the nonsense of family life. The idea is that whoever you are or however old you are, you should make the most of the one chance we are given on this earth. This book is a compilation of my blog posts, from my first coronavirus worries in March through to the NHS unleashing me upon the world a few months later. I've added some narrative, some old posts, some of my personal Facebook posts and some unseen bits along the way. The posts were never written with a book in mind but looking back through them they reflect a family journey* through some very strange times. I hope you have plenty of 'oh, me too' moments and a few laughs as you read.

I'd like to thank my husband, daughter, son and my wee hairy boys for everything they have done to keep me safe and sane. Also, for putting up with the nonsense, the loud singing, the inappropriate humour, the leg hair, the tantrums, the day pyjamas, the night pyjamas, the day to night to day oh FFS change them now pyjamas, the endless online shopping, the demands for ice cream and the disappearing Jaffa cakes.

A massive thank you to all the people who read the blog, leave comments and encouraged me to write this book. Some may say it is the wine talking but you have no idea how warm and fuzzy I get when I see strangers from across the world having conversations and sharing their experiences. You make Growing Old Disgracefully such a positive, friendly place. My sister, Anette, deserves a medal for all the putting up with angst and all the putting in of commas. She is my rock and I am hers. Big bow and round of applause to my friends Mark, Dawn, Shona and Andy, who have gone out of their way to help/encourage/nag me into getting off my rather too well-padded lockdown backside and tell my story. Finally, thank you to my friend, Julie, who didn't even blink when I asked her to crochet a blue jobbie for the cover photo.

Keep buggering on my Lovelies x

P.S. you can also find me at www.theweehairyboys.co.uk and on insta as theweehairyboys. I'm somewhere on Twitter too but I've just never gotten into it. Maybe when I'm rich and successful, I'll pay someone to do clever tweets for me.

* I'd just like to apologise for using the word 'journey.' I've annoyed myself. A couple of years ago I wrote a list of 'modern day expressions that make me want to punch someone in the tits'. Journey came in at number two (below 'woke'). I was surprisingly brutal when I wrote, "Journey. Definition - life experience, often used by reality TV 'stars' as an excuse to talk about themselves. Reason why people talking about being on a journey need to be punched - it's not a journey you effing wanker, it's just stuff that happened, learn from it and move on. Exceptions to punching are 1. anyone who has had a really serious illness and 2. anyone who

has been on an actual journey which involved leaving and arriving at real places." 'Deep dive', at number four, did not fare much better. I declared that, "managers using this expression are so full of hot air, their farts are like the inside of your granny's oven on cabbage casserole Tuesday." I really am a delight.

THE CAST

....

Me:

I'm Mrs V. Fan of cake, wine, gin, cocktails, ice cream, chocolate, presents, pyjama days and men in kilts. Ooh, I missed out shiny things - them too. Intermittent fan of exercise, hence the large bottom (I don't need spinning classes to convince me I've got the perfect body - I have wine for that!). I hate bras and I'm prone to losing everything except weight.

I'm slightly obsessed with my own body hair but not enough to regularly shave my legs. In my thirties, I expected weird body stuff to get better but it didn't. It just stayed or got worse. I thought if I plucked that chin hair then eventually it would stop growing. Nope. It invited all its mates round for a party and they went wild. By the time I was forty I'd somehow managed to grow an inch long eyebrow hair without noticing and my bikini line was slowly creeping towards my knees.

Then in my late forties my leg hair started growing very, very slowly. This was weird but convenient. I wish somebody had told me I had this to look forward to. But, maybe because there was less competition, my chin hair flourished. And my cheek hair. And my eyebrows. I started to wonder if they put effing fertiliser in moisturising cream.

At fifty, my hairdresser is saying things like, 'There's quite a lot of grey in there, dear.' Sometime soon, I won't be so much bleaching my hair as dyeing it yellow. I used to have to pick a few dark pubes off my lovely bar of creamy white soap after a shower. Now I'm googling 'where to buy black soap' because I need the

4

bloomin' contrast.   Yet the chin hairs are still clinging on, dark and bristly.

The irony is that, as I get older, my eyesight deteriorates in inverse proportion to the number of chin hairs I grow and it becomes more difficult to catch the buggers. If I ever have a stroke or end up in a place where they don't allow you sharp implements, can someone please remind Mr V to pluck my chin hair?

At this point, I have to quote the wonderful Mrs P, a lady who comments on my posts most days, "Don't worry about the lady garden as you get older...there's less grass to trim.'" In response to a few shocked face emoticons she ploughed on, "It doesn't happen to everyone. Some are just a bit threadbare, so I'm told."

So, that's me. Fat, furry and fifty. Or forty nine and seven quarters, as I prefer to think of it.

Mr V:

Organiser of garages, fixer of broken stuff, wearer of tartan lounge pants and Keeper of the PriV Purse. Likes manly YouTube videos, fancy cameras, spreadsheets, lists, his lawn and Jaffa cakes. His mortal enemy is the mole that keeps ruining his lawn. He hates mess, being told about plans at the last minute and most other human beings. He mistakenly believes that shopping involves deciding to buy something, going to the shop which sells it then going home and he once confided in me, 'I'm worried I might be turning into a woman. I have an urge to go shopping but I don't know what I want to buy.'

Mr V worries about money...a lot. There's a 0.1% chance that this is because I spend it...a lot. He is also quite forgetful, which is very handy when I have to sneak illicit purchases into our lives and convince him we've always had them. But it's very annoying too, because he never remembers appointments or highly important instructions. I once wrote that "my mood was not improved by Mr V who has the brain of a goldfish with dementia. Two conversations and two emails asking him to confirm a date with someone. He goes out for a pint with the chap yesterday, comes home a bit merry, I ask if he checked that date, he denies knowing anything about anything at all, giggles, farts and falls asleep. I eyed the sofa cushions and wondered, 'Is it acceptable to murder one's husband in his sleep or would it be more polite to wait until he's awake?'"

The loveliest thing about Mr V is that what you see is what you get. There's no deviousness, no undercurrent, no subterfuge. He is quite grumpy but can laugh at himself for this. I once became exasperated with him and accused him of being a secret teenager. I told him, 'Here is the evidence. You moan at me to get off my iPad because I'm ignoring you then promptly go on your computer for hours. You assume I'm intensely interested in all your television programmes and manly YouTube videos. You constantly argue with the dogs over your spot on the sofa and expect me to sort it out. You won't eat vegetables. And you give very little information, answering all texts or enquiries about your day with "okay"'. He just snickered and happily agreed that he was indeed a secret teenager.

Cherub 1:

Cherub 1 is my gorgeous daughter who has finally come out of her teens and settled on a pair of eyebrows that don't look like she's sporting a couple of slugs on her forehead. Cherub 1 loves egg sandwiches, socialising, pyjamas and zooming about in her little car. Hates being wrong...oh, and her brother. She and her BFF have a pact that if neither of them are married by the time they're 30 then they'll just marry each other. I am slightly worried about where they're going to live because Cherub 1 has declared her intention to never leave home.

I suspect that in Cherub 1's mind she is tidy and extremely helpful around the house. To her parents' minds, however, she has the odd bout of spring cleaning, where she dumps the unwanted things outside the door of whichever room she happens to be tidying. As this is most often her bedroom, upstairs is in a permanent state of armageddon. If there is one thing I have passed on to my daughter, it is the ability to leave chaos in her wake. She also says she got her stubborn streak from me. I have no idea what she's talking about.

Cherub 2:

Cherub 2 is 18, that difficult age where they're expected to do things for themselves but they still need their parents to do some things for them. I'm really proud of how he's handling things like conversations with banks and setting up his own online shopping accounts (as opposed to hacking mine and thinking I won't notice). Cherub 2 loves his grandparents, the dogs, BBQ sauce, watches and asking questions. Hates his sister - apparently she is a buffoon - and his parents, unless he wants something. He is highly intelligent but absolutely does not know how to work the washing machine, despite having been shown seventy billion times.

Conversations with Cherub 2 frequently make me laugh (often despite myself) because he has such a brilliant take on the world. Here are a couple I wrote down last year:-

Cherub 1 was about to go out.
***Me**: (jokingly hands dog biscuit to Cherub 2) Go and give that to your sister in case she gets hungry and needs a snack*
***Cherub 2**: Here, mum says to give you this*
***Cherub 1**: Eh? Why's she giving me a dog biscuit?*
***Cherub 2**: Because she thinks you're a bitch *drops mic**

***Cherub 2**:*
Does every pope get a new ring?

7

Is the Vatican like its own country inside Rome?
How many people live there?
Are they all religious?
Why do they have cardinals?
What do you need to do to be a cardinal?
Me: *I don't know all the answers. I'm not Catholic*
Cherub 2: *Yes, but you're half Catholic*
Me: *No, I'm not at all Catholic*
Cherub 2: *Well, why did you make me sing hymns then?*
Me: *What are you talking about?*
Cherub 2: *At school we had to sing hymns*
Me: *So, let me get this straight, you've gone through life thinking your mother's a Catholic?*
Cherub 2: *Yes*
Me: *And she told the school to make you sing hymns?*
Cherub 2: *Well if you didn't tell them, who did?!*

Biggles:

Excitable Jack Russell. Age 10 but behaves like a bonkers puppy. Hobbies are barking threateningly at everything and running away, chasing the vacuum cleaner, biting the watering can and standing behind the shed. None of us quite know why behind the shed is his happy place but he goes there when he's happy, sad, scared or just fancies a good old bark. He's terrified of the wind so spends quite a lot of time behind the shed on windy days. Hates surround sound, farts, bathrooms and the mail. Sleeps with Cherub 1 and no alternative will do. Refuses to get up most mornings. Mr V calls Biggles 'FOMO', although he recently confessed that he sometimes gets confused and accidentally calls him 'MOFO.'

Vegas:

Elder statesman Jack Russell. Age 13. Portly, deaf, no teeth and follows me around everywhere. Goes the wrong way at the top of the stairs when he comes to bed with me every night, despite having lived in the same house his entire life. Occasionally gets it right, but carries on walking and can be found in the en-suite wondering where his bed has gone. Hobbies are sleeping, eating and licking his balls. Regards Biggles as a nuisance.

Vegas and Biggles are my wee hairy boys. If only they could talk, then I imagine this is what they'd say:

Biggles:*OMG WALK! WALK! WALK! WALK! WALK! WALK!*
Vegas: *Do we have to take him?*

So, that's us. We all live in a village in the North of England and trundle off round Europe in our camper van once a year. We started camping in France because, when the kids were at school, the cost of a couple of weeks abroad during the school holidays was ridiculous. The camper van gave us the freedom to go where we wanted for as long as we wanted. It also gives me a chance to try out my appalling French. I was very diligent about memorising all the French swear words at school and they later came in handy if I ever needed to use a bad word in front of the children. However, it is never a good idea to forget that you're in France and announce loudly to your husband (and everyone else in the restaurant) that you're off for a grande merde. Sadly, 2020 made holidays rather difficult but, much to Mr V's delight? disgust? divorce? I made up for it by recreating the experience, as you'll read later on.

At some points during this book you may feel sorry for Mr V, mostly for having to put up with me but sometimes because I'm a bit rude about him. I'm not so very awful and if I think I might be crossing the line, then I run things past him first. You'll see later on that I did once make a thoughtless mistake. He still has sour grapes about that (there's a good pun in there, which is totally wasted on you just now). However, he is also the man about whom I wrote this poem and I hope you'll agree that the love shines through.

An Ode To Mr V - A Legend In Tartan Lounge Pants:

At the tender age of 23,
I kissed a lad called Mr V,
As time went by my love increased,
For this vision in a dog haired fleece.

Now here I am age 49,
Far too fond of cake and wine,
And here he is aged 52,
My margarita, my Irn Bru,
He's all my favourite things in one,
Big grumpy, sticky hot cross bun.

Like Guildenstern and Rosencrantz,
In Marks and Spencer underpants,
We're best of pals whose specialty,
Is mischief, mayhem, twattery.

He's holder of the garage key,
The stacker of our life's debris,
The owner of the holy tools,
Protector of the drill from fools,
Like me who try to build flat pack,
But haven't really got the knack.

Last week he cried out, most confused,
'I cannot find my gardening shoes!'

'The dog peed on them. It soaked right in,
I had to put them in the bin.'
His mourning for their loss was keen,
'Could they not go in the washing machine?!'

Old wires, old jars, old parts and screws,
Are kept in case they'll be of use,
He consults for all things DIY,
A manly YouTube video guy,
And if you're lucky, six months later,
He'll fix the leaky radiator!

He's every man, he's him, he's me,
He's us, he's just my Mr V,
No gold or jewels, fine wines or Rembrandts,
Could match the man in tartan lounge pants

Enough of this slushy nonsense!

THE BEGINNING

....

Let us go back to The Beginning. Long before pandemics and viruses made us hide in our houses. Long before technology took over and we learned to ignore each other in favour of small, shiny boxes that let us communicate with people across the world. Let us go back to simpler times....

When God was giving out superpowers, She looked at woman and wondered how She could make her any more perfect. Then She was struck by an idea. 'I know!' She exclaimed, 'I'll give the bit between her boobs the power to detect the tiniest crumb.'

Then She went back to creating man, a project She'd left until last because She needed a nice simple job to do over a glass of heavenly ambrosia. She hadn't actually created weekends yet but this is what gave Her the idea.

By late Saturday night, She'd had a bit too much ambrosia. She looked around Her at all the discarded bits of men on the floor. 'Ooh, hang on a minute,' She said, picking up a funny looking floppy tube from a dusty corner of heaven, 'I seem to have missed a bit.' She wasn't quite sure what to do with the bit, so She just plonked it in the middle of man and shoved a couple of bobbly things underneath for a laugh. She stood back and admired Her work, still wondering what superpower to give men.

On Sunday morning God woke up, created painkillers and thanked Herself for having had the foresight to create water on day 2. She stumbled blearily into Her workshop and surveyed the chaos. In the middle stood man. She was very pleased with man and decided to leave the dangly bits in place because She'd become rather fond of them. However, what was She to do with all the leftovers? She asked man if he had any ideas.

'Make a list of all the bits and we will do something with them. I am not sure what,' said man, giving his dangly bits a good scratch. 'Or I could just throw them away,' suggested God, 'are you any good at putting bins out?' Man looked at Her in horror. Nothing could be thrown away because surely they might need the bits some day! This gave God an idea. She had fallen asleep last night before giving man superpowers (why She'd fallen asleep She didn't know but She was fairly sure it was nothing to do with all the ambrosia). She would give man the powers of hoarding and organising.

She told man to go forth, make lists and stack all the things neatly. As it was a day of rest and She was feeling a bit delicate, She was off to create Netflix and ice cream. Later that day man asked God to come and admire his neatly stacked piles. 'Piles,' thought God, 'That gives me another idea.' But before She could think any further on it, man told her he needed somewhere to put all the useless junk..ahem..carefully curated items they would probably never need.

And that is why God created garages and sheds. And shelves. Then She created tools because man would need to put up the shelves. Then She gave man empty jars and boxes that he could hoard screws and tools in.

She felt a bit sad that She hadn't given woman very much, so She shared the restorative powers of wine and ice cream with her (whilst still recognising that woman was totally capable of putting up her own shelves if she chose to).

Then God sat down, quickly created swearing and said 'FFS, this was supposed to be a day of rest. If anybody bothers Me again there will be a day 8 where I invent wasps!' Sadly, at this point man asked if he could please have some ice cream too.

MARCH

1st March 2020

THIS IS GETTING SERIOUS

I've become a bit obsessed with the coronavirus. Being of middling years and on immunosuppressants, I'm worried. No amount of reassuring posts that I have more chance of dying from many other illnesses (thanks for that!) will make me not worry. When I started to stress about how I'd work from home 'and what if my computer broke and there was no IT department to fix it?!', Mr V said I needed to calm down and reminded me that I could get run over by a bus tomorrow. 'That's precisely why I always wear clean knickers! What if the coronavirus ambulance comes and I have no clean knickers because we've been too ill to do washing?!' I wailed, perfectly reasonable as always and completely forgetting that there are reasons to wear clean knickers other than dire warnings from my mother about ambulance men finding me wearing dirty ones. I'm not quite sure why she thought ambulance men would be removing my knickers anyway. I once went in an ambulance. I wasn't wearing any knickers at all and nobody even checked! Although in my morphine induced haze I probably reassured them that they didn't need to.

Anyway, I digress. I suspect I might be Making A Fuss, but when Mr V announced he was going to attempt to cut his own hair (usually my job) I seriously asked, 'Are you practising in case I get coronavirus?' He also claimed to have cleaned the bathroom. I decided that I could file this under *Miracle* rather than *Preparing for My Death*.

So far, Mr V has managed to prevent me from blowing our life savings on hand gel and antibacterial wipes. A space suit is apparently out of the question - and not just because they don't come in BBBB (big boobs big bottom) size. Yes, I actually Googled *space suits for well-padded ladies* and discovered that

NASA ran out of women's sizes last year. So, we have done the best we can for now - imposed strict hand washing and sneezing into your sleeve rules.

I'm trying to make light of things and laugh at myself for being such a fusspot, but underneath there's a real streak of worry. I'd say I was wearing my heart on my sleeve in this post, but my sleeve is a bit too crispy right now.

***

And so we marched on from day to day. We started obsessively cleaning door handles and shouting at people to wash their hands.

I had The Talk with Cherub 1 and her (then) boyfriend. You know, the one where you tell them that pretty soon they might not be able to get up to all the things they think I don't know they get up to because we'll have to ban visitors to the house. Little did I know that by July I'd be fondly looking back at a time when we had Visitors. A time before blogging, when I wrote:

"We have Visitors for lunch today. This means being creative in the kitchen and looking like we eat a selection of obscure vegetables every day. Whereas we don't even eat normal vegetables every day. Having Visitors also means pretending that my house looks this clean and tidy every day and praying the kids don't say something stupid like, 'Come and see my room,' because I only tidied downstairs and it's like f***ing Armageddon up there. Fortunately, it's a very good and very old friend coming today. He knows I'm not perfect because neither is he. I'm just trying to make his new lady friend like me. I don't know why, but food and clean sinks seem to be the way to go.

16

A few hours later:

Quick update on the Visitor front. They brought wine and chocolate (how well does my friend know me!). I suppose some of it was meant for the other members of my family too but f**k that. I successfully bribed my daughter's boyfriend to help me clean (microwave curry and 2 cans of red bull - bargain!). I bought biscuits, extra chocolatey posh ones, as I thought serving biscuits on a plate might be an impressive thing to do, but then I forgot about them. We went for a walk in the afternoon and Vegas didn't pee in the National Trust dog water bowl this time. All was well until I drank two cocktails, was accidentally rude to a waitress at dinner and talked too much. However, the lovely lady friend talked about coming back, so I think it was okay."

Ah, Visitors. Even if we could have them, pretty soon we couldn't have fed them anyway.

At the beginning of March, panic buying, other than toilet roll and hand gel, hadn't really kicked in yet. I didn't need to buy toilet roll because, thanks to a miscommunication with Mr V in February, we had each bought loads. A few weeks on, I could have sold the lot on eBay and paid off the mortgage. Hooray! Dirty bums all round but the house is finally ours.

Buying 8 litres of antibacterial liquid was a bit bonkers, though. I have no idea what was going through my head. Mind you, it did come in handy when Cherub 2 threw up in the kitchen sink a few months later. Much to his disgust, I made him remove the chunks and gave the whole sink a good douse. When the bottle is empty I may use it to hide the gin from my thieving little angels. As they are cleaning-product-blind, they'll never know.

Mr V is vegetable-blind. I hide his birthday and Christmas presents in the food cupboard or the vegetable drawer in the fridge. As far as he's concerned, if it's not chicken and chips then it doesn't exist. In almost 25 years of marriage he has never stumbled across his presents. I've decided that in my will I shall leave him a handy cupboard guide...and possibly detailed diagrams of how to put on a duvet cover.

Oh well, enough of such nonsense. Onwards and upwards to me stocking up on tinned stuff...

4th March 2020

THE LAST BIG SHOP

Mr V finally lifted the ban and let me go around Costco on my own again. I was banned due to the purchase of "expensive and unnecessary items." I argued that no dining room should be without a couple of 3ft flamingos but apparently ours could.

Whatever, the boot of my car is now full of anti-coronavirus devices. I'm like a doomsday prepper on wheels. If the country grinds to a halt my family will be surviving on a diet of beans, tuna, pasta and paracetamol.

I also bought 8 litres of antibacterial liquid. I'm not sure why, because if one of us gets coronavirus then we'll all get it. Killing every germ in my house probably won't make any difference. But maybe I could douse all visitors in the stuff. I won't make them get naked or anything unseemly (unless they're Jamie Fraser or a sexy Viking, of course) but a good spray at the door should keep the beasties away. I'm 100% sure the Tesco man would appreciate a faceful of Dettol. And Bobb With Two B's from the courier company would probably benefit from it, filthy bugger.

Mr V phoned while I was at Costco to remind me to buy a giant tub of chocolate covered raisins. Well, he said cereal but I'm fairly sure he meant chocolate covered raisins?

Essentially, I have spent lots of money on stuff that we'll hopefully never have to use (except the raisins). I'd have been as well buying the bloody flamingos.

***

There are actually a few reasons why Mr V discourages me from going to Costco without him. Mainly because he doesn't want to declare bankruptcy. However, looking through my old posts, we have had many happy adventures in Costco.

18th October 2018

I think I might be in danger of being barred from Costco for calling a code brown in aisle 20. They really shouldn't leave their walkie talkies lying around unattended.

20th October 2018

Mr V wore his Star Trek trousers yesterday. 'Why Star Trek trousers?' I asked. 'Because they look like trousers from Star Trek,' he replied. Obviously. The upside of this was that I got to say things like, 'Get your card out and pay, Number One. Make it so.' This did not dampen his enthusiasm, possibly because in addition to the Star Trek trousers he has also bought some waterproof trousers. I have yet to figure out why and, if I were to ask, the reason would no doubt be 'so my legs don't get wet.' Again, obviously

Anyway, we jumped into hyperspace (alright, my pithless little car, but a girl can dream) and found ourselves at Costco. Mr V wanted to go there because at any moment there may be a world shortage of chicken nuggets, chips and San Pellegrino and I might make him eat...shudder...vegetables. I wanted to go because they've opened an ice cream parlour and because shopportunities.

As ever, we went in for a few things and came out with a trolley that looked like it was filled by two people with ADHD who had just won Supermarket Sweep. I was particularly taken by the giant Christmas baubles, shouting excitedly 'Oh look! Big balls. I do love big balls!' Sadly, I was not allowed to buy the big balls, as my trove of shiny things hidden in the boot of the pithless car has been discovered and the budget for Christmas decorations has now been re-evaluated to £0. I don't think I could even sneak these in under the radar and claim we've always had them because Mr V would surely notice he had such huge balls.

Before we left Costco we went to the cafe. I resisted the ice cream but somehow a mince pie fell into my mouth. I have no idea how these things keep happening to me. While we were sitting there I got a call from the company that sold me my car. Had I thought about gap insurance? It was my last chance to buy gap insurance and had I seen their fifty gazillion letters and texts about it? I set phasers to stun, put my deflector shields up and politely told the caller to please go away. Mr V said I should have asked the salesman if he had eff off insurance. I said he'd only be going, 'You can't say that to me! I have eff off insurance!' Then we had a lovely conversation about all the times telephone salesmen would make claims on their eff off insurance. Because, as grown ups who own Star Trek trousers and covet big shiny balls, we like to discuss serious topics.

On returning home with a car boot full of sugar, alcohol and chicken nuggets, Mr V decided to try on his waterproof trousers. As he stood there in the living room in his underpants, I looked at him and said, "We really should have got the big balls.'

13th December 2018

I was let loose on my own in Costco yesterday. Do you think 12 bottles of wine, 4 bottles of Prosecco and 3 litres of Baileys is enough for 6 people on Christmas Day? Will it even last until Christmas Day? Ooh, I do love a bit of suspense.

Anyway, turns out that I'm quite capable of a modicum of Costco twattery on my own. Though it's a lot more fun with Mr V.

First I visited the taster stall, where they were giving away free chocolate. I ate one piece and the chocolate gremlins in my frontal lobe staged a protest march straight to my hippocampus carrying large banners which demanded 'MORE CHOCOLATE NOW!' Do you think 12 boxes of chocolates is enough for 6 people on Christmas Day?

Next I went on a Prosecco hunt. Round and round the booze section like the freaky child catcher from Chitty Chitty Bang Bang, nose twitching, Prosecco net at the ready. Not a bottle to be had. So, of course I quizzed a random stranger. My chocolate gremlins patted their wee tummies and assured my alcohol gremlins, 'That woman has a Prosecco gift set thingy in her trolley. She must know where there is Prosecco'. She didn't, but she helpfully pointed me in the direction of the Prosecco gift set thingies and I headed there on the basis that there must be more Prosecco nearby. And there was!! Because my alcohol gremlins are geniuses.

On the way I came across a parked trolley containing a giant teddy, who was looking just a little too relaxed. So, because I'm a grown up who can shop for Costco stuff on her own, I did the adult thing. Looked around for the trolley's owners, quickly popped a bottle of Baileys on top of teddy and took a photo. Then I ran away and texted the photo of drunk teddy to all my friends.

I eventually reached smelly things and slippers. I wanted to buy something for a lovely coworker who can't do alcohol or food this Christmas. I read the word coworker as cow-orker. I'm always quietly amused that I work with cow-orkers. On my bad days, I just remind myself that work is like some sort of bovine Lord of the Rings. So, obviously I thought about buying my cow-orker some body milk. But in the end I backtracked through the store and bought her a poinsettia.

Finally, I paid for everything, worked out how much I'd spent on chocolate, had a quick conference with the chocolate gremlins to agree that this was perfectly reasonable and Mr V would totally agree with this conclusion, nearly died at how much I'd spent on booze, hid some of the booze in the footwell of the back seats in my car where Mr V won't find it and destroyed the receipt. I can't see how I'll ever be found out.

13th April 2019

Mr V and I spent quality time together yesterday. We started in Costco, where I joined the enormous cafe queue while Mr V went to the Mr V section and emptied the freezer of chicken nuggets and chips. Before he toddled off to do the shopping, he asked if I wanted anything. 'Wine please.' He reminded me we were skint, so I bravely said I could live without the wine. Once he'd left, the woman in front of me commented that she couldn't live without the wine. I reassured her that it was okay because I'd just go to the shop later when he wasn't looking.

I queued for about 10 minutes and that short time was all it took for my brain gremlins to dig an escape tunnel for Mr V's lunch order. By the time I got to the front, all I could remember was that chicken and tea were somehow involved. As the brain gremlins sat there smugly high fiving each other for once again effing up my life, I randomly chose something chickeny and hoped for the best. Needless to say, I'd got it wrong and Mr V was not best pleased with me. However, when I checked the trolley and saw that, despite there being no money for wine, he had bought the kids yet another enormous pot of Nutella to join the 546 half eaten pots in the kitchen cupboard, I found myself feeling distinctly sorry not sorry.

25th April 2019

Mr V came shopping yesterday on condition that we go to Costco. His idea of a proper shop is Costco. He tried to tempt me with the offer of a Costco hotdog but dangling a big sausage in front of me was not going to make me bite. I was determined to go to the real, proper shops. So, we compromised and did both.

We had a wander round the bedding section in Costco. Just a word of advice - the bedding section of Costco is not the place to tell your husband that you want to play with the pillows, realise you've just dropped a brilliant innuendo and decide to emphasise it by doing a sexy dance and groping your own boobs. Other shoppers come round the corner and notice. They have no context. They just see a deranged middle aged woman waggling her boobs at a middle aged man who is saying, 'Yes they're very nice pillows but I don't want them.'

2nd May 2019

Mr V did not buy me wine yesterday. That's at least 3 visits to Costco and I have not benefitted. I have put in a complaint to the management but his mother says it's nothing to do with her.

I met up with Mr V for a coffee after work yesterday because I've barely seen him in days. He was queuing up when I arrived and I gave him a big hug then removed bits of lawn from his face (our lawnmower sprays like a drunk at a urinal). As I did my best impression of a mummy monkey grooming her little monkey, the man next to us said he was jealous. Which was quite sweet, but if he was after a kinky monkey threesome in the coffee queue then he was out of luck. I like my men dressed head to toe in Marks and Spencer with a face full of garden.

We did a bit of food shopping afterwards. Armed with a list from our teenagers, which contained cryptic items such as "fizzy type drinks" and "not the things you usually buy, I'm sick of eating the same things", we headed into the store. We didn't get much food shopping done because we are not very good at this adulting *business and decided to crawl into a pallet of coffee beans instead. It smelled heavenly. As I hugged all the beans, Mr V had his face in a bag and announced 'Look I'm sniffing pure Colombian!' It is probably just as well we can't afford a posh bean to cup machine otherwise we'd never leave the house.*

I eventually sent Mr V off to do the shopping while I went to the loo. There's an unwritten rule about ladies loos. The cubicles nearest the door are for peeing. The cubicles at the very end are for pooing. I decided to be rebellious and go for a wee in the second last cubicle even though all the others were free. Then a lady came into the last cubicle. I was daydreaming about cake and, after a few minutes, realised that things were very silent in the cubicle next door. It occurred to me that the lady was waiting for me to leave in case she made...noises. An evil part of me really wanted to stay to see how long she could hold it in. The nice part of me considered doing a big fart to show some solidarity. But the grown up part of me took pity on her and left. Maybe I'm better at adulting than I thought?

Karma did eventually give me a kick up the backside because, by the time I'd finished dithering in the loos, Mr V had done the shopping and "forgotten" to buy wine. Next time I shall give him a list and the top item will be "Mrs V type drinks, the not fizzy ones with alcohol in them."

13th October 2019 *(we had a posh coffee machine by this time, yay!)*

We went to Costco yesterday. We're a tiny bit broke after paying the vet, so we had to buy less rubbish than usual.

I only went along so I could mentally pee on all the Christmas things and mark them as mine. We walked down the Christmas aisle, past the giant Nutcracker soldiery guy standing guard over creepy Santa. Past the big shiny balls and the light up reindeer family. Past the pop up snow man, forlorn in his dusty corner because he is a leftover from last year and nobody wants him now. The trolley was drawn, almost of its own volition, towards a warm glow at the end of the aisle. And there it was. A big glittery lamppost, softly twinkling in the lights of the warehouse, crying out, 'You know you want me!'. I did an extra big imaginary pee on that lamppost, just to make it mine.

Finally, I know what I want for my special 50th birthday. And to think I was going to ask for earrings!

Eventually, I tore myself away from the lamppost and caught up with Mr V, who was doing sensible shopping. He declared he was not buying chocolate cake because he was sick of wiping up chocolate flakes. I declared I wasn't buying Coco Pops because I was sick of cereal boxes being left out. So, we compromised and bought an enormous box of chocolate biscuits. There is surely no way our teenagers can annoy us with chocolate biscuits, we thought. This morning I wiped chocolatey crumbs off the kitchen counter and put six wrappers in the bin.

There was a pause in the alcohol section. Mr V has taken responsibility for buying a present for a member of his family. This is a very unusual state of affairs and he has spent three days asking me which vodka they like. I have spent three days telling him, 'I don't think they like vodka, I think they like beer.' I even asked Lovely Granny yesterday and she didn't think they liked vodka, she thought they liked beer. The corroborating wisdom of Lovely Granny finally convinced Mr V that his relative doesn't like vodka - and the hissy fit of Mrs V finally convinced him to phone his relative's wife and just bloody ask. She said she didn't think he liked vodka but beer would be good. Message finally received.

Just to be clear, Mr V, I like sparkly lampposts.

The coffee aisle was the scene of much debate. Which South American country was going to feed our addiction this time? Eventually we bought a kilo of Colombian and experimented with a bag from Guatemala. Then we stood in the check out queue trying to work out how much our habit costs us every week.

I texted Mr V that I had a surprise for him. There was a long pause, where I could see he was writing a reply, and I pictured him, his little face bright with excitement, desperately hoping that I was going to be dressed as Mrs Santa Claus who'd lost her knickers on the way down the chimney. Then I pictured him remembering who he was dealing with. 'Is it the giant wine glass you saw in Costco?' he texted back. It was actually more shiny things for the Christmas tree but I had to make it mysterious so as to distract him from the money I'd spent.

***

8th March 2020

FAKE NEWS

Had a chat with the kids last night about coronavirus. There are plenty of articles about how to explain coronavirus to younger children but I haven't seen any articles about explaining it to teenagers, who get most of their news from social media. My two thought the coronavirus causes all sorts of things like spasms and fits and madness. I had to tell them, 'No that's your mother when she has just put the dishwasher on and suddenly fifty cups, stored under beds since 2015, mysteriously appear on the kitchen worktop.'

Teenagers face a different set of problems because their lives revolve around going out with friends. Cherub 1 wanted to know if she should still go to Manchester with with her pals next week and would music festivals be cancelled this summer. Cherub 2 was most disappointed to hear that coronavirus doesn't make you headbutt the pavement. I think he'd been quite looking forward to watching his friends batter themselves senseless.

My wee darlings were very surprised to learn that if you get coronavirus, you don't definitely die. We talked about symptoms and the importance of washing your hands and not touching your face. Cherub 2 proudly announced that he is more hygienic than his friends. Given that they're all teenage boys, this is not an achievement. Teenage boys are a seething mess of bodily functions and if my mother had warned me about this, I would never have kissed Nigel the milkman's son after the school disco in 1983.

Anyway, back to my motherly advice. I told the Cherubs to avoid snogging and if they buy expensive tickets then they should get the insurance in case all events are cancelled.

Their worries were:

Will we get it?

Will you die if you get it?

Will Lovely Granny and Grandad get it?

Will we be quarantined?

Will the hospitals run out of beds?

Will the dogs get it?

How can it get passed to dogs?

Oh no, our lovely wee hairy boys, what will we do if they get it?

Is there a vaccine and does it work on dogs?

Will the dogs die?

Should we wash the dogs?

By this point, the wee hairy boys were thinking, 'I have no idea what's going on here but I'm enjoying the big hugs.'

I took the approach of being honest and sensible. Yes, we might get it. No you can't get your inheritance now. Yes, Lovely Granny and Grandad are more at risk of complications if they get it and no, we can't install surveillance cameras in their house to make sure they wash their hands. Yes, hospitals will be under serious pressure. Yes, cities may be quarantined so, yes, life could become OMG BORING. No, I don't think washing the dogs twenty times a day will do anything other than ensure the living room carpet gets a deep clean as two Jack Russells roll about enthusiastically drying themselves off. And, Cherub 2, the answer to your top ten million most important and highly detailed questions about vaccines is 'Google it'.

I think I've managed to dispel some of the rubbish they've picked up. Although, as chief purveyor of Facebook nonsense in our family, I was aware of the irony when I exclaimed incredulously, 'Do you believe every bit of nonsense you read on Facebook?!' To be fair, my nonsense is mostly about the benefits of cake, cocktails and men in kilts which, in these dark times, is surely   what   we   need.

***

Explaining the coronavirus to my 18yo and 20yo was complicated by the fact that they get most of their news from social media. None of us had ever lived through this before, so there was no playbook. I decided to be honest, encourage them to get their news from reliable sources and try not to scare the pants off them. Afterwards, I high fived myself for excellent parenting and got off my tits on wine.

Sometimes I think my kids are past the worst of the teens, only for them to throw a monumental strop about something important like who gets to sit in the front seat of the car. They each think that I never tell the other one off about anything. Here's a post I wrote in January:

"How to drive your teenager. A manual for parents, grandparents and anyone else who thinks they're in charge. Although you shouldn't need a manual because your teenager knows everything.

1. *Your teenager will refuse to start on cold mornings. Or any mornings. To start your teenager, try a combination of threats, promises and junk food. Cash also works.*

2. *To avoid breakdowns, DO NOT offer your teenager vegetables.*

3. *If your teenager is low on fuel, immediately go to your nearest McDonalds filling station.*

4. *Once started, select a gear. If your teenager opens the (full) fridge and roars, 'THERE IS NO FOOD IN THIS HOUSE,' you may wish to select reverse and get out of there.*

5.   *During the drive be prepared to have no control over the music playing. You will find that the volume has only one setting (very loud) and any attempt by you to turn it down will result in it mysteriously rising again within a few seconds. The lyrics will be intended to shock. Channel your inner Stephen Fry and provide a commentary. In a posh, polite voice say things like, 'Oh that's very good. Your father also likes to call me a slutty ho.' This is particularly effective when done in front of their friends. You will find that playlists are moderated in future.*

6.   *Be sure to check your mirrors. They tend to attract rather a lot of pus.*

7.   *A bin is useful for any detritus accrued on the journey. Your teenager will not know what a bin is and you may have to regularly text photographs to remind them. On a similar note, you may keep snacks in the glove compartment but, when hungry, be prepared to find the snacks gone and the empty boxes left behind.*

8.   *Your teenager will frequently tell you that you're a terrible driver and they hate you. Sometimes they will act out to the point where you worry that your teenager is right and all the other drivers must also think you're a dreadful driver. Don't worry about what other drivers think or do. Stick to your lane and keep on trucking. But please be aware that any accidents or other disasters your teenager causes are all your fault. Don't worry if you forget this, your teenager will remind you frequently.*

9.   *To maintain your teenager you will need to look after the bodywork. If male, apply a thick layer of designer sportswear then finish off with a £200 hoodie. If female, apply eyebrow pencil liberally. Possibly too liberally. You will also have to do a regular deep clean. 3 litres of spot and blackhead wash per teenager per day should do the trick. If your teenager is a boy then it is recommended that you follow this up with at least 5 cans of Lynx. You'll know when you've used the*

optimum amount of Lynx because you will no longer be able to breathe.

10. *Your teenage boy may have unexpected emissions from the exhaust pipe. Regular changes of bedding and a box of tissues will help. Remind your teenagers of the importance of covering up the exhaust pipe before parking in lady garages. Nobody wants an unplanned Mini."*

***

10th March 2020

NOT DUVET DAY

I had a lie in this morning. Well I say lie in, it went more like this:

6:00

Mr V: *switches light on and toddles off to the bathroom to clean his willy or whatever he does in there for ages every morning*.

6:15

Cherub 2: Hello are you awake? I'm up. I've let the dog out for a wee. He kept sitting on my head and it woke me up!

Biggles: *sitting on my head* Hello I've been out for a wee, I'm very cold and I need cuddles.

6:30

Cherub 2: *switches light on and toddles off to the bathroom to clean his willy or whatever he does in there for ages every morning*.

6:45

Biggles: There's a draught. The blind moved. Woof. Bad blind. Woof woof. Stop moving. Woof woof woof...

Cherub 2: There's a draught. The blind moved. Biggles is freaked out.

Vegas: *dog shaped lump under blanket at bottom of bed* Is something happening? Maybe I should woof too. Woof. Right, back to sleep now.

7:00

Mr V: I thought you were getting up early for work. Are you getting up? You should get up now.

Me: I am TRYING to have a lie in *much effing and jeffing*

7:15

Vegas: Hello, I know I said I was going back to sleep but I'd like to pee now. I'll wait for you by the back door.

Biggles: Oh me too, me too! I haven't been outside for ages and something might be going on out there that I ought to know about! I'll wait for you by the back door.

7:20

Biggles and Vegas: Hello, we've been waiting by the back door for a very long time and you didn't come. Hurry hurry hurry!!

7:30

Me: *stomping round the back garden in my dressing gown and Cherub 2's sandals, trying not to inadvertently flash George next door lest he have another stroke* FFS Vegas where are you?

At this point, I contemplated telling my family that I was self-isolating in the bedroom and if they got within one metre of the door I'd sneeze on them. In the end I went through knicker mountain in the laundry room, located a pair of undercrackers that Biggles had failed to render crotchless and, rather grumpily, got dressed.

11th March 2020

SHENANIGANS TIME ZONES

I'm having a bout of insomnia at the moment. I tried counting men in kilts, but not even that did the trick!

My insomnia has plagued me all my life. It drives Mr V crazy (and not in a sexy shenanigans way, as I found out). I tell him, 'if you find it annoying, how do you think I feel?'

So, when Mr V found me (and my hairy disciple, Vegas) in the kitchen at 2am, mum-dancing to ABBA, he was not surprised.

'Am I your wee dancing queen?' I asked, trying to reel him in on an imaginary rope.

'No, you're my giant pain in the arse,' he said, resisting all my wifely hotness. 'Do you want a cup of cocoa?'

'Yes please. The insomnia instructions say to get up and start your routine again. I'm on 10am Saturdays, twerking to Waterloo and cleaning the kitchen,' I announced, shaking my bum at him. Yet he would not be tempted by the sight of my big bottom, firmly encased in a pink, fluffy dressing gown, waggling wildly in his direction. I fear we have reached a stage in life where we might be on different shenanigans clocks. Where rolling your eyes and handing your wife a cup of cocoa is preferable to sexy disco. I was starting to wonder if I should fast forward my routine to Saturday night, a bottle of Sauvignon Blanc and me snoring like a baby elephant on the sofa. That's usually when he's up for shenanigans and I'm up for him buggering off so I can sleep. Far preferable to me being wide awake and perky and him wishing I would bugger off.

Anyway, we agreed I could fast forward my routine to 7pm on a Sunday and he sat with me on the sofa watching Countryfile, until I pronounced it so boring that I was going to bed now, thank you very much.

Life may be full of problems but there's a lot to be said for someone who is there for you, no matter how inconvenient you are.

***

By mid-March, I was feeling increasingly unsafe going to work and being around other people. I knew that taking immunosuppressants meant I could become seriously ill if I got the virus. The lovely range of snacks in my desk drawer had been replaced with hand gel and antibacterial wipes. I was slowly perfecting the art of pulling one wipe out of the packet instead of a block of six. Hashtag winning at life.

I asked my doctor what other steps I should take to keep myself safe, but the poor bugger just sat there looking knackered and confessed he didn't have any more information than me. His only advice was that if I caught coronavirus, please stay at home and FFS don't come to the GP practice. He didn't actually swear, but we both knew he wished he could.

I made sure I got my flu jab and the nurse stayed late to give me a pneumonia jab. The nurse is called Lisa and she's absolutely lovely. Every month she pricks me full of holes for a blood test and we both get really excited if she finds a vein on the first go. When she was getting the pneumonia jab out of the fridge, I couldn't help asking if she ever stashed a bottle of wine in there. She said no, but we both knew she wished she could.

The news was full of doom and gloom (and infected people wandering into their local GP practices). We were watching with horror as bodies piled up in Italy and people sang from balconies. I found three bottles of vinegar in the cupboard and concluded that Mr V was stockpiling in case he had to live on a diet of oven chips. Also, it was quite unsettling to discover that he did, after all, know we had a food cupboard. Perhaps I could now risk introducing him to the vegetable drawer in the fridge without him having an aneurism?

***

14th March 2020

ALWAYS KEEP YOUR GLASS HALF FULL

I've found it difficult to be happy this week, as every day just brings further blows. So, I've tried to focus on the little things that make me smile. Here are some of them:

- Overhearing a colleague telling someone, 'Well, I used to wash my hands before it became trendy.'

- Being particularly proud of my morning hair. I appeared to have sprouted a mohican. Selfie duly taken and texted to Mr V. It's been a while since I popped the big question - 'Dontcha wish your girlfriend was hot like me?'

- Becoming momentarily outraged because 'A nice lady used to leave bottles of posh hand wash in the ladies loos at work. Now I have to use the boring stuff that work provide!' Then realising I was being a bit of a shallow twat.

- A friend lamenting the dire choice of Mother's Day gifts in the shops:

Friend: I'm in ASDA and the Mother's Day gifts are depressing. It's all pyjamas and dressing gowns and trays for breakfast in bed. What mum has time for that shit and who's going to make it for her?!

Me (wondering if I should confess to the inordinate amount of time I spend in my pyjamas): I've asked for a wine rack. More useful.

- A conversation about whether we'll all be told to work from home ending in general agreement that, when things return to normal, they'll have to chisel me out of my pyjamas.

- Choking slightly on something and being unable to stop coughing afterwards. Then feeling everyone's eyes on me.

- Realising I had just answered the door and had a whole conversation with the Amazon man, completely forgetting I was still sporting my morning mohican.

16th March 2020

THE DAY GRANNY DIDN'T BREAK THE INTERNET

The coronavirus (or Covid-19 if you're down with the kids) has made many differences to our lives. None of my family is self-isolating yet, but already changes to our behaviour are creeping in.

I rang Lovely Granny yesterday because I want to visit, but I don't want to visit, if you know what I mean. LG was feeling overwhelmed by the media reports and not sure what she and grandad should be doing. 'Wash your hands and make sure anyone who visits washes their hands as soon as they arrive. Wipe your door handles and bathroom regularly,' I told her.

I'm quite relieved that over the years Lovely Granny has tried to use the internet for things. Despite her best efforts to break it, the internet has survived and I'm hugely proud of her for figuring out how to order groceries. I realise that what comes instinctively to me is a massive challenge for LG. However, not everyone is as dogged in their determination to conquer things digital and lots of older people are potentially facing months of self-isolation, cut off from the world.

With this in mind, I emailed the local council offering my help if they are organising people to do deliveries and I joined the village Facebook page in case there is anything going on locally I can pitch in with.

I'm not telling you this to get comments saying 'how kind'. I mean we've already established in previous posts that I'm a delight. I'm just saying that it was brought home to me yesterday that not all people have the window on the world that the internet brings and, despite all this talk of social distancing, if there was ever a time to get involved with our communities it is now. And remember, for every selfish person out there hoarding toilet roll, there are probably 10 decent people asking, 'What can we do to help?' The world hasn't really gone to hell in a hand basket just because the media says so. Or if it has, then I expect Satan to be standing at the gates of Hell, shouting at people to wash their hands before they come in.

***

16th March and Britain was on tenterhooks. Big announcement expected from Boris. Do we all have to come in to work tomorrow? Possibly no and possibly yes. Hurrah? 'Avoid non essential travel,' was the advice. My employers were brilliant and quickly made the arrangements for everyone to work from home. In fact, they were brilliant throughout. I was relieved to finally be able to hide from the virus, but a tad worried that I didn't possess enough pyjamas for all the pyjama days ahead. Little did I know just how many pyjama days there would turn out to be! Also, I didn't realise that the day I left the office on 16th March would be the last day I properly ventured beyond the confines of home for 4 months. I did get released once a month to go for a blood test and got very excited about turning right. There was no traffic! Turning right was easy!

***

17th March 2020

I HATE WORKING FROM HOME

Day 4003 of working from home and being a person at risk. Well, day 1, but I prefer being in the office, so I've had enough already.

The morning commute was a nightmare. Nearly tripped over a dog on my way to the dining room in my pyjamas, laptop tucked under one arm and hot coffee sloshing from cup to feet. Does this count as an accident at work? Should I fill out many many forms to report it? Should I set out a yellow warning sign, like the cleaners do when someone spills something at work? I actually own one. Except I bought it as a joke for Mr V and it says, 'Do not enter, deeply satisfying poo in progress.' Maybe best not to put that in front of the dining room door.

Here is how my day went:

07:30

Clear dining room of clothes mountain. Decide that if my darling Cherubs continue to use the dining room chairs to dry clothes then their chances of surviving this pandemic will be drastically reduced.

8.30

Have sent approximately 5000 texts, made 700 phone calls and sent 3 million emails, just to reassure myself that there is a world outside. Think I might be lonely.

8.35

Have promised my boss I'll stop being a nuisance for the rest of the day.

9.00

Contemplate getting changed out of my pyjamas. Manage to distract myself from this dreadful thought with chocolate biscuits.

10.00

Work computer system screams, 'There are too many people working from home!' and promptly dies. There is nothing else for it. I will have to spend the rest of the morning being a nuisance. This must be why work gave me an iPhone.

12.30

The network comes to life because all the home workers are making lunch. I can stop attempting to read tiny documents on my phone. Have lost my proper reading glasses. My varifocals have only a slim 'reading glasses' strip along the bottom, which means I have to prop them up to read things. Remove chewing gum from bridge of nose and get laptop going.

Cherub 1 appears with friend. They make stinky sandwiches and are deaf to my protests that stinky food is not allowed in the workplace.

15.15

Work computer system rolls over and dies again. Take a break and head for the living room, disinfecting door knobs as I go (am top multi-tasker!). Mr V very happy because he has created some notebooks to sell on Amazon. Check news. Amazon has halted selling non essential items. This is completely understandable and not a problem. Break news to Mr V. 'Well that's your Mother's Day present scuppered. I only ordered it this morning,' he tells me. Decide Amazon is being completely unreasonable and scuttle off to check if I can still use Prime Now as my personal Ben and Jerry's delivery service.

15.45 to 17.00

Working, with short bursts of checking BBC news (or coronawatching, as I call it). Ring boss to say thanks because she's had a crappy day trying to work out what to do about coronavirus things, IT issues and me being a nuisance. We agree that, going forward, I will have to change out of my pyjamas in case someone video calls me. I suppose I'll have to brush my hair too. Jeez, work is almost as unreasonable as Amazon!

Finish work. Everyone in family asks what's for dinner. Everyone in family most confused because nobody has put the dishwasher on today. Everyone in family has had the day off, except for me. Everyone in family decides to socially distance themselves from me until I have stopped shouting, 'Bugger off!' at them.

18th March 2020

THE INVASION OF THE COCKWOMBLES

Day 2 of working from home.

8.30

Am outraged. Nobody has noticed that I've put non-pyjamas on! Not one video call! Due to have a conference call at 10:30. Am tempted to switch my laptop camera on so that everyone can see I'm dressed.

10.00

IT connection says, 'Eff you,' to all the home workers and storms off in a huff until 4pm. Watch video of penguins on a field trip to an aquarium. Feel mightily cheered up.

10.30

Attempt to join conference call. App keeps kicking me out. Everyone is texting to find out why I haven't joined meeting. Am in panic mode. Dentist phones about Cherub 2's appointment. Bugger off dentist, I don't care if Cherub 2 needs a full set of falsies, do you not know I am trying to join a meeting?! Take a deep breath and think of cute penguins. Start again. App works, meeting attended. Did not turn on camera - hair a mess, have run out of moisturiser and appear to be slowly turning into Ann Widdecombe.

12.30

Call dentist back. Apologise for being grumpy. Tell Cherub 2 his dentist appointment is cancelled. Cherub 2 manages to conceal his disappointment behind a wide smile and a pile of sugary snacks.

13.00

WhatsApp chat with team, who are also working from home. We reminisce about the good old days when we shared a biscuit tin and Barry came in wearing a hat because he tried to shave his head when he was drunk, i.e. Monday.

13.30

Take a break and clean door knobs on way to living room. Family is getting used to my daily (and hilarious) 'Clean knobs!' announcement.

16.40

Stop work to watch Boris doing his daily announcement. Sadly, he's not allowed to do knob jokes.

17.00

Check Facebook. People are up in arms about government advice to only burn dry wood in stoves, rather than be allowed to exercise their right to create toxic air pollutants. Half of them (who we shall call the cockwombles) are spouting nonsense, convinced it's a conspiracy to stop folk using stoves, and the other half (who we shall call the sensible people) are earnestly posting links to scientific evidence. The cockwombles apparently know better than any darn scientist and give many reasons as to why they should be allowed to pollute the air, all of which can be summed up as "because I'm more important than other people". I ask if they're having a *heated* debate. Everyone ignores me. I decide that the cockwombles are probably the people who are stripping our supermarket shelves bare.

A couple of months ago, I wondered how we'd cope in the event of a zombie apocalypse. Not at all well, it seems. I can't quite get rid of the image of a world devoid of human life, except for a few remaining cockwombles huddled around a wood burning stove, debating whether to burn that last toilet roll.

***

By this stage, hoarding and panic-buying were well underway. At one point, we went three days without bread. Some would say that this was a good thing for my hips. Some would point out that this was a #firstworldproblem. Yes, but it was still a pain in my very large arse. I'd bought a few days worth of tinned stuff, nuts, dried fruit and long life milk earlier in the month, just in case it became impossible to shop. I was buying with basic nutrition in mind. My family would probably wonder why I was punishing them with these vitamins.

Everyone was vaguely doing social distancing and avoiding contact with strangers. So, it was very odd when two people knocked on our door. Cherub 1 answered and reported back only that they were carrying clipboards, didn't say who they were and told her they couldn't talk to her. It all seemed very strange and I agonised over what to do. Anyway, the long and short of it is that I called the police on Amnesty International. Straight to hell Mrs V, do not collect £200, do not pass Go.

Facebook was full of quizzes and games, as more people spent time at home. I completed only one - the one where you name a bunch of things using the first letter of your surname. Some may say it was only so I could write 'body part - vagina', but I couldn't possibly comment. Later on, social media became choked with people sharing album covers, pictures of special moments, pictures of being a mum etc etc for 10 days. I probably offended all my friends by declaring my intention to ask Facebook for a 'snooze for 10 days' option.

I was nominated twice to do the 10 days of albums which influenced you. I posted the same one as I did the first time I was nominated a couple of years ago, Russ Abbot's Madhouse. Fond memories of a caravanning holiday in the 1980s with my parents. It was the only tape they had and the cheeky chappie with his novelty songs was on repeat for three weeks. Three effing weeks. It influenced me to buy a proper album full of proper music, Now That's What I Call Music! II, which led to a lifelong love of Queen Annie of Lennox. Who can resist a feisty bit of 'Sisters Are Doing It For Themselves' of a morning?

***

21st March 2020

THE SHELVES ARE BARE

I'm not sure how I'm going to get through the next few months if my family are in charge of shopping.

I sent Cherub 1 to the shop for bread yesterday and she came home with cheesecake. Mr V is delighted because he no longer has someone to strong-arm him into the vegetable section in Tesco. He can march straight to oven chips without so much as a cucumber in his path. Nevertheless, I'm hopeful that at some point all the hoarders and panic-buyers will have bought everything they "need", things will calm down and I will once more be able to order a delivery and force vitamins upon my family. In the meantime, I'll consider this an ideal opportunity for my family to howl, 'Stop poisoning us with this food that didn't come from a packet,' as I make my own bread and create weird soup from anything I can find in the freezer. Broccoli and burger anyone?

22nd March 2020

HAPPY LOVED ONES DAY

Happy Mother's Day to all the mums in the UK and other countries who celebrate it today (just adding that in there to be inclusive and not confuse all the Americans, who would otherwise think they'd forgotten and panic buy some flowers. None of us wants to see an item on Fox News explaining that the reason the shelves in New York have been stripped bare of flowers is not linked to coronavirus, but is the result of a rumour started by a well-padded Scotswoman sitting in her kitchen in pyjamas, wondering why no bugger has bothered to get up and make her breakfast in bed as a reward for being such a delight).

Mr V wished me happy Mother's Day yesterday and was most disappointed to learn that he was a day early and had to go to work. He followed this up with, 'Darn it, this was the year that I was going to take you out somewhere special and make a really big fuss of you but what with everywhere being shut...' I peered at him over the top of my glasses and said, matter of factly, 'No you weren't.' As I write, I'm still waiting for him to get up, so I can see if he actually bought me the wine rack I suggested or if he's gone with something he likes. Normally I'd bet on the latter, but an extra crate of wine appeared after his last Costco run, so fingers crossed.

It is a more poignant Mother's Day this year as so many families around the world can't spend it together. My heart usually sinks a little when I see the "Happy Mother's Day but so sorry for those who don't have a mum" messages on Facebook because, while I appreciate the thoughtfulness and sensitivity, I hate to think that me not having my mother any more would make someone else pause in shouting loud and proud about their's. I usually just pop a photo of my lovely mum onto Facebook and raise a glass to her. However, this year is different because we are all going through such a rotten time together. I realise that this year people may feel even more sensitive around Mother's Day, but I do hope that, if nothing else, this virus gives us all the perspective to cherish our nearest and dearest that little bit more, whatever role they have in our lives. Perhaps in future there will be a day when the world remembers how this pandemic drove us together even when we had to stay apart.

So, I will raise my morning cuppa and say Happy Loved Ones Day to you, wherever you are. Mind you, I still want that wine rack.

23rd March 2020

THE ONE WHERE WE CHEERED OURSELVES UP

Is there a special place you can put teenagers to self isolate? Asking for a friend. I found myself having a rip roaring row with Cherub 2 yesterday and I realised it was because we were both anxious and scared. From his perspective, being under house arrest with your parents is torture and everything they say and do is just further evidence of them being complete [insert favourite swear words here]. From my perspective he won the numpty cup for doing something stupid. Really, we were both just scared and ground down by the endless avalanche of depressing news.

Well I refuse to be beaten by the bug. The bug can bugger right off and when it gets there, it can bugger off some more. Mr V has offered to go round all the supermarkets to find bread, which we haven't had for days. It's just as well I have a bag of strong flour which, if you squint and blur your eyes a bit, is definitely possibly not past it's sell-by date. But I'm quite looking forward to a sandwich that's vaguely edible.

As we sat on the sofa last night (four of us, two of whom were small, furry and blissfully unaware of social distancing), I recalled that one of my favourite ever posts was where everyone shared a picture of their pets. Cute animals never fail to cheer you up. So, today I thought we could share our pet pics and put a smile on everyone's faces.

I'll start you off. Here's Biggles creating a dilemma for his human last night. Mr V wanted to go to the loo, but didn't have the heart to move his arm. How long could Mr V hold in a wee?

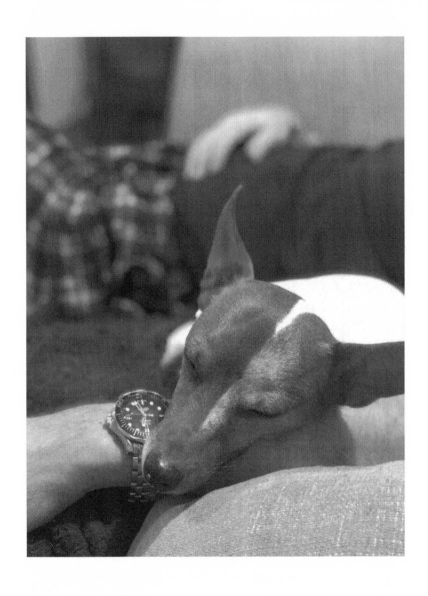

Hundreds of people shared pictures of their pets that day. The next day I almost posted that I'd spent the day before clicking the love button. Until Mr V pointed out that I could be a bit of a wanker at times, but there was no need to shout it to the world.

24th March 2020

WHEN LIFE GIVES YOU LEMONS...

Mr V went out foraging yesterday. With a list. The problem with Mr V being in charge of groceries is that he doesn't do fruit and veg. I could write a list comprising bananas, apples and pears and he'd come home with six chocolate bars and a courgette. Yesterday's offering was 3 lemons.

'Erm...what were you planning to do with 3 lemons?' I asked.

'They're good for your immune system,' said my wise husband. 'You can cut them up and put them in boiling water.'

I was quite surprised. We are talking about the man who objected to my healthy eating fad on the basis that his diet was already healthy because he ate lots of chicken, thank you very much. The fact that each piece of chicken came with a generous portion of fries somehow slipped his mind.

Fast forward a few hours and Mr V went to make a lemon infusion. I heard the fridge door slam and a confused Mr V appeared in the living room.

'I thought I bought 3 lemons!' he exclaimed.

'Yes but you also bought tonic water,' I said, rattling my glass of G&T complete with ice and slice, at him.

Somehow I will struggle through this lockdown.

***

Here's the one that I never posted. I must have been having an apocalyptic day. Mr V said it made me sound like I used the dark web and drank too much. All a bit doom and gloom. I'd like to assure you, dear readers, that I drink at most two bottles of wine a week (one, if my doctor is reading this) and all my drugs come from Boots the Chemist. To be honest, I think he was a bit shocked that I know what goes on on the dark web, but I assured him that my days of queuing at the village post office to mail a cheeky AK47 were far behind me.

25th March 2020

CHEER UP LOVE, IT MIGHT NEVER HAPPEN

Call me Nostradamus, but I predict that by May the most common phrase heard in tele-conferences across the land will be, 'Good morning, oops I've spilt my wine.'

Since the closure of the Apple stores the dark web, once home to drug dealers and weapons sellers, has been overrun by the now illicit trade in iPhone chargers. By June half the women in Britain are howling, 'I didn't know I had THIS MUCH grey,' as they frantically try to buy a packet of L'Oréal on the black market.

Boris doesn't know it yet but he's going to have to form a chisel squad to get us out of our pyjamas. All these wonderful people he's marshalling to deliver food and medicine will have to be kept on, to force hundreds of thousands of functioning alcoholics to once more wear a bra. One summer morning we will emerge, blinking into the sunlight, and the air will be rent with the sound of a million car batteries spluttering and dying. And possibly an awful lot of swearing at whoever forgot to keep them charged.

But everyone will have very organised tins cupboards. So, every cloud...

We have a long and terrible road ahead but it won't always be like this. I pray we all make it to the joyful chaos on the other side. Chin up my Lovelies and stay safe.

***

26th March 2020

IT'S BEGINNING TO FEEL A LOT LIKE CHRISTMAS

Day 6023 of working from home. I've taken to wearing my special work headphones and pretending to be in a meeting so that nobody will talk to me. When I'm in a meeting I have to go on mute, just in case the wee hairy boys spot a leaf invading the end of the drive and bark themselves hoarse. So, I spend every meeting on tenterhooks in case someone asks me a question and I have to fumble around to click unmute, thereby causing an awkward pause. Yesterday I was mid flow, imparting Very Important Information, when Cherub 1 swept through the room with the vacuum cleaner.

I've also discovered that 5pm is the new wine o'clock. Does this count as day drinking? I've always aspired to day drinking during the week. It seems so decadent that I feel it's something I ought to do.

I have asked Mr V to get the Christmas tree out of the garage so we can have secondy Christmas. I figure that I've lost track of what day it is and I'm drinking more than usual, so I may as well get some presents out of it. Mr V is not nearly as keen as me on secondy Christmas, mainly because my plans mean disrupting the feng shui of his garage.

In between meetings I tried making Mr V a face mask with a bra. Sadly, Mr V has a very small head and I have very large boobs, so it was more of a head basket. Plus it was a front fastener and he nearly took an ear off on the catch.

As I write, he is grumbling about something. But it's okay, with these big headphones on I can't hear a thing.

27th March 2020

THE CLAP

Day 7046 of working from home.

All the chocolate raisins have accidentally fallen into my mouth. This accident seemingly took place over 4 days and approximately 5000 online meetings. I have no recollection of it whatsoever.

I have stopped looking at the BBC news. Too much doom and gloom. Instead I'm watching the local news, where the reporter is standing with a microphone on a 6ft pole, shouting questions at elderly people outside Tesco. 'Have you queued for long Mrs Peabody?' Mrs Peabody has forgotten to turn her hearing aid up and thinks he's asking her to sing a rude song. She obliges with a filthy rendition of Mary Mary. And, just like that, it's back to the studio.

Cherub 1 came outside with me last night to do the national clap for carers. She was hesitant because she thought nobody on our street would do it. I told her I didn't care and I was going to clap, whoop and holler, even if I was the only person out there. Apparently this wasn't an incentive to join me, but I did eventually persuade her. We started clapping, I duly let out a big loud whoop, Cherub 1 died a little inside and told me to pleeeease shut up, then we heard everyone else around the village begin to clap. So, I whooped some more. As people started to feel less like prize prats, the clapping got louder and the pots and pans were clanged. It was honestly one of the most uplifting things I've ever heard. For a few minutes, millions of people across the country, separated for so many days, were part of something together.

In all my ramblings about working from home, I'm conscious that others don't have that choice.

Thank you to the NHS workers. I can't begin to imagine the strain you're under right now, the fear that you'll bring the virus home to your families and the courage it takes to keep going back to work day after day. Thank you to all the carers, the teachers, the supermarket workers, the farmers, the drivers, Mr V and his colleagues, the pharmacists, the police officers, the firefighters, the armed forces personnel and the myriad of other key workers and volunteers who are keeping us safe, fed and looked after. Thank you.

28th March 2020

SHIELDS UP - COVID CORNER IS BORN

Day 8412 of working from home fell apart a little when I opened the post.

Dear Mrs V,

We know you like cuddles and presents and tasting other people's cocktails just in case they're nicer than yours but for the next 12 weeks you're to have no face to face contact with anyone. Now lock yourself in a quiet room with a bottle of gin, binge watch Netflix and don't come out til June.

Yours sincerely,

All the amazing people at the NHS xxx

At least I think that's what the letter said. I panic texted a lovely lady I know who took time out from doctoring proper ill people to send me useful links and calm me down. Then I gave the letter to Mr V who said sensible things like, 'It says you have to have your own bathroom, but it can't be the en-suite because how then will we continue the family tradition of waking you up at stupid o'clock by trooping in and out of the bathroom, switching lights on and off and loudly complaining that we can't sleep?' Or at least I think that's what he said. There may have been a trifling concern about needing to use the shower. Cherub 2's main worry was, 'Does this mean I can't do my poos in your bathroom?' I pointed out that we are fortunate enough to have a family bathroom, a downstairs loo and, if he's desperate, an effing garden.

Anyway, I am one of the unlucky few who are at high risk and have to distance even from the people we live with. It's called shielding. I've commandeered the dining room, bedroom and en-suite. And the garden, but only on sunny days. I've made a little nest for myself in the dining room and christened it, probably very inappropriately, Covid Corner.

I checked with all my Facebook friends whether the no face to face contact instructions apply to the wee hairy boys. I can cope with not being allowed to sleep with Mr V, but if I had to consign Vegas to the spare room I'd be devastated. I don't sleep with Biggles because, despite being terrified of farts, he cuddles into your bum. I'm not a fan of being woken up twenty times a night by a terrified Jack Russell shooting out from under the duvet. I'm fifty, night time is my deflation time.

Mr V was feeling quite sorry for me, all alone in Covid Corner, until I pointed out I'd taken the one room in the house where all the alcohol is stored. I currently have seven bottles of gin, six bottles of wine and some dodgy liqueur that Cherub 2 bought in France last year. Although I'm not sure what I'm going to do after Tuesday.

I'll be honest, I felt a bit tearful when I got the dreaded letter. I also felt quite scared because, until now, I've been very careful, although not to the point of making my own meals alone in the kitchen and eating them in my room or having a go bag packed in case I need to be hospitalised. So, I had a word with myself. Sensible me told anxious me that there are people working flat out under the most horrendous pressure in hospitals across the country and all I'm being asked to do is sit on my arse in Covid Corner for 12 weeks. Everyone can still shout at me from the door. Plus, as I said to a friend, I'm fortunate to have rooms to make my own - there will be some people who are a lot worse off than me.

I have a week's leave booked in April. I'm thinking of going somewhere exotic. Like the downstairs loo. Brace yourselves for the postcards.

***

We had to adjust to me shielding in Covid Corner. It felt a bit odd that yesterday I could snog the face off my husband, but today I couldn't touch him. Not even a friendly pat on the willy!

Nobody was allowed in the kitchen at the same time as me, which led to traffic jams and Cherubic moaning. Over the proceeding months, it felt like every time I was in the kitchen, someone else needed to be there. They would arrive and declare a kitchen emergency, assuring me that they would only be a few seconds. I would then meekly stand in Covid Corner for 10 minutes, putting my own lunch on hold and wondering if I could Google 'how to commit the perfect murder' without the police finding out. However, I reasoned that they were doing all the shopping and jobs around the house, so I shouldn't make a fuss.

Over time, I started to suspect they were doing it on purpose and I realised I'd quite forgotten that I enjoy making a fuss. If I were on Mastermind and they asked me for my specialist subject, I would confidently declare 'Making A Fuss.' 'So, Mrs V,' the lovely Bamber Magnus Humphrys would ask, 'Question 1. You are in the kitchen making lunch and a Cherub says they need to make a drink, otherwise they will "literally die". They then proceed to also make a sandwich and raid the biscuit tin. What is the correct course of action?'

At this point, I snapped and stormed out of Covid Corner screeching, 'Out! Get out! No, I'm not arguing. I was here first so you can bugger off and wait your turn!' The mummy had turned. She was not going to go meekly to her covid infested grave, leaving behind a legacy of doormattery. If this virus got her then far better she be remembered for Making A Fuss, with a possible second specialist subject of Being Easily Distracted By Shiny Things.

Cherub 2 stood at the kitchen door waving the Lakeland catalogue at me. 'Ooh, lovely things I never knew I needed,' I said. Then I wandered back to Covid Corner, my lunch forgotten.

***

29th March 2020

WOMANNING THE BARRICADES

Greetings from Covid Corner. I've created havoc among my offspring by stealing an armchair to furnish my little slice of isolation. Apparently, now that I have the chair, the sofa has suddenly become far too uncomfortable to sit upon. Could I please buy another armchair? Yes, I'm fairly sure that furniture makers are offering an uninterrupted service to the bottoms of Great Britain at this time. Problem duly noted and filed under First World.

Cherub 1 breached the sanctity of Covid Corner in search of sticky tape yesterday. I have had to shore up defences. Mr V said I wasn't allowed to dig a trench through our lovely wood floor, so I took a tip from Les Miserables and put dining chairs at the entrance. I'm now womanning the barricades like a 21st century Valjean in Winnie the Pooh pyjamas. If anyone tries to breach my defences, I shall sing at them.

Vegas is doing his bit. I've moved his bed nearer the door and fed him a pork chop. He is obligingly farting like a trooper. If they get past the barricades and the fat lady singing, intruders will have to make it through the silent but deadly zone. Eat your heart out Indiana Jones!

Mr V went to the supermarket in the village and came home confused. There's a rule that you can only buy up to three of the same items. Now, I'd assumed this meant up to three loaves or three tins of beans. But the lady at the till told Mr V he could only buy three frozen items. Out of the whole range of frozen items, he was only allowed to choose three. Is this correct? We're a family of four. Six, if you account for the appetite of a teenage boy.

The one saving grace of being 'the person at risk' in this family is that if anyone has to share a tub of ice cream, it won't be me. Every cloud and all that.

30th March 2020

MRS V IS IN THE BROWN STUFF

That sense of relief when there's something brown under your fingernail and you realise it's Nutella...

I inadvertently started World War 3 yesterday by making pancakes and not knowing where the Nutella was.

I'm allowed out of Covid Corner to make food, so I got up early and made a batch of Scottish pancakes for breakfast. Cherub 1 knew where the Nutella was and suffice to say that Cherub 2 had to apologise for approximately 50,000 sins, real and imagined, before she would tell him. Cherub 2, meanwhile, embarked on a campaign of door slamming, presumably in an effort to make the Nutella magically appear. I entered the fray from my perch in Covid Corner, with UN level peacekeeping along the lines of 'stop behaving like a couple of twats'. Then I put my work headphones on and pretended to be in a meeting, even though it was Sunday. Eventually the Nutella was found, peace was restored and chocolatey knives were left for me to clear up during my next snack run.

I really think they should send mums into countries to do peacekeeping. I'd have North Korea mumbling a sullen apology within a day. I'd do it in my quiet, 'mum's a serial killer in her spare time' voice.

'Kim Jong Un, I am very disappointed in you. If I hear of any more nuclear testing, then you're grounded and there will be no ice cream for a month. Now, go and apologise to Japan and put your Nutella knives in the dishwasher.' He's a big lad so an ice cream ban would probably do him no harm.

Anyway, back to internal affairs. Lovely Granny phoned to find out how we were coping with me being separated from the rest of the family. Mr V told her it was respite. Normally I'd batter him to death with a giant chocolate bar for such cheek, but Covid Corner contains no chocolate. Only gin and wine, neither of which can be wasted. So, I just smugly reminded him that I have custody of the alcohol and at some point he'll want to negotiate visitation rights.

APRIL

***

After what felt like the 99th of March, suddenly it was April. Easter beckoned, with all its chocolatey loveliness. We didn't have many Easter eggs, but Mr V and Cherub 1 made up for it after Easter, when the local supermarket sold off all their posh eggs at half price. Suddenly, Covid Corner was awash with the sweet stuff.

The sun was shining and the lockdown-breaking numpties were out in full force. Most of Britain seemingly descended on Snowdonia, firmly convinced that nobody else could possibly have the same idea this fine Spring day.

Boris got both the virus and a new baby. The BBC reported "the baby is Ms Symonds' first child while Mr Johnson is known to have fathered five." 'Is the BBC really slut-shaming Boris?' I wondered. Did he keep millions of illegitimate children in a cupboard at 10 Downing Street? Just like half the world is descended from Genghis Khan, would historians a thousand years from now be marvelling at our Prime Minister's prowess?

We were all fiercely proud of our NHS, key workers and carers, so we gamely turned out every Thursday night to clap. God help you if you forgot. Tales of neighbourly spats abounded, as people cried, 'But I was in hospital with coronavirus!', which was clearly no excuse at all. As a nation, we stood on our front doorsteps and peered down the street to sneer at the absent Mr and Mrs Goodbody from number 3, who were obviously complete arseholes, never mind that nobody had ever actually talked to them.

Looking at my own social media for April, I appear to have spent the month binge watching reruns on telly and saying 'Aww that was in the days when people were allowed to touch each other.' I didn't join in with the collective horror at folk in parks or driving hundreds of miles to collect something they bought on

72

eBay.   I was just quietly thanking the gods for Netflix and wondering if I really had to wear a bra to go for my monthly blood test.

***

1st April 2020

I LOVE WORKING FROM HOME

Still beavering away, working from home in Covid Corner. Slight mishap when Siri came on mid meeting and loudly played Bolero, but the advantage of not switching your computer camera on (and having slidy wooden floors) is that you can have a wee Torville and Dean moment to yourself and nobody is any the wiser.

There are, of course, other reasons for not switching the camera on. Mr V asked yesterday, 'Are you wearing your work shoes?'
'Yes.'
'With your tartan lounge pants?'
'Yes.'
'And your work blouse?'
'Yes.'
'And your pink dressing gown?'
'Yes, I'm 50% dressed for work.'
'You haven't brushed your hair.'
'Yes, but I've brushed my teeth, so that's 50% of my brushing done.'

I feel I should have been praised for making the effort. I might even, at some point, have a shower!

I'm having weird thoughts in the shower since taking up residence in Covid Corner. Like should I shave my legs? What if I end up in hospital and I haven't shaved my legs? Please tell me I'm not the only person in the universe whose coronavirus precautions are isolation, hand washing and shaving my legs because I don't want a mortician exclaiming 'My! She was a hairy one!'

I have to obsess over the daft stuff. It makes the big scary stuff seem a bit less big and scary.

Anyway, I think I need a hobby to distract myself. I've ordered a Lego Steamboat Willie, which I'm looking forward to building. I'm storing all the Willie innuendos to use on Mr V when it arrives. Although I'd like to pass on one piece of advice - never accidentally search for Lego willie in Google images. There's a whole subculture right there.

*** *Friday is Wineday. Monday, Tuesday, Wednesday, Almost Wineday, Wineday, More Wineday, Sunday.* ***

3rd April 2020

WINE AND WAZZOCKS

Hello and happy Wineday. We did the national clap last night. There was a palpable air of "I feel slightly less like a wazzock standing outside clapping this week". Thank you to all the amazing people who are keeping us safe. On the inside we are clapping for you every day.

I went into the garden this afternoon and Old Ivy Next Door was out. It felt very exciting to talk to someone who isn't related to me and we had a nice chat. At 2pm I waved her cheerio, saying I had a meeting to do. It wasn't until I was indoors that I realised I was still in my pyjamas and sporting a fine hedge of hair. I've written her a note to explain:

Dear Old Ivy Next Door,

I just wanted to explain that I don't normally wear pyjamas all day, but today is Wineday. Also, I brushed my teeth. Hope you are well.

Yours sincerely,

Smokin' Hot Mrs V Next Door

Mr V is being very unreasonable and has refused to deliver the note on the basis that it's a big fat lie - I do wear my pyjamas all day, far more often than I should, and my hotness is more likely to be a menopausal flush.

I'm back in Covid Corner now. The weekend has begun. I've no idea why I'm looking forward to sitting in the same four walls for two days but I am. I'll raise a glass to the NHS and all the other wonderful people who are keeping things going and I'll raise a glass to you. Stay safe.

4th April 2020

#SAVEGEORGE

A few people enjoyed my use of the word wazzock yesterday. My mum used to call me a great wazzock. I was just pleased she thought I was good at something.

Here in Covid Corner, myself and the wee hairy boys have been catching up on Outlander. Jamie Fraser has turned 50 but doesn't look a day over phwoarty. Yes, you can roll your eyes. I'm full of nonsense today.

I'm not allowed in the living room, but I've been standing in the garden in my dressing gown, gazing longingly through the window. Mr V told me to stop as it's freaking him out. So, I've taken to banging on the window and scaring the sh*t out of him instead. Apparently this too has to stop.

There is further marital strife because a spider has moved into Covid Corner. I've named him George. Mr V hates spiders. He is in a tizz because I refuse to banish George and he's not allowed to breach my barricades to kill George. I've made a whole 'Save George' campaign. Sadly, I'm not allowed in the room where the printer is and Mr V is refusing to hand over my Save George posters. We are at an impasse.

I'm also using my time in isolation to learn new skills. I had two large gin and tonics last night, stood up to go to bed and burped the alphabet all the way up the stairs. Yay, go me!

And that brings you up to date with all the exciting developments in Covid Corner. Stay tuned for tomorrow's thrilling report.

5th April 2020

#SAVEGEORGE NEWS

Breaking news from Covid Corner. George the spider is missing two legs. The brave little arachnid continues to wander around the ceiling, but concerns have been raised in the House that George may need additional support in spinning and catching flies. Chancellor Mr V, who has done a disability assessment and declared George fit to work, released a statement last night saying, 'There are plenty of opportunities for good web designers out there.' The Prime Minister, Mrs V, has publicly backed Mr V but rumours continue to circulate that she is considering a reshuffle.

In international news, Old Ivy Next Door has been out in her garden again and diplomatic relations have resumed. The brief appearance of Mrs V in her pyjamas at 2pm the other day was shocking, but all parties have now agreed to try to be dressed by midday on week days. This does not apply to hair brushing and Wineday.

Our economic affairs correspondent reports that the Chancellor has voiced concerns that the Prime Minister spent £80 on a Lego Steamboat Willie. The Prime Minister has hit back at the Chancellor's purchase of yet another coat, particularly as he has nowhere to wear it to. Questions were raised in the House as to the exact number of coats that the Chancellor now owns and a committee has been formed to consider which old coats he should throw out. It is recognised that robust legislation may be required to make him discard the denim jacket from 1989.

And finally, the weather. Britons are being warned to stay indoors this weekend as temperatures climb and the sun shines. Covid Corner will be dull with intermittent showers of Netflix. In the living room, temperatures will rise as teenagers cheat at Monopoly. A storm will sweep in from the east when Mr V gets up at lunchtime and discovers that nobody has done the dishes...again. It is recommended that occupants seek whatever shelter from his wrath they can find.

My Save George poster. Poor George. I was rooting for the underspider.

#SAVEGEORGE

MEET GEORGE. HE'S MY ISOLATION BUDDY. NOBODY ELSE IN MY FAMILY LIKES SPIDERS AND GEORGE IS ONLY SAFE AS LONG AS THEY CAN'T COME IN. THE QUESTION IS, HOW LONG CAN I KEEP CONVINCING MY FAMILY THAT I'M STILL SELF ISOLATING? #SAVEGEORGE

8th April 2020

THE PASSING OF GEORGE

George-watch update. George has disappeared! I'm praying that he has wandered off the ceiling and is hiding somewhere. However, I've been joined by a new spider, Brenda. I'm slightly worried that Brenda may have eaten George. She's looking a bit pleased with herself, dangling from the ceiling there and rubbing her belly with her eight chubby little legs. Oh poor George. I hope big Brenda didn't get him. I fear we can no longer #savegeorge

Some good news. If anyone was wondering where I've been the last couple of days...my Steamboat Willie arrived The dining room table became the centre of Lego operations. It's impossible to build Lego without narration and I invented my own naming system for all the bits. My family took to secretly listening to me as I muttered things like, 'I need two big jobbies and a knobbly. Stick two shinies onto the jobbies and pop a knobbly on top.' Anyway, the Willie went up quickly, although it's much smaller than I thought it would be. Such is life.

I have a couple of thank yous. Firstly, thank you to the makers of Magnum double dark chocolate and raspberry ice cream. You have made a well padded Scotswoman even more jolly.

Sadly, there is no room in our freezer right now, due to the fact that two grown ups living in the same house managed to each do a grocery shop. Mr V went to the supermarket, then I helpfully sent him back again to collect the online shop I did a few weeks ago but forgot about. I can't believe I have to keep reminding him that I'm a delight. You can tell he's getting used to being in charge of shopping. The man who, until last month, thought a giant bag of Costco chicken nuggets was enough to sustain a family of four for a month and assumed vegetables were for other people, queried my every purchase. 'And where am I supposed to put these carrots?' he demanded. I had a few suggestions.

And finally, thank you to the lady who tagged me in the kilt face mask photo. Making face masks that resemble kilts is genius. I was looking for a new project and now Mr V is looking for his tartan lounge pants.

9th April 2020

THE MYSTERY OF THE DISAPPEARING JAFFA CAKES

DCI Mr V was on the case again last night. Who ate his Jaffa cakes? Was it Mrs V in Covid Corner? 'Absotively posilutely not!' cried Mrs V, who was very busy on FaceTime with her friend and did not have time for this nonsense. Was it Cherub 1 in the living room? 'No', said Cherub 1 and helpfully pointed him in the direction of the recycle bin. There he found the damning evidence - an empty box.

DCI Mr V knew his Cherubs well. They would never put the empty box in the recycle bin. They would leave it in the cupboard next to all the empty cereal boxes they couldn't be bothered binning and the out of date, expensive breakfast bars that they once insisted were the only thing they could ever ever eat but never ever ate. For a generation that seems to be on a perpetual "journey", they never seem to be able to manage the effing 2 metre stretch to the bin.

DCI Mr V considered all the evidence and did a lot of muttering about Jaffa cakes. He revisited his suspect list. Mrs V had denied everything. Surely Mrs V would not lie about something so important. Meanwhile, back in Covid Corner, Mrs V was on FaceTime with her friend making this face…

***

There have been quite a few DCI Mr V Mysteries over the years. Crimes against domestic harmony which must be solved. He gets quite confused as to how these things keep happening to him. I kid you not, he does actually go around the house quizzing suspects and when the kids were little he threatened to fingerprint them. Here's a DCI Mr V Mystery from Christmas 2019:

"T'was Christmas Eve and things were in a parlous (or as autocorrect would have it, parkour) state of affairs. Mr V's cooked chicken legs had disappeared. 'And not even the horrible ones covered in bbq sauce!' he howled. Mrs V had been having concerns of her own. She had haphazardly filled the fridge with less important items such as turkey and highly important items such as pudding, so now there was no room for alcohol. Mrs V was very worried about this parkour state of affairs because how was she supposed to get her Prosecco chilled in time for Christmas morning breakfast?! Perhaps it was time to get Detective Chief Inspector Mr V on the case...

DCI Mr V applied his razor sharp deductive reasoning and hunted for the chicken legs receipt, to check that he hadn't left them at the checkout. The receipt for every item he had purchased in December was carefully filed in his coat pocket. Except the receipt for the chicken legs.

There was an interrogation of the chief suspects (both Cherubs and a friend of Cherub 1, who didn't know the family well enough yet to empty their fridge like all the other visiting teenage hordes). All denied eating the chicken legs. In fact nobody had ever seen the chicken legs.

Mrs V was suspicious. 'Did you actually buy the chicken legs?!' DCI Mr V was affronted. 'I don't just go around imagining chicken legs you know!' he huffed and stomped off, accompanied by his trusty sidekick, PC Cherub 2, to search the fridge.

Now, DCI Mr V is an organiser of things. Dishwashers must be loaded in the most space efficient manner. The garage is full of neatly stacked old crap, which he fully intends to take to car boot sales and display on our old wallpapering table for other folk to admire, before returning the whole lot to the garage.

Mrs V, on the other hand, is very very sneaky. So, on hearing the news that the fridge had been searched, it was with Christmas joy in her heart that Mrs V grabbed 2 bottles of Prosecco and ran to the kitchen to find all the food neatly reorganised with plenty of room for wine.

Quietly, Mrs V extracted the chicken legs from their hiding place and slipped them on top of a pie. And so it was that upon Christmas morning there was great jubilation when Mrs V, chilled glass of Prosecco in hand, announced that she had "found" the chicken legs in the fridge."

There weren't many mysteries to solve during lockdown, but there was teenage angst over people eating other people's food. It was like living in a student house. Not only did the place descend into being a complete tip but, because we couldn't just pop to the shops any more (ah those were the days - remember when we used to pop to the shops?), we had to create a separate food zone for Cherub 2, just to keep the peace. A couple of months later I had a senior moment and put his 5000 tins of tomato soup in the food cupboard. He still hasn't forgiven me. I did, however, steal all his chicken noodles and he didn't notice. There were also minor explosions in the Mr V department when people kept using his favourite cup. At one stage someone used it for chicken noodles. I have no idea who did this.

11th April 2020

THE WALTZER CHAIR

Facebook has been serving up some weird ads recently but beard balm?! Come on Facebook, I know the chin situation has been a bit lairy since lockdown but things aren't that bad...yet.

I decided to have a clear out in Covid Corner yesterday. I started with the wine. That was it.

The Covid Corner armchair is quite difficult to get out of (especially when you're mid "clear out"). The chair is not made for short people, it is on wheels and I have a wood floor, so it's like the effing Waltzers every time I try to stand up. The effort was causing some minor explosions in the tartan lounge pant department last night. Basically, my bum decided I'd get out of the chair more easily if I turned into a hovercraft. Thanks for that, bum.

Cherub 1 has declared she wants Easter eggs for as long as she lives at home. My offer of an advance payment of £20 if she buggers off now didn't go down too well.

I was joking - I love her and I love that she likes pyjama days, sexy Vikings, Jamie Fraser and gin as much as I do. Well, maybe not the gin. But the rest is down to a fine mix of nature and nurture.

Mr V will be fixing the downstairs toilet today. When he fixed the cat flap, he put it on upside down. When he fixed the light switch, he put it on upside down. I'm quite looking forward to the toilet being fixed. I've never owned a bidet before.

I really do appreciate that he tries DIY. In fact, I appreciate that he's doing far more than his fair share right now, while I'm in splendid isolation, and he definitely deserves a reward. Maybe, when all this is over, I'll let him have a wee go on my Waltzer chair.

***

I do like an interesting chair. Lovely Granny used to have dining room chairs that made a fart sound when you sat down. I'd amuse everyone at dinner by standing up and sitting down a lot. Well, maybe not everyone. Okay, me and the kids. I was quite sad when LG got some new chairs, although I'm 80% sure I wasn't to blame. When you encounter a good farty chair, it helps to have no shame and the sense of humour of a 12 year old boy. I had my eyes tested last year and came across one of my favourite farty chairs:

"Went to the opticians yesterday and he acted like I was the only person who had ever asked him to stop mid-eye examination so they could take a selfie and text it to their husband asking, 'Dontcha wish your girlfriend was hot like me?' He totally does.

I finished work early due to the crippling symptoms of cash withdrawal. The urge to splurge was upon me, so I withdrew some cash and met Mr V at the shops. He was on a mission to get glasses. I was on a mission to get shiny things and chocolate. Somehow our missions got confused and I ended up seeing an optician, while Mr V sat in the waiting area clutching the bar of Dairy Milk I bought him to compensate for the fact that his big jar of jelly beans had accidentally fallen into my mouth. It was a very big jar, so this accident happened over the course of a few weeks.

I was delighted to find that the optician has a farty chair. One of those vinyl things that is like bum roulette. Not only does it fart when you sit down but there's a risk of leaving bum sweat on hot days (of course I have never left a bum sweat imprint on a chair - it is something that only happens to other people). When sitting on a farty chair, one has a few options:

A - explain that 'it wasn't me, it was the chair' (nobody will believe you now you've tried to blame the chair)
B - pretend nothing happened
C - bounce up and down a lot, enjoy the fart noises and hope it's obvious that it's the chair
D - brazen it out by saying 'better out than in' (preferably in a gravelly Danny Dyer voice).

I briefly considered option D, but remembered I'm a sophisticated lady, so chose option C. Both fun and exercisey.

Once I'd stopped farting, the optician got down to work. He made me read letters and try lots of lenses. He tricked me by varying the letters so I couldn't learn them. Opticians from the olden days, who used to spend a fiver on a board, would be stunned to learn that, in 2019, opticians spend thousands on computers so they can trick unsuspecting, well-padded, farty Scotswomen into saying ERFP when it's actually VNTD.

Dontcha wish your girlfriend was hot like me?

All in all, I had a lovely time at the opticians and I have ordered a new pair of spectacles to lose. My early Christmas present to Mr V is the opportunity for a rant - 'You've only had the effing

9

things a week, how could you lose them already!?' It's a skill!"

Some people collect stamps, some people collect china; I appear to collect farty chair experiences. Well, a girl has to have a hobby, I suppose. Hospitals often do a good farty chair and in 2018 I found a classic of its genre:

"Yesterday I went to the eye hospital and was delighted to find it was just as good as rheumatology. There were three areas, A, B and C, where the receptionist sent you to wait. A bit like Argos but with specs.

I was in A (obviously) and parked myself at the end of a row, where I wouldn't need to squeeze past people to get out again (knees not happy after spending yesterday on a train). I settled myself in for an extended Candy Crush session and didn't look up until my name was called. At which point, I realised there had been a wheelchair invasion and I was now boxed in. I had an internal debate and decided that asking people in wheelchairs to move because I had sore knees might be a wee bit insensitive. So, I braved the obstacle course of handbags on the floor and went the other way.

After various tests I got taken to the children's department (obviously) to see the optician. I sat in the big fancy chair while he read my notes. As I moved in the chair it did a little fart noise. *Dilemma!! He's going to think I farted. What do I do?* So, I did the only thing possible; squirmed around loads and made very loud fart noises so he would surely realise it was the chair, not me. Although, on reflection, he probably thought I was engaged in a monumental battle with my bowels.

90

My dilemma was a bit like when someone has had a poo in public toilets, but you're the only person in there now and while you're washing your hands someone else comes in. You can't really turn to a complete stranger and say, 'Just in case you were wondering, it wasn't me who made the smell.' If you're a man, you can probably get away with saying, 'You might want to light a match,' before wandering off, hands in pockets, contentedly fiddling with your balls and nary a care in the world. If you're a woman, you know there will be someone out there who thinks you're the poo monster and has told all her friends and you just die a little on the inside. What is the best way to deal with this poo etiquette situation?

Anyway, the optician sent me for more tests and I managed to get lost. He eventually tracked me down back in A, Candy Crushing, and escorted me back to the children's department. I got diagnosed with things I didn't even know were things and they had absolutely nothing to do with why I'd gone in the first place. I'm now the owner of a variety of drops and creams and so many instructions I made the optician repeat them 3 times. He eventually sent me on my way, even going so far as to see me out of the entrance, although I suspect that was just to make sure the mad farting woman actually left the building."

Right, well, after that little diversion into my 'inner' world, on with the next bit.

***

12th April 2020

CLEARLY OFF MY TITS ON CHOCOLATE

Happy Easter everyone. I wanted to sing you a song but the reactions of my family were 'nooooo!' 'that's too cheesy' and 'if you do that, I will never forgive you.' So, I'm giving you the words and encouraging you to pretend you're a well padded Scotswoman and sing as dramatically as you can (the boys can miss the bra bit out), I Dreamed A Dream* :

I dreamed a dream of times gone by,
Of days before coronavirus,
Of haircuts, pubs and hugs goodbye,
Before 'stay home' became desirous.
When I was free to have a snog,
Sometimes with tongues, sometimes just pecking,
And I was free to use the bog,
Then wash my hands for just 10 seconds.

Since the virus came, it's shite,
My hair's all grey and quite demented,
So many Pringles, so much wine,
And every day is much the same.

My nipples gently graze my thigh,
My bras lie lonely and forgotten,
They used to hold my boobs up high,
They've gone since corona came.
In online meetings I am scared,
That I will activate the camera,
That my pyjamas will be there,
For all to see, some office drama.

I had a dream my life would be
So different from this isolation
But thank the workers who are key
Because of them we can still dream

*Obviously the proper I Dreamed A Dream lyrics were written by Herbert Kretzmer (based on the original French libretto by Alain Boubil and Jean-Marc Natel) without any help from me.

***

Here are my eight golden rules for a happy family Easter:

1.   *You will budget £4 each for your family members' Easter eggs. You will budget £10 for your own luxury chocolatey ovoid of deliciousness. This is perfectly reasonable. Nobody can appreciate chocolate like you.*

2.   *You will spend ages devising clues for an Easter egg hunt. Unless you have a degree in cryptology your family will solve them in three minutes flat.*

3.   *If it is 9pm and your family are still wandering around the garden, compasses and codebooks in hand, you may have taken things a little too far. Pour yourself another wine and resolve to unlock the back door and let them in around 10.*

4. *If you try to explain to children the true meaning of Easter eggs, don't be offended if they're too busy running around off their tits on sugar to listen.*

5. *You will have a primeval urge to panic buy food because the supermarket is going to be closed. For a whole day! This is known as a hashtag first world problem. If, on Saturday, you find yourself buying six loaves and a case of wine to last you until Monday, then give yourself a stern talking to and put the bread back.*

6. *Easter Sunday is like a less glittery version of Christmas Day. One minute you're having chocolate for breakfast, the next it's 7pm and grandad is sound asleep on the sofa, while everyone else is arguing over what to watch on telly.*

7. *If you are a teenager, you must try to convince your parents that ALL your friends' parents buy them extravagant gifts. Your parents will thank you for this information and give you a £4 chocolate egg.*

8. *If you are visiting family on Easter Monday, you'll buy Easter eggs on the Monday, hoping for a bargain. Only the rubbish ones will be left. Granny pretends to be delighted with her milky bar egg and very considerately waits until you've left, before smashing the accompanying milky bar mug against a wall and wailing, 'I wanted a posh one from Thorntons.' You can go home, happy in the knowledge that you've fulfilled your familial duties, and tuck into the luxury chocolatey ovoid of deliciousness you bought in Thorntons last week.*

Over the 2020 Chocolate Season, I looked back at Easter 2019 and wished I could have Lovely Granny and Grandad round for lunch again. I missed LG & G. I tried to plot ways to see them but just had to be content with the weekly closeup of grandad's nostril hair on FaceTime. Here's what happened last year:

18th April 2019

Has anybody eaten their kids' eggs and sneakily replaced them yet? Have a gold star if you've resisted, but have a bigger gold star if you've spent the last 2 days running around supermarkets in a blind panic, trying to replace like with like and wondering whether you can convince your family that Lovely Granny definitely bought them these boring Kit Kat eggs. Obviously, I have no experience of this, but being that greedy and disorganised takes effort, so I applaud you.

I'm looking forward to the big day known to most people as Easter Sunday, but known to me as the Day of Chocolate for Breakfast. I've been having a staring competition with a gorgeous pink chocolate creation in my dining room for two weeks now and this Sunday I'll finally win.

Easter Sunday is also the day when there's a risk of new additions to the family mug collection. I have posh mugs by a designer I love (Emma Bridgewater anyone?) and these are what I call 'the mugs for using'. I also have a cupboard full of mugs from Easter eggs and Christmas presents. These are 'the mugs for lemsip' (because there's no point in wasting a posh mug on a lemsip). There is an overflow box in the sacred man-territory of the garage called 'my name is Mr V and I can't bring myself to throw away a useable mug'. It's comforting to know that our legacy to our children is a fine collection of Kit Kat and rude Rudolph mugs. However, I do have a cunning plan to reduce the collection...

I have invited Lovely Granny and Grandad for Easter lunch and I'm going to make everyone do an Easter egg hunt. The prize will be five Kit Kat mugs and a hilarious one with a naked Santa on it. My plan is to set clues that only LG & G can solve. If I keep this up for the next ten Easters, I reckon I might be able to shift the entire mug collection to LG & G's house by stealth.

21st April 2019

I was mopping floors in my pyjamas and a glance in the hall mirror told me that, for some reason, my boobs had decided they were quite happy with this uncharacteristic bout of housework. The headlights were on, even though nobody was driving. I wondered if I could be menopausal and Googled whether the menopause causes very happy girls, but all the results were people complaining of very sad girls.

I love Google. Google has been there for all the important events in my life, like the time I urgently needed to know why Galaxy chocolate tastes so much nicer than Cadbury's. I nearly wrote in the blog the other day that nobody had ever died from want of a potato. Google took me to one side and pointed me in the direction of the Wikipedia article on the potato famine. Thank you Google. I could have upset a few Irish folk there and, more importantly, made a right fool of myself.

I don't know how I coped before Google. I seem to recall my parents saying, 'I don't know, look it up,' quite a lot. I have been connected to the internet since 1996, when I innocently tried to plan a trip to Amsterdam and decided that Johnny's Pink Pussy Palace was definitely not going to be on the agenda. Therefore, I live in awe of how my parents ever managed to haul four children and a cat around what felt like every campsite in the UK and make it back home to Scotland every summer, with only a map and a vague sense of direction to guide them.

Anyway, I digress. Lovely Granny and Grandad arrived on time for lunch yesterday, which is unheard of! I'd said lunch would be at 1.30 but it was looking more like 3. I was still at the 'cleaning stuff so granny doesn't think we're completely feral' stage and had to do an emergency run upstairs to put the girls away. LG offered to help with the cooking, but I lied and said, 'It's all under control. Easy stuff, just a matter of timing.' Then I silently prayed for Dr Who to come along and mess with the space time continuum. Then I stopped cooking to Google 'what is the space time continuum?'

Eventually, we sat down to eat. A teenager appeared and pronounced everything 'lifting', which I think must be teenage speak for 'nutritious' Said teenager proceeded to eat enormous amounts of turkey and pretend temporary deafness when LG offered vegetables. I believe the vegetables may have been considered very lifting indeed.

After lunch, Mr V pretended we were normal people, who load dishwashers immediately and don't leave it until everyone discovers there are no clean breakfast bowls in the morning. For once, all was clean and tidy (downstairs only - upstairs was still like effing Armageddon) and we could all sit down to argue about what to watch on telly, while grandad snored his head off in the corner.

All in all a lovely family day, topped off with some Easter eggs (about which the girls pronounced themselves most pleased).

***

15th April 2020

TIME ON MY HANDS

Anyone else a bit bored? I think I might be spending too much time reading rubbish on the internet. I call this 'having an enquiring mind'. Mr V calls it 'being a nuisance'. Either way, I have questions:

On home decor - What is a cocktail chair? I quite like the idea of having a special chair for cocktails. Might the armchair in Covid Corner be a cocktail chair if you count the amount of wine and gin spilt on it? Also, can I have a Baileys chair?

On celebrity chefs - Who says 'housewives favourite' any more?! Have I inadvertently slipped back to 1973? I think housewives might be quite rare these days, so is this the equivalent of saying, 'Hardly anyone likes you'? If so, I have a whole list of housewives favourites, starting with my maths teacher circa 1984 and ending most recently (and temporarily) in Biggles. I didn't know Biggles had eaten a hole in the crotch of my pyjamas and I spent Easter Sunday curled up in my cocktail chair wearing pyjamas and no knickers. Like pushing giblets through a polo mint. An Easter treat for all the family.

On medical advice - How many wines is too many? My doctor said a bottle a week is 1000 calories and above the recommended limit. I came away from that conversation quite glad I hadn't mentioned the gin. I checked with Dr Google, who says a bottle a week is low intake and it's about 600 calories. Normally I don't trust Dr Google, but I'm prepared to take a leap of faith this time.

On life - Is life like Candy Blast? When I reach the pearly gates, will St Peter offer me another go if I just watch a 30 second ad?

On economics - If a blouse costs £50 and you tell your husband it cost £30, how much did the blouse actually cost? Also, can you still buy that lovely skirt and pretend you've had it for years?

On time - hey Siri, what day is it?

Stay tuned for more exciting updates from Covid Corner tomorrow.

***

By mid-April, I hadn't been anywhere in a month. I was commenting on absolutely everything my friends posted on social media. A lovely friend posted a picture of Fanny Cradock and I somehow morphed into a snickering 12 year old. I did, however, look into Fanny and discovered things I never knew. If you're ever bored, I suggest you Google Fanny. You might be surprised.

I love my family dearly, but we were getting a little tetchy with each other. Cherub 1 was walking the dogs for about 3 hours a day; not really in the spirit of government guidance, but it was keeping her going. I was only allowed out in the garden and, with one eye on my ballooning bottom, Mr V was nagging me to exercise more. I didn't fancy the dog shit minefield that is our lawn, so I bought myself an under the desk exercise bike. I also bought some new pyjamas. As my lockdown hobby now appeared to be 'standing by the oven door waiting for the ping', I allowed room for expansion and the new pyjamas were a size bigger than normal.

What I didn't mention on the blog at this time was that a member of my family was going through some health issues and I was desperately worried. On top of this, a restructure at work meant that I had to look for a new job in a climate where new jobs were few and far between. I wasn't going to be out of a job but I was a bit 'minister without portfolio' and I desperately needed to move on. I was very aware that many of my readers might be in a far worse employment situation, so I certainly didn't want to moan. Nevertheless, I think it's fair to say that there were a few tough days in the second half of April. Days when I wished Boris would get up on his wee podium and announce, 'As of now all people called Mrs V are allowed one hug a day.'

There were plenty of good days too. Most of them involved chocolate raisins and ice cream. I had to fit into those pyjamas!

16th April 2020

YOU MIGHT WANT TO LIGHT A MATCH...

We are descending to new lows now. There was an argument yesterday, when Mr V accused me of sneaking off for a poo just before he went for a shower. 'I had a wee!' I cried, outraged.

'You had that *just sneaking off for a poo* look on your face,' he declared, 'I even had counter-measures ready.' Sure enough, there was a can of air freshener on the stairs. I was a little annoyed but, more importantly, I had questions.

'What sort of look is *just sneaking off for a poo*?' I asked.

Mr V took a moment to think about this. 'Quiet concentration but slightly shifty, like you hope nobody notices you going,' he eventually declared.

'But that's my *going for a poo at work* face!' I exclaimed, confused at how I had managed to take a work face into the home. Then it hit me - lightbulb moment - I'm working from home, of course. This virus has consequences more far reaching than I'd realised. What other faces had I imported from work? I checked with Mr V. 'Have I been nodding a lot while looking highly interested yet slightly glazed over recently?'

'Yes. That time I told you all my concerns about repairing the shed.'

'That's my *understanding boss* face, for when people tell me about work problems that I don't understand and I'm actually just trying to decide whether 11am is too early to eat my sandwiches.

Have I smiled fixedly at you with a slightly worried face? Yes? That's the face I usually reserve for Sandra who, despite her laughing claims of 'I don't wanna be that guy', always has 'a couple of quick questions' at the end of every training course. It's the look of a woman within whom an inner battle is raging, because if I batter Sandra to death with an office chair there will be nobody to do all the leaving collections.'

Mr V has been working from home too and wanted to know if he'd imported any work faces. Turns out his *eff off and don't talk to me until after 11am* face is the same at work and home. Who knew.

18th April 2020

SOURPUSS

Could lockdown be getting to me? I had a hissy fit over 'the wrong type of sour cream' yesterday and refused to make dinner for myself. I think this might be the finest example of cutting off my nose to spite my face I've ever managed.

Mr V did not understand my angst.

'What's wrong with the sour cream?' he asked.

'It's NOT sour cream. It's sour cream SAUCE!' I bellowed.

'What's the difference?' he wanted to know.

'The difference?! The difference?!' I spluttered, deciding that my outrage was sufficient to convey all the nuanced differences between sour cream and sour cream sauce.

Mr V knew better than to argue and scuttled off clutching a plate of fajitas. However, he did not know when to just shut the eff up. He came back half an hour later and told me, 'The sour cream was actually rather good.' Then he saw my face and was quite glad that I have to socially distance myself from my own family. I may not be able to convey the difference between sour cream and sour cream sauce, but I'm very good at telepathically signalling precisely where I'd like to shove the bottle of sour cream effing sauce.

Am I alone in having a moment of lockdown lunacy? Whether it's making mountains out of molehills or doing something wonderfully weird to relieve the boredom, please share your stories of how you're getting through this.

*** *People did share their stories. My heart broke for the lady who lost her husband less than a year ago and was going through lockdown alone. Someone else had a meltdown when her husband put BBQ sauce on her bacon sandwich "never mind that he was making me breakfast in bed." And one poor man just said "No, you're not alone. Didn't know there was a right way and a wrong way to put milk in the fridge."* ***

19th April 2020

BANANA BOLLOCKS

Today, the gods of baking sent me a message along the lines of 'Mrs V, you are a lady of a certain girth in the bottom department - do you really need more banana loaf in your life?'

I defied the gods, waving a wooden spoon and my iPad at them and shouting, 'Begone and bugger off, for I have her Maryness of the Berry on my side. She has a simple recipe which serves eight people (or one Mrs V eight times).'

The gods of baking were angry, but I took no notice. I had a bunch of over-ripe bananas and I was going to use them. The gods, however, were not to be thwarted. I triumphantly slammed my big drawer of baking things shut, somehow catching the lid of the baking powder. The baking powder duly exploded all over me, the floor, the cupboards and, most annoyingly, the inside of the drawer. Oh, how the gods laughed.

But they were not finished with me yet. I got the vacuum cleaner out. The vacuum cleaner decided it didn't like baking powder and promptly died. As I cleaned up the mess, threw it in the bin then cleaned it up again because I'd missed the effing bin, the gods cried, 'Do you give up? Oh please, for the love of elasticated waistbands, say you give up!'

But I did not give up. I got the ultimate weapon out - the electric mixer. Round and round went the mixy spinny things, until all was as her Maryness decreed. Then I unplugged the mixer and tried to eject the mixy spinny things. Nothing happened. The gods smiled knowingly. I held the mixy spinny things up to my face, peered closely at them and plugged the mixer back in. The gods peed themselves laughing. Top tip - before unplugging a mixer do not leave it set to top speed. I swear I heard the gods whisper,

'Now pour yourself a glass of wine and we'll say no more about it.' Or at least that's what I told Mr V when he found me covered in gloop, sitting with a large glass of Sauvignon, in the centre of the banana loaf Jackson Pollock that used to be our kitchen.

Maybe next time I bake, I'll have the wine first. Then the gods can throw what they like at me and I really won't care.

21st April 2020

PYJAMAS AND PUDDINGS

Today's bulletin from Covid Corner:

In local news, there was much excitement when Mrs V's new working from home uniform arrived. There was less choice than usual in the Marks and Spencer pyjamas department, presumably because all the other ladies are now size 'slightly larger bottom than last month' too.

In currant affairs, there is a worldwide shortage of chocolate raisins. Or a least that is what Mr V, Minister for Essential Items, has announced. The residents of Covid Corner suspect this may be linked to local issues with pyjama sizes. Mr V has released a statement, saying that, while the growth of Mrs V's bottom is of concern, the economic impact of her chocolate raisin consumption also needs to be tackled. Mainly because she likes the expensive Belgian chocolate ones. Mr V presented graphs, showing that the growth of the Belgian economy was (very) broadly in line with Mrs V's bottom and coincided with a downturn in household finances from mid-March onwards.

And that neatly covers international affairs too! Mrs V is very good at multitasking.

Our war correspondent reports that a minor explosion occurred in the kitchen last night, when Cherub 2 discovered that there were no 'nice puddings'. All offers of nice puddings were deemed 'not nice enough'. A truce was reached, following the discovery of some ice cream in the back of the freezer. However, it is expected that hostilities will resume later, when Cherub 2 finds out that the Minister for Essential Items has imported the wrong type of hob nobs.

Finally, the weather. Mostly sunny, but with a risk of a few showers around 7pm. The dishwasher is broken and it's Mr V's turn to do the dishes. Residents are advised to take cover from a hail of swear words this evening, when he discovers that Mrs V used the big dish and didn't leave it to soak.

22nd April 2020

HOW DO I LOVE THEE? LET ME COUNT THE WAYS

I was feeling sad yesterday and had to remind myself of the wise words of a certain sophisticated, genteel, well-padded Scotswoman (yes, you guessed right, it is me!):

When the world seems set against you,
And you're feeling kinda glum,
Just stick two fingers in the air,
And holler "UP YER BUM!"

Of course, wise words are always better if washed down with wine. And maybe cake.

To cheer myself up, I pondered all the things my family love about me. Let me count the ways:

1. I create mysteries for them to solve. Like who ate all the Jaffa Cakes, why do we have no money and who bought all these shiny things?

2. I give them opportunities. For example, shopportunities when I need presents.

3. I have taught them useful life skills such as ice skating backwards, all the swear words in French and cheating at monopoly.

4.   I can economise. I buy the dogs' Christmas outfits in August and and and…well, I'm sure there are other things.

5.   I make a contribution to our family. Sometimes it is charcoaled pizza. Sometimes it is hugs. Always it is love.

Just to check that I was getting this right, I asked Mr V what he loves about me. Let me count the ways:

1.   Sense of humour

2.   Boobs

25th April 2020

HANDS OFF MRS V

Residents of Covid Corner have found mysterious notes saying 'Hands Off Mrs V' attached to every packet of Jaffa Cakes over the past couple of weeks and have welcomed this timely reminder to attractive men in kilts of the importance of not touching Mrs V. A spokesperson for Mrs V said, 'While Mrs V is pleased that an unknown admirer has championed her right not to be touched, if Jamie Fraser would like to put his hands on her then she is willing to take the risk and come out of isolation.' Locals have expressed concern that the notes may simply be a warning from Mr V not to eat all the Jaffa Cakes, but Mrs V says this is stretching the interpretation a bit far.

In other news, our domestic affairs correspondent has a shock report from the kitchen. On learning that the dishwasher was broken, Cherub 1 asked 'Well, what are we supposed to do when we run out of clean dishes?' The parents were contacted for a response, but unfortunately it is unprintable.

And now, a special report from our consumer affairs correspondent. Following the purchase of multiple tubs of chocolate raspberry ice cream, Mr V has just noticed that there are instructions on the lid to wait 10 minutes, then press the side of the pot to break the chocolate shell. Our intrepid reporter asked Mrs V whether she intended to follow the instructions to wait 10 minutes. Mrs V responded, 'What instructions? I can't see any instructions!'

A worldwide hunt began yesterday for Mrs V's glasses. The government minister for Lost Property, Mr V, has released a statement saying that everyone is getting fed up with Mrs V denying everything on the basis that she didn't have her glasses on. The crisis reached a peak yesterday, when she accidentally bumped into one of his little apple pies with her mouth and posted a laughing emoji on the picture of a friend lamenting her frosty roots.

And finally, in sports news, Mrs V has bought an under the desk cycle and travelled many miles during online meetings this week. However, it has been a struggle not to sound like a telephone sex pest every time someone asks her a question and she has to unmute her microphone.

26th April 2020

SORRY SAM. IT'S NOT YOU, IT'S JAMIE.

We have sent Cherub 1 to the shop for snacks. Mr V dictated the shopping list and I was in charge of texting it to her. I may have added one or two essentials. I wonder how long it will take her to notice.

Today 14:15

Bread 🧊 ice cream 🍦 Chocolate 🍫 crisps , Swiss roll , Chicago pizzas, mince, bbq sauce Heinz, ▓▓▓▓ s, Jamie Fraser, chocolate angel delight, butter (lurpak but the lighter kind)

Delivered

Also, please note my restraint in requesting lower fat butter.

I suspect this is everyone's lockdown shopping list.

In other exciting news, George may have appeared last night. I say 'may' because the worldwide hunt for my glasses hasn't been completed and I couldn't tell if he had six legs or eight. Mr V couldn't tell either, but I'll let him off - many men seem to have trouble understanding the difference between six and eight (sorry boys - I couldn't resist that one).

If it turns out to be a new spider, what shall I call him? I was thinking maybe Ringo - I reckon I can get the full set by the end of lockdown.

*** No, I won't tell you what the blanked out thing was. That's between me and a body part beginning with the first letter of my surname. I have a slight fear that some day the lovely actor Sam Heughan will hear about this middle-aged lady who never shuts up about Jamie Fraser. Just to be clear, I read the books long before Outlander appeared on our screens and I fancied Jamie in the books too. So, it's definitely not you Sam, it's Jamie. This is what my life has come to - I fancy a fictional character. ***

27th April 2020

USING YOUR BLOG TO DROP SUBTLE HINTS

I ventured out of Covid Corner and went into the downstairs loo today for the first time in a month. I was met by the sink swamp monster, who growled, 'Whaddaya want?'

'I'm just popping in because the door was open. Can I ask when anyone last ran a cloth over you?'

The sink swamp monster looked at the layer of grime coating his surface and said, 'What month is this?'

Suddenly, there was a loud bang and the toilet troll appeared. 'Who dares disturb my slimy slumber?' roared the toilet troll.

I averted my eyes, for the toilet troll was a fearsome, odious beast. I asked it, 'When was the last time someone chucked some bleach over you?'

The toilet troll looked at the matter splatter coating its surface and said, 'What month is this?'

A crunching sound to my left alerted me to the presence of the towel of doom. 'Hello,' I said. 'Are you the same little towel I put here in March?'

The towel of doom unfurled its crispy corners to reveal its damp underbelly and cried, 'Please rescue me from this hell!' The stack of fluffy, fresh towels I'd placed under the sink many moons ago puffed themselves up and twittered, 'Ooh, please pick me, pick me, give me a job to do.'

The liquid soap dispenser gave a little cough and spluttered, 'The filthy feckers have been frantically pressing my head to get the last micro drop of soap out for the past day. Please fill me.'

It is as I've always suspected. I am the only person who ever cleans the downstairs loo. Either my family are breeding bacteria in the hopes of finding a cure for the coronavirus, or they've gone feral. Why am I even debating this? They're feral.

In tomorrow's exciting episode of Covid Corner, I'll be sneaking into the living room to write "clean me" in the dust on the telly.

***

Using the blog to drop subtle hints to my family is a wonderful by-product of being a social media unfluencer. I say unfluencer because I am fairly sure the world will never take its cue from a short, plump lady in Winnie the Pooh pyjamas.

Mind you, I did once launch a revolution at the local chemist. I was like a fearless leader of middle-aged people clutching pile cream and indigestion tablets. As the queue to pay got longer and still only one person was serving, the very British part of me whispered, 'Mind your own business and keep buggering on.' The Scottish part of me countermanded this with, 'Bugger buggering on, at this rate I'll never get my messages done.' So, I marched to the front and said to the solitary lady behind the till, 'Excuse me, you have a queue half way to the door here. Would you be able to summon some help please?' I may have been a raging Scot on the inside, but this was a very polite revolution. I apologised profusely to the customer I'd interrupted and returned to the queue.

On my return I was a conquering hero. The people beside me were overjoyed. One lady kept exclaiming, 'Ooh, look, another one!' as new people appeared at the till. More than once she expressed her surprise at 'What a difference it makes when you say something to them.' She seemed so excited about someone speaking out that I imagined her going home to her husband that night and telling him, 'From now on I'm in charge of the remote control. And what's more, in future you can get your own damn pile cream.'

This was peak unfluencing.

Sometimes I do make a tiny difference through the blog. For example, ladies in America now know you can get Jaffa Cakes in Aldi and that there is no such thing as just one Jaffa Cake.

During the last election I came up with my own manifesto and we all (okay, I) agreed that it was far more sensible than anything that the political parties had come up with:

A vote for Mrs V is a vote for cake.

(P.S. the manifesto works best if you sing it to the tune of Michael Finnegan...you didn't actually expect anything less, did you?)

First there will be lots of twattery,
Shenanigans and top chit-chattery.
Cake and wine and gin are free for all,
Vote for me and we will have a ball.

Could of, would of, should of grammar crimes,
Will be subject to the harshest fines.
Christmas decor, Yuletide provender,
Outlawed 'til the first of December.

Every man will have a cave or shed,
Every pet will have a comfy bed,
Every school will offer this degree:
Theoretical mixology.

The Bra Removal Act will simply state,

Underwire's illegal after 8,
A Three Day Weekend Act will also say,
Saturday, Sunday and Pyjama Day.

Here we are, the final master plan,
Every street will have an ice cream van.
Raise a glass and say this after me -
"Vote for Growing Old Disgracefully!"

There you go, a free ear worm for the rest of the day. I'm a good unfluence.

Mr V has always said I should make more of the blog but I've been oddly reluctant. I'd never criticise other people who do adverts and sell things, because it takes work and dedication to write or make videos all the time. Why shouldn't they benefit? For me, though, it has always felt like a lovely hobby that somehow blossomed and it's a privilege to put smiles on a few faces. It feels wrong to make money out of it (says the lady who is hoping a few people buy her book).

Mr V once asked, 'If you were to advertise something on the blog what would you advertise?' I replied, 'Marks & Spencer, but only if they offered me a year's supply of free knickers.' 'Weeeeell,' said Mr V, with just a hint of self-interest, 'You write about them anyway so maybe you could advertise the camera shop?' Perhaps if I ever do make the family fortune, I shall treat him to a new camera lens. But only after I've treated the dog to a can of posh air freshener up his rear end. Cut out the middle-man and go for a straight insertion. Honestly, my main memories of writing this book will be the cloud of rotten eggs emanating from his bottom.

***

29th April 2020

TESTICLES AND VEGETABLES

I read an article about unusual coronavirus symptoms in kids and teenagers, so I phoned Cherub 2 (who was ill in bed) to check. It's perhaps testament to our relationship that he didn't bat an eyelid when he answered the phone and his mother bellowed, 'Hello, how are your testicles?'

In other news, I have been battling the bus company to get a refund for a ticket that couldn't be used due to the current state of play. The bus company was very rigid and refused any refund, so I was getting a little annoyed. So annoyed that I buggered up the autocorrect and signed off as Mrs Vegetables. All subsequent correspondence has been addressed to 'Dear Mrs Vegetables'.

Mr V came home from the shop in a bad mood after a man leaned over him to get some bananas. Apparently Mr V was taking too long. Did he not know that Mr V was new to the fruit and veg section?! Had I been there I'd have told the man that if he thought a few seconds to choose bananas was too long, then he should try asking him to make a decision on buying a new vacuum cleaner! That man was lucky Mr V didn't whip out a spreadsheet comparing the features of every banana on the market and bore him to death with it.

So, another exciting day in Covid Corner has passed by. Tomorrow is Almost Wineday, then it's Wineday. Something to look forward to.

Stay safe and may your testicles be fine.

Mrs Vegetables x

*** What I didn't mention in the post about Banana Man was that there was an exchange of words, witnessed by Cherub 1. 'Yes,' said Mr V proudly, 'and I won when I called him a dickhead.' 'No,' said Cherub 1, rolling her eyes. 'You called him a fucking dickhead.' Mr V, role model and excellent parent. ***

MAY

MAY

***

Ah, the merry month of May. The month when social media exploded because the PM's aide appeared to breach lockdown. The month when you couldn't escape pictures of people having a lovely day out, spreading the virus at the beach. Boris pleaded with everyone to stay home over the sunny bank holidays and parks were shut to prevent a repeat of Easter, when many judged a game of frisbee to be absolutely worth dying for. We all got very confused about how far and where we could travel for exercise and the newspapers pounced with glee on every penalty issued. Name 'em. Shame 'em.

The nation was consumed with self-righteous indignation and the parents of roving groups of teenagers were firmly to blame for all that was wrong with the world. I was horrified that one of mine went awol and only let him back in the house on condition that he self-isolated in his bedroom for two weeks. After which, he promptly got a bug and had to spend the next 4 weeks in bed. I went from wanting to wring his neck to wanting to cuddle him and wrap him up in cotton wool forever. I think it's called being a mother.

Locked down and outraged, little did we know that just around the corner a far bigger issue was about to hit us that would put 'Twats-on-the-beach-gate' into perspective. If I'd told you in May that, by June, almost everyone would care deeply about statues which, until that point, they'd never heard of, you'd have said, 'Have you been on the wine again Mrs V?' There's a fairly high chance the answer would have been yes, but that's neither here nor there. On May 25th, the tragic death of George Floyd was the trigger for anti-racism protests and unrest in cities across the world. Far finer minds than I will no doubt dissect the events and I don't presume to judge as, at the time of writing, the battles rage on. However, like most people, I want a better world and the Black Lives Matter protests made me listen, take stock of my own attitudes and think about how I can improve. Suffice to say that I've had some good conversations with the Cherubs.

May was the month of the new 'caring' emoticon on Facebook. I started to wonder if I was a complete cow because I hadn't found a use for it. Facebook also introduced avatars. I felt I needed to make mine as realistic as possible…

Barely worn a bra for weeks. Can you tell?

1st May 2020

HOW TO SURVIVE LOCKDOWN

Forget everything you have read in the newspapers, here is Mrs V's guide to surviving lockdown:

1. Under no circumstances wear a bra. Unless you are a man who secretly fancies a go - in which case, this is the ideal time to indulge your inner Glenda and give those moobs your full support.

2. If you have to isolate, do it in the room which contains the most alcohol.

3. Learn a new skill. A proper life skill. Like cocktail making (see 2 above) or advanced online shopping.

4. Don't be fooled by all the exercisey, fabulous people, who are excelling at home schooling and baking on social media. They're secretly day drinking and their kids are surviving on a diet of home made cake.

5. You're not allowed to sell your family on eBay apparently, so you have to find ways to get along with them or ignore them. I find it helps to wear your work headphones and pretend you're in a meeting at all times. Also see 2 above.

6. If ever there was a time to experiment with personal hygiene, it is now.

7. Grow a fabulous moustache. And if you're a man, feel free to do this too.

8. Take up a new hobby. Top tip - you may not own tap shoes, but you can reproduce the sound effect by letting your toe nails grow out and dancing on a wooden floor.

9. If being cooped up with your nearest and dearest is getting to you, spend time in the garden. Digging can be very therapeutic. Ideally, holes should be about 6' long by 6' deep.

10. Pretend you're on holiday. Make the whole family sleep in one room for two weeks, store your iron in the wardrobe, get up at 6am every day to put a towel on your spot on the sofa and post pics of alcoholic beverages on social media in the afternoons.

***

Everybody loves a list. Here's one of my favourites from August 2018. We'd been staying with a friend in Scotland:

"We're going back to England today. Mr V is relieved to be driving in England again because he thinks all Scottish road signs

should come with a sign underneath explaining how you pronounce the place names. So, we won't be camping in Wales next year then. I think we've been good house guests. We've followed all the rules:

1. Never leave your pubes in the shower

2. Secretly feed the cat treats so your friend thinks his cat loves you

3. Bring an unexpected gift (I chose a houseplant over Mr V's suggestion of sausage rolls)

4. Be considerate by covering your friend's grill pan with foil when you make bacon sandwiches (even though your own grill pan at home rivals a fatberg in a London sewer)

5. Compliment the sensitivity of his smoke alarm when you set the bacon on fire while making bacon sandwiches

6. Be sympathetic when your friend comes back from a run and tells you he has sweaty bits and pits, by telling him that you have sweaty tits (then maybe have a shower - see 1)

7. Kindly let your friend pay for dinner because while you were in the loo he and your husband decided to dessert share, then had such a heated debate over whether they were having custard or ice cream that everyone in the restaurant now thinks they're a couple and it would be nice for people to know that, even after custard-gate, they can still give each other a wee treat

8. Avoid mention of your friend's baldness. Stop yourself mid way through asking him if he has any conditioner because you left yours at home

9. Don't fat shame his pets. Say sensitive things like 'what a jolly cat!' instead

10. Remember that with age comes wind. There are three of you in his new car and it could have been any one of you. Admit nothing.

I feel completely confident that we'll be invited back."

We also had to make an emergency phone call to our friend's family, asking them to just double check we hadn't burnt his house to the ground. He'd gone to work, leaving us alone in his house while we got ready for our journey back south. We were about an hour down the road when Mr V remembered that he'd left the oven on. I felt slightly less confident about being invited back.

2nd May 2020

ZE CHERUB WITH ZE BIG SPEWIES

The peace of Covid Corner has been disrupted by incessant honking. Cherub 2 has been ill and he has not been a good patient. Tempers have frayed and all parties have retreated to their own corners of the house.

I have Covid Corner, which is lovely and full of dogs and booze and chocolate raisins (yes, they're back).

Mr V has Curmudgeon Corner, with its to do lists, spreadsheets, computer games and grumpy old man chuntering on about the price of chocolate raisins.

Cherub1 has Crockery Corner, which is full of manky old plates and glasses, carefully curated over the course of weeks until she is breathing in pure spores and is forced to dump them in the sink when no one is looking. She has no worries about whatever sickness bug has afflicted her brother because she has been inadvertently making her own penicillin for years.

Cherub 2 is, of course, in Chunder Corner. He is utterly miserable and we all feel sorry for him. Except, maybe, when he bangs on the floor like the old lady from 'Allo 'Allo, to demand his fiftieth glass of water of the day. Being a teenager, he didn't have a clue when I asked if he had some airmen and a madonna with ze big boobies stashed under his bed. I thought I was being tres amusant but he just thought I was being a bit of a twat.

Sorry non-British friends and anyone under the age of 30 - you'll just have to Google Allo Allo. It's classic British comedy.

Anyway, between Fanny le Fan upstairs and Mr V being in high dudgeon, it has been left to the residents of Crockery and

Covid corners to try to bring peace and happiness to the house via the twin mediums of online shopping and home renovation. We are absolutely sure that Mr V will be delighted to put up new wallpaper and it will lift his spirits tremendously.

***

Cherub 1 was quite annoyed with me for posting about Crockery Corner because she had just thoroughly cleaned it and was not (in her words) 'a tramp'. She genuinely is much tidier than she was a year or two ago. Let us hope that Cherub 2 goes the same way.

Being a parent of young adults is a minefield. When they're little, you think things will be so much easier once they can dress themselves. When they're in their early teens, you think things will be so much easier when they leave school. When they leave school, you begin planning futures, shouting, 'Go to work!' and 'Go to college!' a lot and thinking of simpler times when all you had to do was convince a four year old that she couldn't wear princess sandals in three feet of snow. Somehow, I find myself in charge of two mostly-grown-ups who firmly believe it's not their job to put the cereal back in the cupboard because they weren't the one who left it out. I have to restrain myself from pointing out that, despite not being the ones paying the bills, they sure are happy to eat my food, use my electricity and watch my telly. My cherubs are not perfect cherubs. But neither are Mr V and I perfect parents.

I once came home to find Mr V in high dudgeon because the house was "full" of teenagers (i.e. our two Cherubs and a friend) lounging around. 'Do they have nothing better to do?!' he cried, sounding like an actual parent of teenagers. Then he gave them chores and told them to focus on the positives. This left me somewhat discombobulated. Faking being proper parents is something that has taken us years to perfect. We are the masters of muddling through. And now the traitor was actually sounding like the real deal!

I worried that, if he kept this up, we would have to stop bribing our kids to eat vegetables and coercing them into pretending to be polite and decent members of society whenever we had visitors. We would have to lay down the law and start saying parenty things like 'if someone asked you to jump off a cliff...' Instead of a quiet life where I just closed the door on the mess, I could see years of yelling at people to tidy their bedrooms stretching before me. Surely our kids were turning out alright despite our best efforts?

I had to nip this in the bud before it got out of hand and we all found ourselves, with not a trace of irony, posing in matching jumpers for next year's Christmas cards. I was prepared to take extreme measures but in the end I didn't have to do anything. Cherub 1 would only let Cherub 2 have the broken slice of cake. Cherub 2 was absolutely not having this disgusting piece of patisserie with its filthy break in the middle that tasted exactly the same as the unbroken slice. Cherub 2 suggested cutting the unbroken slice in half and sharing it. Cherub 1 objected on the grounds that this would be breaking the unbroken slice.

Within minutes World War 3 had broken out and Mr V was storming into the living room saying, 'I can't deal with it. You deal with it.' Thus normal service was resumed. We both hid in the living room, turned up the volume on the telly to drown out the teenage swearing and agreed that surely some sibling rivalry was character building.

Some day they will leave and we will miss them because, despite all the daily frustrations of living with two young adults and despite all our failures as parents, there is a bottomless well of unconditional love.

Also, cake is so good on so many levels, isn't it?

6th May 2020

MORE WINE PLEASE

A side effect of lockdown is that the boys of the house appear to have synchronised their man periods and have been doing a lot of stomping. One of them wanted to know who stole his shoes. There was much slamming of things and general grumbling. Meanwhile, I sat in Covid Corner wondering whether to fess up or wait for him to notice me wearing them.

Mr V clattered around the kitchen, bellowing about how 'it's like managing a bunch of prima donnas.' I had to tell him there were only two prima donnas in this house and one of them was about to try pricking holes in a microwave meal with a teaspoon.

I am down to my last bottle of wine. I don't know how I let things get to this perilous stage. Tomorrow is Almost Wineday, so I'm working on persuading Mr V to go to the shops again. He went yesterday. I suggested he get a couple of ready meals and that I quite liked the carbonara he bought before. I am now the proud owner of about ten carbonara ready meals. So, I was thinking that if I tell him I quite liked the wine he bought last time...

The good news is that Mr V was finally successful in finding flour in the supermarket. It's wholemeal flour and that means I can now eat as much cake as I want. It's all good fibre. If I make banana bread or carrot cake I will officially be on a health kick. Yay, go me!

7th May 2020

WHO IS THIS MAN?

Two of us are working from home in this house. We are each amazed at who the other is at work. Mr V thinks I spend far too much time being nice to everyone, whereas I think I've achieved a good work/life balance.

Me on the phone:

'How are you doing? Have you been managing to get out at all? Are you in touch with your friends and family? Hang on I'm just going to put you on hold...WILL YOU STOP ACTING LIKE AN EFFING 2 YEAR OLD. I AM ON THE TWATTING PHONE YOU INCONSIDERATE LITTLE SOD...hi sorry about that, so you were saying you've been FaceTiming your mum...'

Balance.

Mr V is full of positive suggestions and when his boss asks him to do something, he doesn't go and hide in the garage, organising his tools, hoping his boss will forget she asked. He also says things like 'Thanks for your valuable input' instead of 'STOP INTERRUPTING ME' and 'Let's put something in our calendars' as opposed to 'Appointment? Appointment?! You never told me there was an appointment! What do you mean you put it in the house diary? You didn't remind me that we have a house diary!'

Sometimes Mr V overhears me in a meeting and, afterwards, offers helpful advice like 'I would have just told them to eff off.' I know this is not true because I overhear his meetings and he says things like 'Make a smooth transition' and 'Do some forward planning.' Which I suspect is corporate speak for 'Eff off and when you get there, eff off some more.'

I didn't think I'd like working from my dining room table, but it has actually been fine. I can watch telly in my lunch break, cuddle a dog when the going gets tough and if I fancy that Friday Wineday feeling all I need to do is wait until the dining room chair cuts off the circulation to my legs and stand up too quickly.

Sorted.

8th May 2020

MUM OF THE YEAR

Even from isolation in Covid Corner, I'm able to do excellent parenting.

Yesterday, Cherub 2 commented that the paracetamol tablets were quite big and difficult to swallow.

'Is that the kind you're supposed to swallow or is it the kind that goes up your bum?' I asked, donning my most innocent expression.

'What!' exclaimed Cherub 2, outraged, 'I've been swallowing these for weeks. Do you really get ones that you put up your bum?!'

'Oh yes,' said I, knowledgeably. 'It's all to do with how your body absorbs it into your bloodstream. Check the packet. Does it say they're the swallowing kind?'

Cherub 2 looked closely at the box. 'It doesn't say anything,' he said.

'Then they must be the up the bum kind,' I confidently assured him.

Cherub 2 was horrified. He checked the other boxes to see if any were the swallowing kind then, seeing none, marched off declaring that there was no way he was sticking anything up his bum.

I really, really wanted to tell him to try it, but I couldn't keep a straight face for long enough. I like to think that I'd have stopped him at the bathroom door.

***

When the Cherubs were little I bought a fake dog poo and left it next to Cherub 2's chair at the kitchen table. In the morning, he came down for breakfast, spotted the poo and howled, 'The dog has done a poo on the floor!'

'Are you sure?' I asked. He was very sure. I said I wasn't so sure. I picked up the poo and gave it an experimental lick. 'Yes, you're right, it's definitely dog poo,' I said.

That was my favourite prank – the one where I scarred my Cherubs for life.

***

9th May 2020

EXTENDED SENTENCE

I got a text from the NHS yesterday:

Dear Mrs V,

We know you are missing things like shops and cuddles and Mr V's willy, but we have heard how comfy Covid Corner is and that you've taken custody of All The Wine, so we need you to stay there in splendid isolation until 30th June. Maybe you could ask Mr V to flash you from a safe distance, just so you know he still has a willy. Thank you.

All the lovely people at the NHS xx"

Or I think that's what it said. I may have read between the lines a tiny bit.

So, I shall definitely be reporting from Covid Corner for a while yet. It will be very odd being imprisoned while the world comes out of lockdown, but at least if I ever develop a menopausal bout of kleptomania and get myself arrested, then I know I can do the time. To be fair, I'd probably get a longer prison sentence because I'd make sure I stole proper things. There would be little point in having kleptomania if I didn't put it to good use and pinch a Ferrari. 'Sorry officer, I have no idea how my bottom accidentally got in the driving seat!'

It looks like we'll definitely be having a staycation this year. There's a lovely North East expression for that - going to Worgate - which means going to our garden gate. But as the alternative is a potential trip to Pearlygate, I'll take Worgate any time.

Under no circumstances feel sorry for me. There are folk far worse off and I can't begin to imagine how people living in apartments are coping. I have a garden in which to enjoy sunny days, a family to bring me ice cream/replenish wine supplies and a fine array of online shops. I have a good supply of pyjamas and I don't have to wear a bra for another seven weeks. Plus, by the time I get out there will be hairdresser appointments again. My boobs may require a visit to the Marks and Spencer scaffolding department, but my hair will be instantly fabulous.

Of course I feel anxious and helpless in the face of this awful virus. Frustrated that I can't do more to make a difference. Scared that when they do finally release me into the wild I'll be struck down (please god let it be after I've been to the hairdresser). But I'm cheered by seeing so many successes every day. So many fabulous people doing amazing, funny and kind things. Keep looking forward my Lovelies. It won't be like this forever.

10th May 2020

EGGERTON V COVHENTRY CITY

For the VE Day celebrations on Friday Mr V and I shared a bottle of Prosecco. Or, as I like to think of it, half a bottle was wasted on Mr V.

Mr V has kindly replenished my wine supplies. For some bizarre reason, he also came home with 26 chicken thighs. They're enormous! The chickens must have been footballers. I've got the full bloody team and the reserves here. Who did they play for? Liverpoulet? Manchickster United? Tottenham Cockspur? I can't help thinking that, somewhere out there, there's a little chicken coach wondering why none of the team have turned up for training. And now I have to explain to Mr V that I'm too sad to eat them.

I cooked (okay, incinerated) dinner last night but left Mr V to serve himself. He has been binge watching Mad Men, which is set in the 1950s, and may have had his expectations raised somewhat. 'And how do you expect me to serve myself?' he asked, 'According to Mad Men there's a lot of things you're supposed to be doing that you're not doing. According to Mad Men I can put my foot down. I can have the final word!' Oh, how we laughed. Oh, how I imagined exactly where I'd like to stuff those 26 bloomin' chicken thighs. Anyway, I've been watching Outlander for years but he's yet to don a kilt, call me Sassenach and take me into the woods for a bit of rumpy pumpy!

And that, m'dears, brings us up to date with all the exciting goings on in Covid Corner. With the problem of what to do with the chicken thighs resolved and the wine supplies replenished, for now all is good in my little world. Cheers.

***

Oh bollocks

😋👍😲 23   14 comments

Here's my personal Facebook post from 9th May. I didn't do the chicken thighs because Mr V had also bought (eye roll please) a monster pack of 18 sausages which were about to go out of date. The wee hairy boys thought all their Christmases had come at once.

I'm no cook. I do my best, but the culinary world will remember me for charcoaled pizza. I have my old faithfuls that I trot out about fifty times a week, spag bol being chief among them. To be fair, it's so bloody hard finding something that everyone likes, so when I do hit upon a universally approved family meal, I tend to repeat it until they tell me to stop.

The thing I don't do is eggs, mainly because I don't like them. Mr V once made the mistake of putting me in charge of the fried egg part of bacon and eggs for the family. All my previous attempts at cooking eggs had been cunningly concealed in sandwiches, so nobody had ever actually seen any eggsamples of my rubbish egg frying before. Nobody has ever shown me how to fry an egg and I had no inner Nigella whispering vague innuendos about getting things hot and oily to help me. Just an inner Gordon Ramsay shouting, 'FFS you're a bloody grown-up. How can you not do this?!' I told Mr V that I couldn't fry eggs. He said, 'Nonsense. It's very easy. When I was a student I used to do it all the time!' and left me to it.

The eggs were misshapen lumps. The whites spread thin and the yolks broke. I even tried pouring them into an upside down cookie cutter so they'd come out in a vague circle shape, rather than looking like the poos of a very large, very sickly bird. There were bubbly bits, burnt bits, torn bits and a bit that bore an uncanny resemblance to an ex boyfriend with a lazy eye and acne (I was 15 and under strict instructions from my hormones to practise snogging the face off any boy who would snog me back).

Ten minutes and six eggs later, I proudly presented my culinary efforts. Mr V surveyed the dripping mess on the plate and said, 'You're right. You can't fry eggs. Even my dad can cook eggs better than you.' By this time, bacon-gate had started between the crispy camp and the not crispy camp, so I made a hasty eggsit, saying I'd have a bacon sandwich when anyone decided the bacon was ready.

Fifteen minutes later, Mr V came to find me - they'd eaten all the bacon! Did I want an egg? Almost a quarter of a century of marriage. A quarter of a century where he has never seen me eat an egg. A quarter of a century of me pretending to throw up on trays of egg sandwiches at posh receptions and complaining about the disgusting Scotch eggs he stores in the fridge until they're six

140

weeks past their sell-by date and I have to throw them out and he gets all miffed the next day because he was sure there was a Scotch egg in the fridge and it appears to be missing. Aaaand breathe...

I'm afraid I had to give him some good wifely advice as to what he could do with the egg, much of it involving the general area it had come out of in the first place.

Maybe I should try an omelette. Isn't there a saying that you can't make an omelette without breaking a few legs? I think I'd be quite good at that.

***

11th May 2020

TICKY TAPE

I've had another text from the NHS, telling me that someone else should be putting the bins out. Mr V has noted that this will cause absolutely no disruption to my life whatsoever.

I discovered a tick on Vegas this morning. Mr V was in full curmudgeon (probably because NHS had the cheek to think I'd ever put the bins out in my life) and just grumbled something about putting sticky tape on it. No further instructions. So, I wrapped a big bit around the dog. Then I thought about it logically. Maybe I was supposed to wrap the sticky tape around the tick? I untaped the dog and went back to get another piece for the tick. By which time the tick had fallen off and was lying on the Covid Corner chair, ready to sink its little teeth into the next big lady bottom that descended.

I'm not ashamed to admit I was freaked out by the tick. I picked it up using the sticky tape and tried to pop it in the bin. But the tape stuck to my fingers and I ended up screaming and frantically waggling my hand in the bin. Mr V came rushing through to see what all the fuss was about, but by that time I'd dislodged the bug. 'What fuss?' I asked him, with all the dignity I could muster. 'I was merely removing the tick using sticky tape as recommended by you.'

I have a feeling that this little tick will metaphorically come back to bite me on the bum the next time I get annoyed with my family for being wimps about spiders. I'm preparing myself for some mickey taking. But at least I won't be the one putting out the bin with the tick in it.

P.S. Vegas was completely unharmed. Just a little confused about why his mummy wrapped him in sticky tape then screamed at the bin.

14th May 2020

NOODLES À LA V

Mr V did haute cuisine the other day. He came huffing past Covid Corner, grumbling about having to make noodles for Cherub 2, who is still ill. I stood on the sidelines, walking him through such thorny issues as 'Where is the jug? I can't see the numbers on it. What do you mean I can just use a half pint mug? Are all our mugs half a pint, well bugger me! Cold or boiling water? Do the noodles go in first?' Cherub 2 came through later to let me know that his dad makes much better noodles than me.

In other news, I was let out of Covid Corner for my monthly blood test today. I was so excited that I put on my going out bra. Thought I'd give my boobs a bit of a treat. I didn't extend the glamour to the knicker department. I figured I didn't need my usual sexy pair of ginormous tuck-your-bingo-wings-in-here-while-you're-at-it tummy control knickers to see the nurse. They'd only roll down under my belly the moment I sat down and I didn't have the cover of a pub table to discreetly roll them back up again. Oh Lordy, pubs. Remember them?

Cherub 2 has been painting her bedroom. Normally I'm in charge of painting but, as I'm not allowed into other rooms, I was in charge of being the UN. This involved relaying a series of cries for help to an increasingly curmudgeonly Mr V. I had to use all my diplomatic skills to obtain cooperation. My opening sally of, 'Can get your arse upstairs and move the shelves please' was unsuccessful, so I added an extra layer of diplomacy and asked if he would, 'Kindly get your arse upstairs and move the twatting shelves NOW please.'

Work has been non-stop. My brain is whirling. The brain gremlins have slammed the filing cabinets shut and hung a 'Full up' sign on the door. They've declared that it may not be Wineday but an exception must be made. So, I am off to pour myself a glass of wine and watch mindless telly. And, now that we all know he makes such brilliant noodles, I'll put Mr V in charge of dinner.

Cheers.

15th May 2020

BIG HANDS, BIG...CLAPPER

Happy Wineday, although for some of us it started yesterday.

We had a fun awards ceremony at work today and I won the *Dressed For Bed - most likely to be wearing pyjamas right now* award. In my acceptance speech I thanked the Marks and Spencer Ladies With Big Bottoms Pyjama Department for their steady supply in these trying times.

The Cherubs have been struggling under the broken dishwasher regime. Cherub 1 was full of complaints last night about the quality of my washing up. I told her that if she wasn't happy with the service at home then she was welcome to move out. 'But I like living here because it's free!' was the reply.

She went on a bike ride this afternoon and I found myself telling her, 'Have a lovely time and don't touch any strangers.' That's probably number two on the list of odd things I've said recently. Number one was when we did the clap for carers last night. Mr V heard myself and Cherub 1 going into the front garden and shouted, 'Where are you going?' 'We have the clap,' I merrily shouted back.

Does anyone else do the same as me during the clap for carers? I clap for a bit, then I make the family stop clapping for a few seconds so I can hear all the clapping from the other streets. I can't shake the thought that, some day, we will all do this at the same time and there will just be an eerie silence. Thanks to clap for carers, I've also discovered that Mr V does very loud clapping. I checked in case he'd grown giant hands during lockdown but they appear normal. A little part of me hoped he had grown giant hands because that might be very useful, especially if I asked him to pass me a handful of chocolate raisins.

Anyway, we have all made it through another week, so let's give ourselves a very loud clap and a little bit of what we fancy.

***

During May the lockdown rules were relaxed, so that those not shielding could exercise with a friend. Cherub 1 chose to interpret 'exercise' as 'gin' and spent a fair amount of time sitting outside, ginning with our neighbour's daughter. We share a drive and they each sat in their own part of the drive, two metres apart, having a good old chinwag every evening. I'm fairly sure this wasn't what Boris meant, but across the country neighbours were chatting over the fence and playing street Bingo. My main objection was that she buggered off with the outdoors chairs then left them in the front garden.

My children are thieves. No phone charger is safe and it drives me nuts when I go to bed, lean over to plug in my phone and the bloody charger is gone. I have lost count of the nice things Mr V has bought me which have subsequently fallen into the hands of my little angels. Here is another DCI Mr V mystery which pretty much sums it up:

The Mystery of the Vanishing Hair Stuff - Part 1

It was 5.30 on a cold December morning. In a dark, rather untidy house in the suburbs, a well-padded Scotswoman rolled over in bed, farted and woke both herself and the dog. As she was awake, she decided that she may as well get up have a shower. The dog objected to the intrusion into his little dreams of finding a giant pizza that he didn't have to share with the other dog, so he buried himself under his blanket and ignored any suggestions that he might like to go out for a wee.

146

The woman (who we shall call Mrs V) padded through to the shower and switched it on. While she waited for the water to heat up, she idly wondered whether she should shave her legs. She weighed up the arguments and, finding herself inventing increasingly outlandish excuses for not shaving her legs, concluded that ultimately she was just a lazy cow. Anyway, surely December was the very best month to sport a fine pelt.

Soon the water was hot and steam covered the mirror, obscuring all of Mrs V's wobbly bits and leaving her free to imagine herself as rubenesque. Glancing into the shower Mrs V noticed a gap in her many, many, absolutely necessary shampoos. She gave gasp. Where had the posh banana shampoo gone? Mrs V asked her brain gremlins to check the 'things I have lost and it's all my own fault' filing cabinet. They reported back that there was no memory of Mrs V doing something ridiculous like sniff testing her leggings and giving the crotch a quick wash with shampoo (all the while swearing she'd put them in the proper wash when she got home yet knowing she would wake up the next morning and reason to herself that a quick wash with shampoo must last at least a couple of days), then putting the shampoo away somewhere it didn't belong. This was a mystery. 'But no worries,' thought Mrs V, 'I have probably just mislaid it.'

Mrs V had her shower and, wrapped in her special fluffy towel that nobody was allowed to touch but which also regularly disappeared, wandered back into the bedroom. She rubbed some frizzy hair oil (or 'calm the fuck down cream' as she called it) into her hair and looked around for her hairbrush. Where was her brush? She looked in all the places it could be and even sent the brain gremlins back to the filing cabinet, all without success. Mrs V was going to have to go to work without brushing her hair. Something Must Be Done About This!

Realising that she couldn't possibly solve all the mysteries on her own, Mrs V decided to call in professional help. She needed Detective Chief Inspector Mr V. She was fairly sure he wouldn't mind at all that it was 6am and he would completely understand *that she couldn't go to work without brushing her hair. She was, therefore, most surprised when DCI Mr V stumbled around in his underpants for twenty minutes with his eyes closed and used some very undetectivelike language. However, DCI Mr V was hoping to have marital relations again some day, so agreed to conduct an investigation. He pulled on his regulation uniform of tartan lounge pants and Captain America t-shirt, declared the house to be freezing and went off to stand in front of the dreaded digital thermostat for ten minutes trying to remember the code to unlock it (Mrs V had optimistically set the code as his mother's birthday in the vague hope that he could remember this number and would stop phoning her at work to ask her to turn the heating up). If you are wondering why the thermostat had a code, then consider yourself blessed that you have never had to yell at recalcitrant teenagers for turning the heating on max then leaving the house five minutes later.*

Mrs V came downstairs and turned the heating up then, ignoring some dark mutterings about 'effing pain in the backside wives' emanating from behind the toilet door, set about making coffee. She hoped that a good morning poo, followed by coffee and crunchy nut cornflakes, would work their magic and turn DCI Mr V back into a human being.

Fifteen minutes later, DCI Mr V pushed his cereal bowl aside and declared himself ready to investigate. Together, he and Mrs V compiled a list of suspects. It was quite a short list:

1. *Cherub 1*
2. *Cherub 2*
3. *Mrs V, because she loses everything and cannot be trusted with items such as passports, keys and small children.*

The witness list was equally short:

1. *Wee hairy boy*
2. *Other wee hairy boy*

3.	*DCI Mr V, who was willing to testify that Mrs V had probably eaten the banana shampoo (it did smell very tasty) and put her hairbrush in the fridge.*

DCI Mr V declared that he would begin by interviewing witnesses and conduct a thorough investigation. The dog appeared and declared that he too would like a morning poo. Mrs V declared that she was off to work and left the house looking like Boris Johnson trapped in a wind tunnel.

Does DCI Mr V discover the culprit? Is Mrs V all fur legs and no knickers? Did the wee hairy boys see the thief? Find out in Part 2 of this thrilling DCI Mr V mystery, coming soon....

The Mystery of the Vanishing Hair Stuff - Part 2

At the end of part 1, we left DCI Mr V promising to investigate the mysterious disappearance of shampoo and a hairbrush, the dog declaring it was time for his morning poo and Mrs V going to work with a hairdo to die (of shame) for.

Mrs V worked very hard all day, even though it was December, the official month of pretending to work. At lunchtime she received an 'only phone me at work in an emergency' emergency phone call.

'Is this an actual emergency or do you just want money?' asked Mrs V.

'It is a real emergency!' howled Cherub 1, most shocked that her mother would think otherwise. 'Someone has eaten the chocolate out of my advent calendar. Something Must Be Done About This! And can I borrow £5?'

'You need to speak to Detective Chief Inspector Mr V immediately!' exclaimed Mrs V.

'Who?'

'Your father. Speak to your father.'

'Why are you calling him detective...is this a weird old people's sex thing...? Ew! Never mind. I'll phone him.'

Mrs V stared at her phone, wondering how, in a few short years, she had gone from being the bestest mummy in the whole wide world to being a wild haired pervert. Then she shrugged it off and went for a sandwich, pausing only to reassure complete strangers in the lift that she didn't normally look this wild. She decided against telling them she was also not a pervert.

After work, Mrs V phoned DCI Mr V for a progress report. He sounded very sleepy. Mrs V could not understand why, because she had woken him up at the perfectly reasonable time of 6am to demand an investigation. What had he been doing all day? Mrs V suspected that he had been napping on the job. She was about to begin an interrogation of her own, when he quickly promised a full report in due course and hung up.

Mrs V arrived home to find DCI Mr V, still dressed in his tartan lounge pants and clutching the 'I'm a Total Fucking Legend' notebook she bought him last Christmas. He licked his finger, flicked the pages importantly and read out that day's progress.

'At precisely 0800 hours I asked the elderly wee hairy boy, a Mr Vegas, if there had been any incursion into our bedroom. Mr Vegas replied, 'Woof,' and explained that he'd spent most of the day sleeping under a blanket, except for the bits where he stuck his balls out because he was getting too hot. The second witness, a Mr Biggles, ran away when I tried to speak to him and I was forced to give chase. By the way, I will be submitting an expenses claim - we have to fix the fence and I've lost a gardening shoe.'

DCI Mr V moved on to his interviews with suspects.

'At 0900 hours I knocked on the bedroom door of Cherub 2. There was no reply, so I shouted, 'Open up!' and kicked the door open. I was overwhelmed by boy fumes and ordered an immediate withdrawal for officer safety. Then I remembered he was at college, so I texted him. He says your shampoo is in his college bag.'

One mystery solved and one to go.

'What about the hairbrush?' I asked.

'Ah, that is an ongoing investigation. What with detective resources being cut and budget restrictions, the case is being moved to another team.'

'You mean you're back at work tomorrow so you're putting me in charge of the department of hairy mysteries?'

'Erm yes. But I will be submitting a formal request for the continuation of marital relations.'

Mrs V immediately decided to put in a complaint to DCI Mr V's management about his lax attitude to hairbrushes and rang her mother-in-law. Mrs V Senior was not in the least bit interested in hairbrush investigations, so Mrs V grassed him up for something else instead, then wandered off to make dinner.

Dinner was a fraught affair. Mrs V had perfected the art of hiding vegetables in sauces but had never quite managed to anticipate the mercurial attitude of her children towards food. 'But yesterday you loved spaghetti bolognese!' she would cry, as her lovingly prepared sauce was pronounced the blood of Satan himself. As a result, the wee hairy boys were looking decidedly portly. Cherub 1 came home and regarded today's offering of sausage casserole with disgust.

'But you love sausages!' wailed Mrs V.

'Yes but only the Tesco ones on the fourth Tuesday of every second month,' replied Cherub 1, completely baffled as to why her mother didn't know these things. She clearly didn't care. Cherub 1 was cursed to have such awful parents.

Mrs V regarded the back of her retreating teenager and wondered how, in a few short years, she had gone from the bestest mummy in the whole wide world to wild haired pervert who starved children. She didn't feel quite so bad for eating the chocolate from Cherub 1's advent calendar that morning. Ooh, another mystery solved.

Mrs V went upstairs to find out what Cherub 1 wanted to eat. She knocked politely on the bedroom door and went in. Cherub 1 was sitting on the floor sorting her makeup. Also sitting on the floor was a hairbrush. Mrs V peered more closely. It was full of blonde hair. Now, Mrs V was no Nancy Drew, but Cherub 1 had dark hair, so only one conclusion could be drawn.

'You took my hairbrush! You took my hairbrush! I had to go to work with Boris Johnson hair today!' screeched Mrs V. 'I've been looking everywhere for it!'

Cherub 1 looked at her unapologetically.

'Well you could have looked in my room so it's your own fault.'

'It was 5.30 in the morning. You were sleeping. It's your fault. You took my hairbrush!'

'It's not my fault. You didn't look properly,' declared Cherub 1, unequivocally.

Mrs V took a deep breath, counted to ten and, grabbing the hairbrush, left. Making her way back to the kitchen she noticed something on a shelf. Very quietly she picked it up and went into *the kitchen. Grabbing a knife she carefully opened the big door on day 24 of Cherub 1's advent calendar, slit open the foil and removed the big chocolate from inside. She smoothed the foil and door back down and put the advent calendar back on the shelf.*

Mrs V was not really a bad parent. But she was very, very sneaky. And she had a funny feeling that on Christmas Eve, DCI Mr V would find himself pressed back into service.

The end"

16th May 2020

KEEPING BUSY

I've been looking for isolation hobby ideas and have realised, to my relief, that there are far bigger twats than me out there.

Mindful cocktail making? 'What is a mindful cocktail?' I hear you ask. No idea. I saw the word wellness, filed it straight under 'sh*t someone made up to extract money from me' and moved on.

One article suggested I clear out my beauty cabinet. A whole cabinet?! I have a bag of doom, which only gets washed once it is fully orange on the inside and anything I touch is mysteriously covered in grey eye pencil. And, most mysteriously, I don't even own a grey eye pencil.

I looked into cheese making, but it seems very complicated. So complicated that I'm not sure how we ever discovered cheese in the first place! The writer of the article recommended getting milk straight from the udder, adding that you would need to be on a dairy farm. Therefore, step 1 of any isolation cheese making hobby is to get out of isolation.

Mr V has suggested that cleaning the kitchen would be an excellent hobby but I just referred him back to the first sentence of this post.

Anyway, I thought we could just have a bit of a chat today. How are you coping with lockdown, isolation, quarantine, whatever? Has the relaxation of the rules helped or are you staying at home anyway because you don't trust the numpties of the world not to start running amok? Whether you're quietly going insane or loving the chance to potter around the house, please tell us all about it. No judgement and be kind x

*** *The NHS workers were looking forward to finally having a day off. Some folk were happily pottering around. Lots of people were missing their families and a bit concerned that they were having far too many conversations with their pets. A lady in Canada was #winning - she had finally managed to buy yeast. A lady from New Zealand said things were getting back to normal there. I was a wee bit jealous because I was missing the outside world.* ***

17th May 2020

THE LAZY REPORTING GAME

As you know, I sometimes write posts in the style of a news article. My articles are always relevant and informative. For instance, who could forget that growth in the Belgian (chocolate) economy is in line with the expansion of my lockdown bottom? That's proper facts right there.

Now, often of a morning I have a WTF moment and I like to text it to my friend. Yesterday it was an advert for a sponge to clean taps, "Your guests will ask how do you get that shine?" (I threatened to buy her one and come over every day to ask that very question). This morning's WTF moment was a news article about a celebrity buying a new house just down the road from his old house. "The move comes two years after he was mugged outside his sons' school." Eh? How was that related? This was just shoddy reporting of a type you would never see in an article written by Mrs V!

So, I wondered what I would write if I was describing what I'm doing now and popped in something I did years ago. I looked through my Facebook memories and here is what I came up with:

This morning a well padded Scotswoman sat on her garden wall sipping coffee. The sipping comes eight years after she lost a false nail in a pot of chilli.

This morning, in shock news, a lady binned a bunch of old bananas because she couldn't be arsed making banana loaf. The binning comes three years after the cat got stuck behind the bookcase and she was somewhat confused because she didn't own a cat.

This morning a little dog refused to get out of bed and go for a wee. The refusal comes four years after his human drank cheap wine out of a plastic cup in a Travelodge in Sheffield.

Are you up for a game of Lazy Reporting?

*** *This morning a lady who was supposed to be writing a book decided that her excuse for everything today would be "but it's sunny outside." This comes five years after she was given a fork with a bent tine and discovered, to her delight, that she could eat and pick her nose at the same time.* ***

19th May 2020

ME: ALEXA, REMIND ME TO GO TO THE GYM

ALEXA: I HAVE ADDED GIN TO YOUR SHOPPING LIST

Some days you wonder why you bothered to get out of bed and change into your day pyjamas. Everyone in my house is tired and grumpy today. I'm in trouble for stealing other people's shoes again, Cherub 2 has banned everyone from talking to him and Biggles has failed in all attempts to have sex with Vegas' head. It's hard being a total love machine and having all your advances spurned. Coincidentally, that's also what Mr V said when I asked him why he was grumpy. I don't know what he's got to moan about, I've had a headache for the past ten hours..days…weeks..months.

I'm not allowed to have Alexa on while I'm working from home, presumably in case she hears any important work conversations, such as what my team are binge watching on Netflix, whose house looks lovely on video conferences and how my headphones aren't working but I'm wearing them anyway so that my family won't talk to me.

I think we need a break from each other. There is just this incessant flow of information from my loved ones about their bodily functions. Then they start comparing their current bodily functions with past bodily functions - 'This is like when I got dehydrated in 2009. Do you remember? It was like slowly firing single bullets.' Honestly, if Alexa was on and really is secretly gathering information about my family, then Amazon would be serving me ads for portaloos and adult diapers.

Anyway, with Alexa being off, I have no way of instantly adding things to my shopping list, so I have taken to using Mr V as Alexa. If something occurs to me I just text it to him. At first he was very confused and asked why I was texting random words - "pasta cheese bleach". He soon got the idea, but drew the line when I asked him to switch the lights off and play With My Little Ukulele.

21st May 2020

HAIRIUS HOBBITUS

Breaking news. There was an emergency phone call to Covid Corner yesterday, when Cherub 1 went for a wee in the woods and accidentally squatted on a nettle. The rest of this story will be brought to you when the residents of Covid Corner have stopped laughing.

An archaeological dig in the living room has unearthed a man cave inhabited by a newly discovered species - Hairius Hobbitus. The Hairius cave is believed to be a fine example of what happens in the absence of female influences. Artefacts include pillows, game controllers, laptops, a beautiful Japanese trunk now being used to display model soldiers and a priceless collection of empty Pringles tubes. The Hairius itself was once a well-groomed, intelligent species, but societal changes forced the sprouting of what appears to be a big hairy scarf. There is evidence of inhabitation by two of the hirsute creatures and a separate expedition to their bathroom unearthed multiple empty loo rolls, a crispy towel and a seat permanently set to up.

Consumer spending has taken a downturn this month, with the announcement that Mr V is sick of going to the supermarket. A brief drop in ice cream sales followed Mr V's realisation that he was in control of Mrs V's diet, but bottom sizes were unaffected when Mrs V realised she could just bribe Cherub 1 to go to the shop for her.

And finally, the weather for Almost Wineday. Mostly sunny with a few woofs as several deliveries arrive. Cloudy with a chance of severe storms later, when Mr V finds out that one of the deliveries is an item of furniture and he has to build it. The warm front experienced yesterday in Cherub 1's nether regions will be replaced by a chill when Mrs V roars at her for getting paint on the good tea towels.

And finally finally, the archaeologists behind the unearthing of the man cave have just reported the discovery of the female counterpart of Hairius Hobbitus. She is known as the Braless Letherselfgoabit.

22nd May 2020

THE GOLDEN RULES FOR LETTING YOURSELF GO A BIT

1. Eat lots of ice cream. Your boobs will need a comfy tummy to rest on.

2. Don't wear a bra. Not many people know this, but bras were invented by evil boob wizards in 1642 to subjugate women. History records some nonsense about ducking stools and burning at the stake but really it was just boob wizards. Fact.

3. Tell everyone you are exercising and having oodles of fun, when really you're binge watching Netflix and posting pictures of a lake you visited in 2012. It's the internet - people will believe any old rubbish. Or at least that's what the chief boob wizard said.

4. The fridge is your friend. Why else would they put a welcome light in it?

5. Don't worry if day pyjamas become night pyjamas then turn into day pyjamas again. The pyjama is not like other clothes. It has an extended lifecycle. However, bear in mind that the knicker lifecycle is much shorter.

6.   Do shower. If you join in the bread making craze, you don't want your friends asking awkward questions about how you managed to get your hands on so much yeast.

7.   Stop worrying about your hair. Unless you're a lady and it's chin hair - in which case tug at your face for three days like a deranged monkey. Men - you may also wish to give up shaving and enjoy days of obsessive tugging.

8.   Lose the ability to count. You were never any good at maths anyway. This applies to wine, biscuits and slices of cake. However, it should never apply to blessings.

9.   Or is it 6? I forget. More wine please.

10.   Remember that, just like any gym membership you ever took out, letting yourself go a bit is a temporary lifestyle choice.

24th May 2020

GLASSES OR GLASSES

I live between three rooms. The bedroom, Covid Corner and the bathroom. So, where for the love of twattery are my glasses?! So far during lockdown I've lost 2 pairs. Mr V has stopped answering all glasses related questions and has refused to look for them. This is fine because next time there are sexy shenanigans, I won't have my glasses on and I can legitimately pretend he's Jamie Fraser. Can you tell I'm a bit exasperated and spoiling for an argument today?

Cherub 2 has removed all his head hair and grown a beard. I threatened to phone Feltham Young Offenders and ask if they were one short, then I told him total lockdown has been extended for another two months until his hair grows back. He kinda suits it though - like a model who mugs old ladies in his spare time.

Mr V and I have taken the coming week off work. He declared that, 'We must do things and get things done!' As he hasn't been clear about all these doings, I have made a list of top priorities:

1. Eat ice cream
2. Drink cocktails
3. Tidy bedroom
4. Take a nap in tidy bedroom
5. More cocktails please

It's important to have achievable life goals.

Mr V disagrees with number 2, but I have told him that I too am refusing to discuss glasses.

25th May 2020

ANYONE FOR GLAMPING?

Because we can't go for our usual camping holiday in France, I have decided to recreate the experience at home. Sadly, I can't bus in a load of nice, strapping Dutch people with well mannered children to make me feel like a short tub of lard in charge of a heathen brood. However, undaunted, I have raided the campervan for camping chairs, charged up the kindles and ordered a packet of Gauloise to waft around the place.

As I'm not allowed to go to the shops, Mr V will have to get up at 7am to source fresh croissants. He is, surprisingly, less keen than I on the idea of camping at home.

Under normal circumstances, I'd ask Old Ivy next door if we could use her bathroom so I could replicate that '100 yard dash to the nearest loo' experience. Obviously this is not possible, but I've still promised to drink litres of Orangina then wake Mr V up three times a night when it makes its inevitable appearance out the other end. Once more, he has pronounced himself less than keen on the idea of camping at home.

Mr V perked up at the idea of pizzas and barbecues. Mainly because no vegetables. Mr V thinks fruit and vegetables are for other people. The only things standing between him and scurvy are myself and Lovely Granny.

Cherubs 1 & 2 are not so enthusiastic because everyone has to take their turn at doing the dishes when we're camping and we all hate cleaning the barbecue.

Finally, I have told my family that, for the full campervan experience, if it rains they must all squeeze into the downstairs loo and play Monopoly for six hours. Of course, I'm exempt because I have to stay in Covid Corner with the gin. My family may have shouted some rude words at me.

We always have such a lovely time on holiday, so I really don't understand why they aren't embracing my whizzy ideas. Once more, I have been forced to remind everyone that I'm a delight.

***

We don't always have a perfect time when we camp in France. I recall one particularly disconcerting toilet block where the loo roll was outside the cubicle, so you had to be absolutely certain that a number one wasn't going to unexpectedly turn into a number two.

Trying to get my family to agree on a campsite in France makes the effing Brexit negotiations look like a mild disagreement between friends. After a referendum on dates and days of discussions I generally find a place that looks like it might do.

The list of family requirements go like this -

Me:
Croissants
Crepes
Wine
Sexy monsieurs

Mr V:
Swimming pool to cool balls when hot
No noise
No other human beings
Good book
Somewhere to take photos

Cherubs:
Wifi
Showers
Wifi
Stuff to do
Wifi
Noise
Wifi
Chicken nuggets
Wifi
Rich parents who could afford to take them on a cruise.

Before we go to France, I have to practice not swearing in French. It is normally my 'go to' language if I have a wee swear in front of the kids or Mr V, but when you're actually in France doing French swears is a Bad Thing. Which is a shame because it's my best French. To not use it seems like a waste of all those years sitting in Mrs Richardson's class, looking up swear words in the French dictionary while she wittered on about 'Ou est la bibliotheque?' I also paid attention to Mrs Richardson sometimes and if I ever find myself in a situation where I urgently require a library, rest assured I will be able to find one.

Before we set off on our adventures, Mr V will spend ten weeks researching all the war museums he can drag us to. And plotting how he can make his recalcitrant wife have a shower and get dressed every day, when all she wants to do is sit in her pyjamas until 11am, munch croissants and make the inside of the campervan look like an explosion in a bakery.

We will forget to take bags every time we go to le supermarche and come home with dozens of SuperU and Carrefour bags for life. None of which we'll be able to find the next year. We will randomly buy weird wines until we find one we like. We will tell each other to remember it for next time we go to the supermarket and, two days later, find ourselves in a Carrefour scanning the rows of bottles, desperately trying to jog our memories.

On our way home, Mr V will make us leave ridiculously early and, the moment we arrive at the Eurotunnel, I will lead the charge into Starbucks. After two weeks of surviving on thimble sized French coffees and not brushing my hair "because we're camping", I am now a feral creature, crouched in a corner of Starbucks, hugging a bucket of latte and snarling at anyone who comes near me - because Mr V made me get up at 6am for an 11am train and I didn't even get a croissant. It was at the top of my list!

27th May 2020

MUMMY'S LITTLE ROBBER

Cherub 2 has gone out to the post office wearing a black balaclava, that incorporates a face mask, and black gloves. This is on the basis that if the post office people see his shaved head, they'll think he's there to rob them.

He'd be the only robber ever in the history of the universe whose mum adjusted the strap on his bag and offered an alternative mask before he set off.

It's hard being out in the world as a teenager. Even in normal times, people automatically view you with suspicion and sometimes go out of their way to make life that little bit harder. Cherub 2 told me the other day that a bus driver once refused to let him use his bus pass unless he produced ID, citing new company policy. Cherub 2 explained he was under 18 and didn't have any ID, but the driver refused to accept this. It was an adult bus pass, so there was no good reason for the check. A friend eventually paid his fare, but my point is that the driver would never have done the same thing to me, a middle aged woman. In these times of face masks and gloves the petty biases are likely to become even worse. Don't get me wrong, teenagers can be utterly horrible. But they're not always horrible and it is difficult to teach your kids to respect people in a society which throws so much disrespect their way.

Fortunately we live in a village and Cherub 1 has been going to the shop that houses the post office since he was little. I'm fairly sure that his polite demands for a first class stamp will be met. Nevertheless, I have waved him a cheery goodbye and told him to use his one phone call wisely.

28th May 2020

ARISE SIR MR V...IF YOU CAN

Being from the north of England, my kids tend to call me mam. I choose to hear it as ma'am, like the Queen. Although I'm fairly sure the Queen has never had to patiently explain to the D of E that the wet patch on the chair was caused by the dog enthusiastically cleaning his balls and was definitely not a leaky regina. Am not quite a Tena Lady yet, although a good coughing fit takes me perilously close to being a Tena Lady-in-waiting.

So, yesterday I was queen for the day. My throne was a camping chair in the garden and my footmen were two useless wee hairy boys who failed to bring me anything but a ball and a ragged teddy they found behind the shed. I sat there happily baking in the sun, my leg hair rippling gently in the breeze.

Over the course of the day, I fulfilled all my queenly duties. I admired Mr V's good work in the palace garden, I gave Cherub 1 royal assent to buy us both ice cream and every time someone said ma'am (or mam) I replied, 'Hello and what do you do?' in a posh voice. Mr V told me I was being a royal pain in the arse. One was not amused.

Unlike the actual Queen, I can't afford my own chef, so I had to make dinner myself. But I did use the good cutlery. The stuff we use at Christmas or to make visitors believe we're proper people instead of heathens with fifteen mismatched forks, which we can't remember how we acquired.

Mr V, presumably channelling the gaffe-prone D of E, came through afterwards to tell me, 'You know the dinner you made? It wasn't...er um er...it was too tomatoey.' I don't own a knighting sword, but I was washing a pan at the time and offered to knight him with it. Very, very hard. Like a good commoner, he slowly backed away and avoided eye contact.

All in all, a good day, but slightly disappointed that I didn't get to smash a bottle off the side of a ship.

***

I love the royal family. It's the glitz and glamour of it. I'm sure there must be downsides to being royal, for example reading nonsense about yourself in newspapers and never being able to so much as fart in an empty room without a paparazzi popping out from behind a 16th century gilt credenza. However, it must be lovely to live in fabulous houses, work part-time, swan off to posh parties and never have to make the difficult choice between buying that lush handbag or eating for the rest of the month.

I sometimes think that gynaecologists are a bit like the Queen. Everywhere they go is well scrubbed and tidy. But no smell of fresh paint because that would just be weird. It must be hard being a gynaecologist's girlfriend. Such high expectations to live up to.

In April, Meghan and Harry stepped down from being HRHs and buggered off across the pond to make their own way as plain old Duke and Duchess of Suffolk. I wasn't sure how I felt about this, or even if I was entitled to feel anything at all. It's not like they're my kids. Although, don't get me wrong, my kids are also brilliant at falling out with everybody and delivering a big eff you before storming off. Nevertheless, I decided that I wished their Dukelinesses the best of luck on t'other side.

Of course, the Queen is my favourite royal. She's still there giving out medals in her 90s. I can't imagine the strength of character it must take to get up every morning and wear a hat.

A couple of years ago, I watched as an elderly man at the next table to me rocked back and forth, trying to get off his chair. His wife was pulling from the front and I was just about to offer a friendly shove from behind when he gathered enough momentum and made it to his feet. I thought to myself, 'The world is full of people who quietly keep going despite everything that life throws at them. People are made Sirs or Dames just for being on the telly or in politics. That's all well and good, but what we need is an award for people like that man. People who just Keep Buggering On.' I decided that, instead of a KBE, there needs to be a KBO.

I imagine the Queen would be delighted to award KBOs. No heavy swords involved. Just a tap on the shoulder with a walking stick and a jaunty, 'Well done, now keep buggering on some more,' required. Although, I'm not sure who would give the Queen her KBO.

***

30th May 2020

BUNNY FREEZER

News just in from Covid Corner. There was consternation when a resident found a stuffed toy in her freezer. A local woman, Miss Cherub 1, is currently being questioned as to why a fluffy bunny rabbit was taking up valuable ice cream space, but has so far offered no explanation other than, 'Ha ha, take it out.' A spokesperson for Covid Corner has reminded the public that taking up ice cream space in Mrs V's freezer could result in serious head injuries.

In fashion news, Britain's most well-padded supermodel, Mrs V, has been too lazy to unearth the bag of summer clothes, so has been making do with whatever she can find stuffed in the bottom drawer. Today's ensemble of flowery blouse, old swimming costume and work shoes has been described by Mr V, world fashion expert and devotee of the dog haired fleece, as 'erm...alright.' Since becoming caught up in the great 'does my bum look big in this?' scandal of 1997, Mr V has been very circumspect in offering opinions on Mrs V's appearance.

Our religious affairs correspondent reports that there has been a flurry of activity in the garden. Mr V has been putting a new roof on the sacred shed and worshippers have been invited to join him in gazing admiringly at it. However, the shed will not be open to the public as it is where Mr V keeps important relics, such as random bits of wood that might come in handy some day, three buckets with no handles and a big piece of plastic that 'you never know, it might be useful.'

And finally, the weather. As hot as a Mrs V in big knickers (smokin'). As windy as a Mrs V after a double helping of chilli (dis-gusty). As changeable as a teenager being told to tidy up (cloudy, with a chance of screaming). And as calm as a Mr V having to stand in a queue at the DIY store for the second time in a day because he bought the wrong nails for the shed roof (so about 9 on the Richter scale).

All is well in Covid Corner. Happy More Wineday.

31st May 2020

MORE MORE WINEDAY

Spray sun tan cream. A gift for those of us with dodgy backs who can't reach our feet.

I'm happily baking in the sun on my last day before going back to work. Mr V decided I was taking the week off to work on the website. I have done nothing but sit in the sun and come up with what he calls 'hairbrained schemes' but I call 'imaginative use of time'. I'm not feeling in the least bit apologetic either. Any queries as to why I'm not doing website stuff have been met with me marching outside shouting,'Weather!'

Big news for those of us who are shielding. As of tomorrow, Boris has decreed that we ladies may once more need to wear a bra. The BBC news, of course, completely missed the bigger picture and focused on us being allowed to take a walk with one member of our household. We have been stuck in our houses since March. Does Boris not think we've seen enough of these people already?! I'm taking my first walk alone!

Mr V is going to see this as an opportunity to 'walk the wife'. He believes he's being subtle, but whenever he thinks my bottom is approaching the size where we may need to buy two aeroplane seats, he starts suggesting we go out on long walks. To be fair, months of self isolation (and possibly ice cream, but I wouldn't swear to it) have not been kind to my bottom, so he may have a point.

For now, I'm going to enjoy sitting in the garden with my wee hairy disciple, who has never left my side for months. I may even have one last hurrah and declare today a More More Wineday. Or more accurately Steal Mr V's Cider Day. He's been refusing to go to the shops so we've run out of fizzy drinks that I like. He hasn't noticed that his stash of cider is slowly depleting.

P.S. Is it bad that when I write the word 'more' my predictive text suggests 'Wineday'?

JUNE

***

June kicked off (and I mean Kicked Off) with Black Lives Matter demonstrations, counter-demonstrations and confused middle aged+ people asking why they couldn't say 'all lives matter'. The best explanation I heard was given by a radio presenter, Tony Livesey, who pointed out that when we see the name of the charity 'Save the Children', we don't assume that saving children precludes the saving of other people; we understand the context. So, in the context of equality and anti-racism, Black Lives Matter. Well put, I thought. During the unrest, statues were being defaced or removed and, afterwards, many statues were taken down by the authorities. There was some outrage at this "obliteration" of our history. There was also some "hooray" and a large helping of "meh". A number of people took to "defending" statues and war memorials and things turned quite ugly. If we didn't think racism had been a problem in the UK before, the Black Lives Matter demonstrations and many of the reactions to it made us think again. So, what was everyone to do next? Why, go back to being outraged that the protesters were breaching social distancing, of course.

Things started to relax towards the end of June. The number of infections and deaths dropped and the protests calmed down. Boris made announcements about shops in England reopening, with pubs and restaurants to follow in July. Queues for some newly reopened non-essential shops stretched for miles. The country celebrated the news that hairdressers would open soon and the cries of 'no more roots' could be heard ringing throughout the land. First to get a hairdresser's appointment wins a thousand Facebook points.

With camp sites set to open at the beginning of July, the vacuum cleaners were out and the men were sent to garages to raid their cable collections for the electricity hook up thingies (I know I'm being totally sexist but, really, how many women hoard

178

cables? How many ladies have the means of charging a flip phone, plugging in an electric typewriter and getting the fax machine up and running?).

People were allowed to form social bubbles and there were very complicated rules around bubbles, which the BBC explained to me and I instantly forgot. All I knew was that I wasn't allowed to have a bubble, unless it came in a bottle of prosecco.

The good news for this shielding maiden was that I could look forward to meeting up with five people outdoors as of 6th July - and they didn't need to be related to me. After over three months of nurse Lisa (she of the monthly blood tests and big needles) being the only person with whom I'd had physical contact, suddenly I had two weeks to think about who I'd meet up with. I had a strange urge to ask nurse Lisa round for a barbecue.

Towards the end of June, groups of up to six non-shielders were allowed to meet outdoors and Cherub 1's gin circle once more became extended. A brief heatwave brought about 'Beach Numpties - The Sequel', starring Ordinary Joe and his partner Joeletta as a couple who believe themselves invulnerable, then wonder how they managed to kill grandma. We temporarily forgot about shopping and pubs, while we worried about a second wave of the virus. Having now been told I had to shield until 1st August and having thus far kept my one star review of Beach Numpties to myself, I looked at the videos of packed beaches and decided it was time to shit on the fence or get off the pot. So I had a good rant. Aaaah, that felt better.

***

1st June 2020

MR V IS LOSING HIS SHIT

Back to work today. This means I get to spend much of the first day/week trying to remember anything...anything at all...from before I took a week off.

The brain gremlins are excellent weeders of information. If it's not used in a week, they file it under 'shit I will never need to know again' and walk away. I usually spend the first week back at work pleading with them to put the information back in the 'sh*t I definitely need to know so I don't get fired' filing cabinet. Sometimes they relent, sometimes they don't.

To continue the sh*t theme, Mr V's efforts at the weekend to paint the shed ended with us now being the proud owners of a structure that looks like someone had diahorrea on it. I kid you not. It quite literally looks like the place where we put all our shit. Mr V spent an hour queuing at Wee & Poo to buy...well...poo. I'll post a pic and we can all shout at him to go back for a nice colour.

Even though Boris said I could go out for a walk today, I haven't been yet. I won't lie, this is completely down to being too lazy to put on a bra. Also, maybe knickers. And possibly shorts that don't come as part of a pyjama set. Otherwise I'm good to go.

I'm off to make dinner now. You don't have to get properly dressed to do that. I may continue the brown stuff theme and do a nice sausage casserole.

*** *Wee & Poo is my name for the local DIY store. I rechristened it in a fit of pique after yet another failed delivery and it sort of stuck in our house. However, I should be clear that Wee & Poo also does good things, like employs a lot of older people. Despite quite a few customer service mishaps over the years, we still shop there because there has been good customer service too.* ***

3rd June 2020

WEE & POO

Thanks for the feedback about the shed the other day. A resounding bleurgh. We now have new paint. As many of you know, following failed deliveries and various other catastrophes over the years, I had a junior moment a while back and christened our local DIY store 'Wee & Poo.' Mr V had a senior moment yesterday which resulted in the following conversation:

Mr V: I'm having a shower then I'm going to pee and poo

Me: why are you telling me this?

Mr V: I'm going to pee and poo to get paint

Me (thinking this was some weird 'make your own paint like they did in the olden days' manly YouTube video he'd been watching): well the shed already looks like someone had diahorrea over it but okay

Mr V: No. I'm going to buy paint!

Me: Oh Wee & Poo! You have to use the correct terminology. It's Wee & Poo. I wondered why you were telling me about your toilet habits

Mr V: and I wondered why you weren't really pleased about it!

So, there we have it. The key to a successful relationship is good communication and a willingness to let your husband experiment with his own excrement.

We settled on blue. Neither of us could think of a blue bodily function, so at least if it all goes wrong again we can call it art.

4th June 2020

I NEED A LIE DOWN

Dear Furniture Store,

We are engaged in a battle with you. It's very one sided because you are completely ignoring us and your customer service department appears to have run away to join a circus. Possibly as a troupe of clowns. In the meantime, we are trying to figure out what to do with an effing king size mattress we didn't order.

I've suggested that Mr V and I build the mother of all forts and hide from our teenagers. We can have a secret password and our own gang called the InVincibles. Mr V disagrees and has taken the ludicrous step of storing the mattress in the bedroom. In front of the bedroom window. Blocking out the best light for plucking chin hairs. I have tried to contact you to complain about this, but suspect that by the time I find any means of contacting you, I shall have turned into Gandalf.

I expect you'll think I'm being quite rude about your store or a bit hashtagfirstworldproblemy. Particularly as deliveries are bound to be affected by the covid situation. I've actually been very patient and didn't complain when you told me the day before delivery that I'd have to wait another 3 weeks. Then on the day of delivery told me it was delayed again. However, you delivered the wrong thing and if I am to avoid having to join your customer services department at the circus as the bearded lady, I really do need you to take away this effing mattress.

Kind regards,

Mrs V

5th June 2020

ONE-LOVE TO MRS V

News flash from Covid Corner. The Great Battle of The Mattress has been won. For two days fighters were trapped in the enclave of the Covid Corner armchair, desperately seeking a means of opening negotiations with the Mattressian authorities. However, this morning there was a major breakthrough when General Mrs V discovered a brief window of webchat service. The Matressians are making arrangements to remove the giant mattress from in front of Mrs V's bedroom window and have offered war reparations. With the unwanted mattress soon to be gone and the refund on its way, Mrs V has declared a day of celebration for all Covid Corner residents (which happens to be only Mrs V) and pronounced today Double Wineday.

In other news, Covid Cornerwide shortages of ice cream and Jaffa cakes have led to Mrs V inadvertently redirecting Mr V's stash of chocolates to get her sugar fix. Mr V is yet to discover that the chocolates accidentally fell into his wife's mouth and Mrs V is considering just leaving the empty box there, then blaming the kids when he eventually finds out. Mr V is well known for being a big weirdo who can hoard sweets for months, so it may be some time before the mishap is noticed.

In domestic affairs, there has been some discord over who is responsible for washing the dishes. The Cherubs have claimed special dispensation on the basis that they once did something helpful, can't remember what or when, but it was definitely helpful. The parents have pointed out that they've been doing the washing up for weeks. In the meantime, the teenage cries of 'there are no clean knives' ring out across the land and the parents are seeking scientific advice on exactly how many fucks to give.

And finally, the weather. Showery with only a 10% chance of shed painting this weekend. Storms will quickly gather when Mrs V says, 'Ooh lovely colour, could you paint all the fences the same?' There will be a brief burst of sunshine when Mrs V discovers a new box set to binge, followed by a hard frost when she shushes anyone who makes her press pause by having the cheek to initiate a conversation.

Happy Double Wineday

*** In the end it was deuce. I never got the refund they promised and they haven't come back for the mattress. However, I now own a mattress that is far more expensive than the one I ordered. ***

8th June 2020

THE BIG BLUE JOBBIE!

This weekend I've been very busy, pulling together all my lockdown posts into a book. I also had the grand idea of putting in some extra bits that never made it onto Growing Old Disgracefully. Now, you'd think this would be easy - a copy and paste job. However, you have not accounted for the brain gremlins and all the shiny things that distract your average Mrs V and make her disorganised.

I do all my writing on my phone and I cannot describe the muddle in there. I have everything in a folder, but that's as good as it gets. It's a bit like the time my granny tried to teach me to crochet. In my head I was making a neat blanket, but in reality I produced a giant straggly, blue jobbie*. In my head I had an organised folder full of lovely posts. In reality I have a big blue jobbie made of things I've posted, marvellous prose I abandoned because I sobered up and discovered I wasn't a hilarious genius after all, things out of date order and odd musings that have occurred to me as I bumbled through the days. Happy lockdown thoughts such as, 'I no longer know where my bikini line ends and my ankle hair begins.'

Cherub 1 either has complete faith in me or is planning on doing me in because she asked if she could inherit all the money from the book. I hadn't given any thought to actually selling the thing. I'm feeling very British about even mentioning it. I'll put a lot of work into something in the firm belief that I'm about to make a complete twat of myself, but I'll still give it a go. It's the Mrs V way. Without it, we would never have discovered that a purple and green bedroom is not for us and that we can navigate a campervan around Paris, even though we never needed to be in Paris in the first place and are never putting Mrs V in charge of Google maps again.

Anyway, I have to unravel the jobbie and turn it into a neat blanket before I hand it over to Mr V to do clever things on Amazon. At this point I'm only on page 35.

Maybe I shall call the book The Big Blue Jobbie.

*jobbie means 'thing' in England but it's a child's word for a poo in Scotland. I'll let you decide which I meant.

***

I'm writing this bit on 25th July. I'm almost finished the book and I was going back through June to check I hadn't done anything daft, like put the same date down twice. I started out with the expectation of finishing the book by the end of June, but ended up aiming for 70,000 words by 1st August. I broke the 60k mark yesterday. Woo hoo! I told anyone who would listen and was on a high all day. Then I came crashing down to earth, confessing to Mr V, miserably, 'What if nobody buys it?' Nevertheless, I got back on my distinctly bi-polar horse and texted my sister, 'Even if nobody buys it, I've still written a book. Not many people can say that. Well, only a few million. But still...' You can knock Mrs V down, but she gets back up again. I'm like a Weeble, both in attitude and shape. Remember them? "Weebles wobble but they don't fall down."...

...Right, I'm back from a quick break to Google whether they still make Weebles. They do! I'm so happy! Childhood memories of contented hours spent trying to make Weebles fall over, just so I could disprove the advert. Turns out Weebles were remarkably robust.

When you do fall down, often it's enough to just give yourself a good pep talk. Back in January, long before I ever imagined being incarcerated for months on end and writing what will probably be described as an 'unconventional' book, I was suffering from sciatica of the bum. The sciatica is no more, thank goodness, but I wrote at the time:

"Sometimes the temptation to do a Shirley Valentine is almost too much. I would have said Lord Lucan but apparently they've found him (and, despite some pretty murderous thoughts this week, I haven't followed through). Today, the only person who is speaking to me is the dog. I am going axe throwing later and I'm considering taking along photographs of my nearest and dearest to use as targets.

Mr V was harrumphing around downstairs earlier. 'I had my day planned. My day is not going as planned,' he grumbled. This is because I bagged the shower before him and found Cherub 1 already in there, so Mr V went from first in the queue to last.

While I was in the shower I considered my problems and the words of Margaret Thatcher sprang to mind; "this lady's not for turning." Although I'm fairly sure Maggie wasn't suffering from sciatica and trying to reach to wash her bum when she said it.

So, with fresh resolve and other bits, I grabbed Cherub 2 and made him come to the shops. On the way there I gave him the same pep talk I'd given myself. I don't think it had the same impact. I probably should have left out the bit about my bum. We went to the camera shop to order a picture and they gave me a voucher for 50 free photograph prints. I immediately started adding to my axe throwing list.

When we got back Mr V came to tell me how grumpy he was feeling. Being a kind and understanding wife, I gave him the pep talk. He was not impressed either. Perhaps I should have left out my thoughts about how Britain would cope in the event of a zombie apocalypse. And the bit about my bum. 'I am trying to tell you how I'm feeling!' he exclaimed. I did the only reasonable thing. Offered him a picture of me to take to axe throwing.

We're on the way now. Quick pub stop first. Pretty sure it'll help with accuracy. Or at least numb the pain of the sciatica! "

So, if you take anything away from this book, it is 'be a Weeble.' Or do what I did, throw axes, get pissed on cocktails and make your other half take you to Nandos.

***

9th June 2020

DILEMMA DAY

I'm full of important dilemmas today.

This morning I missed fresh croissants straight from the oven, like I used to get from the shop on the way to work. I wondered if it would be reasonable to wake Mr V at 7am and ask him to go to the shop. He told me I was being entirely unreasonable and to bugger off. I felt quite annoyed that he hadn't divined my need for fresh croissants and set his alarm. This was a crisis! Could you divorce someone on the grounds of failure to supply baked goods? I asked Google, who also told me I was being entirely unreasonable and to bugger off. But oh how I miss making the inside of my car look like an explosion in a bakery. And, later on, a bit of bra mining for a mid-morning snack. And finding a big bit stuck to the gear stick on the way home in the evening. Croissants really are the most versatile of pastries.

All is calm in Covid Corner today. There was sibling World War 3 last night, when I tried to do responsible parenting and discuss Black Lives Matter with the Cherubs, both of whom enjoy being more right about something than the other. We agreed on the main points - racism bad thing, challenging racism good thing - but failed to thrash out the finer points of whether Cherub 1 was a buffoon and Cherub 2 a little twat.

I haven't been out for a walk yet, even though I'm allowed, because I don't quite trust that it's safe. However, the covid numbers have dropped dramatically, so I will emerge from my cocoon like a beautiful well-padded butterfly and go for a tootle round the block later. I might even take off my dressing gown for the occasion! .

I've worn my dressing gown every day for the past 3 months, like a big fluffy comfort blanket. If I'm honest with myself, one thing putting me off venturing outside is that I've become rather attached to my dressing gown. Possibly too attached. Yesterday it threatened to walk itself to the laundry basket if I wear it for much longer. 'But you have pockets and magically absorb spills,' I wailed. However, my dressing gown was having none of this and shot back with, 'Yes, but I smell of dogs, gin and old ice cream.' 'Noooo, those are all the good stinky smells!' I protested, hugging Vegas and watching him burrow his nose into a patch of ancient Ben and Jerry's. Anyway, I have relented and agreed to wear my emergency cardigan while the dressing gown gets a wash. It's held together by a finely balanced mix of chocolate and carbonara sauce, so I'm slightly worried that I'll open the washing machine door only to find a pile of gloop.

Finally, I shall leave you with my burning question of the day:

When you're doing the breakfast dishes and come to last night's wine glass, do you (a) drink the last wee bit or...(a), it's (a) isn't it?

10th June 2020

THE VOMITY TOWEL

So, I did the dishes last night with Cherub 2 hovering by the kitchen door, grumbling that I was taking too long. I dried the last of the cutlery, threw it in the drawer and told him the kitchen was his.

Five minutes later he picked up the tea towel and said, 'I hope you washed this before you used it.'

'No, it was lying on the counter so I just used it,' said I, thinking I was about to get the usual teenage lecture on my dishwashing failures (as I do every time they find the merest speck on a plate, despite never washing an effing dish themselves).

'Ew gross,' exclaimed my little angel. 'That's the one I used to wipe my fingers on when I was sick the other day!'

There followed a moment of stunned silence, while my brain processed this information and concluded that cheese grating the bollocks off your own child is probably against the law. Also, I'd just washed the cheese grater.

'Well why didn't you put the towel in the laundry basket?!' I exploded.

My darling boy just looked at me and, in a tone that implied he was clearly dealing with a complete idiot, said, 'I was busy being sick. Duh.'

Being an altruistic little fecker, he then took time out of his busy day (time clearly too valuable to waste on a five metre trip to the laundry basket) to check the dishes I'd washed and give me valuable feedback on all the tiny infractions of his personal dishwashing code.

He's now washing the dishes for the next week. And under instructions to Google the word 'irony'.

I don't swear at my kids (or assault them!) but I sincerely hope he some day marries a woman who's handy with a cheese grater and has the sense to tell him to just eff off.

But I still love him.

13th June 2020

OOH, PRESENTS!

Mr V asked me to wake him up this morning, only I couldn't remember what time, so I woke him up at 7am to ask. It was 10.

When I got back to the bedroom, I found Vegas curled up on Mr V's work coat on the floor. He looked pleased with himself and proudly declared, 'I left you some gifts during the night!' And so he had. Little brown parcels all over the bedroom floor. Then, being too old and creaky to jump back onto the bed, he had given Mr V the gift of a fur coat.

Taking advantage of the fact that the dog wasn't on the bed (a bit like his master, he likes a lie in), I decided to change the sheets. And that's when I found the bit of regurgitated something with sweetcorn. I looked at the dog with a mixture of awe and disgust. 'How can so much stuff come out of something so small?' I wondered.

Anyway, the clean up operation was so revolting that I was sick. Mr V came through to ask what all the fuss was about, only to find a well-padded backside winking at him as, snot and tears running down my face, I frantically scrubbed the carpet. Vegas put on his most innocent face and whined, 'Nothing to do with me. She was sick on the carpet. And look at the mess she's made of your coat!'

Eventually I dry heaved my way downstairs, arms full of sheets, and opened the back door to let my wee hairy tardis out. He just looked at me like I was a complete idiot and said, 'Nah, I'm empty, thanks.'

***

I normally like presents and by mid-June, with only four months to go until my birthday, I started scouring the online shops for ideas. I had no idea when all the proper shops would be open or whether I'd ever be out of shielding, so I planned ahead for Christmas as well. This resulted in many happy hours in Covid Corner and a full Pinterest presents board (for surely that is the purpose of Pinterest!). Mr V only discovered Pinterest this year and has previously resisted my attempts to make him look on my presents boards for ideas. He has instead gone with the safer option of buying me something he likes. Happy birthday me?

When people ask how old I am, I tell them I'm in my farties. You know you've reached your farties when, every time you get off the sofa, you're accompanied by your own trombone section. The order is generally teens, twenties, thirties, forties, farties, death (although some unfortunate souls skip the forties and just go straight to their farties - for them, farty is the new forty).

Your farties is an age where life begins to rob you of a tiny bit of dignity. Like it's giving you a taster of what's to come. Prodding you gently in the direction of the day when strangers wipe your bum, God forbid. It's also an age of discovery. The discovery that many older people are physically capable of bending down to pick up a dropped pen. They just don't dare. The realisation that choosing your breakfast cereal is like bowel roulette. The fun to be had when you walk upstairs, farting to the rhythm. The thrill of clenching and taking tiny steps in public places. The tense waiting game, as you accidentally let rip in public loos then sit patiently in the cubicle, waiting for everyone to leave just in case a complete stranger realises that you're the farty lady and tells Sky News. Boys don't have that problem - in the same scenario in the gents, the farty man proudly exits the cubicle to a chorus of 'good one mate' from five strangers and tells anyone who'll listen that they may want to light a match.

But do not despair. I have found the cure!

I've taken to watching TV with my headphones on. Sometimes I even forget I'm wearing them and just wander around shouting at people. But the real miracle is that when I wear headphones I never fart at all! It must surely be some sort of acupressure. Coincidentally, prior to me shielding, Mr V had taken to glancing over and giving me a thumbs up every time I got off the sofa. He's such a supportive husband.

As I get older, I become more fond of my Scottishness. I love the humour and the fact that we Scots are often 'what you see is what you get'. Over time I have had to learn to be better at diplomacy. Many years ago a manager (older man, who was quite surprised that they let people with jumper potatoes be in charge of stuff) told me I was aggressive. My inner woman said, 'If you were talking to a man you'd have said assertive'. My inner Scot said, 'Aggressive?! You want to see aggressive?! I could never tire of punching you, you big twat.' My mouth said 'Do you mean assertive? Oh you do? In that case I shall take the feedback on board'. NOT.

I might become a lovely wee Scottish granny someday, with a headscarf and brooches. I'll have a cute little dog called Angus and hit unruly teenagers assertively with my walking stick. I'll drink gin in the week and drive a Ferrari at weekends. I'll eat shortbread and bake rubbish scones. And, even when I'm 102, I'll still fancy men in kilts. So, maybe not such a lovely wee Scottish granny.

***

14th June 2020

FISH AND CHIPS AND FAST CARS

We had fish and chips last night, for the first time since lockdown. Normally Mr V is highly resistant to spending money, but he does love his fish and chips. So, last night was like:

Me: I really fancy fish and...
Mr V: *grabs wallet, gets in car, breaks world land speed record for backing out of drive*
Me: ...chips

He rang me from the chip shop queue to ask if he should call the Cherubs, in case they wanted something too. I smiled at him calling our kids 'the Cherubs' because in the real world we normally call them by their proper names or, if they're being annoying, The Twats. But they don't know that last bit so, shh

Have you read Roald Dahl's The Twits? Mr and Mrs Twit's battles are like minor skirmishes compared to the inter-Twat bickering in our house. Sometimes I sit in Covid Corner fervently praying they get the effing Shrinks.

The latest battle is of the bands. Cherub 1 enraged Cherub 2 by playing music and wakening him up at the most unreasonable hour of 2pm. Cherub 2 has today taken delivery of an enormous speaker. I suspect revenge is being planned. Oh well, life would be boring without a bit of drama.

Mr V has been on tenterhooks because he's waiting for the plants he ordered to arrive. So far we've had two Amazon deliveries. He ran to answer the door and each time came away looking like a child with no Christmas presents. The second package was addressed to me, so the Amazon man checked the surname. 'Yes, that's correct,' said Mr V. 'Are you a woman?' asked the Amazon man.

Mr V came slouching back into the kitchen and said he was never answering the door again. I was, of course, a kind and sympathetic wife, reassuring my unhappy husband, 'Don't worry. It was probably the moobs that confused him.'

Life is not all fish and chips and fast cars. Some days it is just buggering along together.

15th June 2020

OH MY, THAT'S A BIT DEEP

I

Love your life.
Take pictures of everything.
Tell people you love them. Talk to
random strangers. Do things that
you're scared to do. So many of us
die and no one remembers a thing
we did. Take your life and make
it the best story in the world.
Don't waste it.

don't normally post memes and the like, but I'm quite taken with this. It echoes thoughts I've had about how transient our existence in the world is and that the best things I've done have been to love my family and give people a few smiles along the way. I doubt I shall ever set the world alight, but, through Growing Old Disgracefully, I've been able to tell my story and hopefully, long after I'm gone, someone will stumble across it and still have a chuckle.

Ooh that was slightly maudlin for a Monday afternoon. I'd better balance things out with a quick raid of Mr V's chocolate stash while he's at work.

*** I don't know who created this meme or took the lovely photograph. I got it from the Scottish Women's Walking Facebook page. A quick Google reverse image search shows that it's widely circulated on the internet. I love reverse image searches. They have helped me weed out many a tosspot from Growing Old Disgracefully; generally people who set up fake accounts to go catfishing. The moment I see 'hey baby' in my G.O.D. messages, I check they follow the blog, do a reverse image search, discover that the person in the photo is actually an innocent truck driver from Gdansk, report them to Facebook and ban them from the page. One man just wouldn't eff off. He set up about eight different fake accounts (different name, same photo). It got to the point where I was catching him before he had time to 'hey baby' me! Creep. ***

17th June 2020

NORMAL SERVICE IS RESUMED

I posted something a bit different on Monday. You were probably confused. Who is this woman with her deep thoughts? And where is all the cake and gin?

All I can say is that this is clear evidence that wearing a bra is not good for you. It was a sports style bra, so I could take my top off in the sunny garden without giving George next door a stroke. But a bra nonetheless. Don't worry, shallow me is back today.

I'm covering for the boss this week at work. She's going to come back next week and spend her whole time wondering, 'Which idiot agreed to that?' It was me. I am that idiot. Normally the hardest decisions I make are between wine or gin, cake or biscuits. And that's just breakfast! (joke!!)...(mostly)

Mr V is conducting a positive reinforcement experiment on me this week. He thinks I don't know when he does these things. The other day I was very busy writing the book. He stood at the door of Covid Corner and said he had something to show me. I looked up, honestly thinking it was going to be either his willy or ice cream, but he just clapped and said, 'Well done.' What use is that?! I put on my disappointed face and said, 'Oh, I thought it was going to be your willy.' Then I realised that Cherub 2 was standing behind him, dying a little inside at the thought of his parents having rude bits. Suffice to say that, unless Mr V comes up with some decent presents or a willy helicopter, this experiment is doomed to fail.

Has anyone been to the non-essential shops this week, or are we all still looking at the pictures of queues outside Primark and deciding that we're not quite that desperate for a pack of knickers and a pair of cheap sandals?

*** To the wonderful, wonderful lady who didn't know what a willy helicopter was, but said she'd like one and did it come with a remote control - it took all my willpower not to suggest you Google it. I couldn't stop giggling at thought of Mr V's look of surprise if I clicked the 'spin' button. Of course, I'd wait until he was in a work meeting. ***

18th June 2020

ONE WEE HAIRY BOY AND ONE BIG HAIRY BOY

Normally at this time of year we are on leg-watch. This involves Mr V making us all look at his legs for signs of a sun tan every day and announcing, 'They're definitely getting darker!' even though by August they're still paler than a ginger Scotsman who has spent the last decade in a cave. When he visits his parents he makes them look too and I've even heard him describing his leg colour in detail to Lovely Granny on the phone.

So, that's leg-watch. However, this year we also have belly-watch. This is because Mr V is a big weirdo who has actually lost weight during lockdown. I suspect he has secretly been giving it all to me - maybe slipping a bit of muffin top into my tea or doing some reverse liposuction when I'm asleep. Every day his Budweiser baby comes out and he stands in profile, declaring, 'It's definitely getting smaller!' Then there is the ceremonial Grabbing of the Muffin Top. 'I used to have this much!' he says, grabbing a doughy lump of flesh that he believes was once the size of a tractor tyre but now resembles a deflated bicycle tyre. Meanwhile, every day I have to risk standing up with the Covid Corner armchair still stuck to my ever-expanding bottom so that I can marvel at his beach body breadiness.

I love him dearly, but he never had much weight to lose in the first place. He's one of those people who can eat a ton of chocolate without putting on an ounce and if he doesn't shut up I'm going to shove a packet of chocolate Hob Nobs where the sun don't shine. Actually scratch that, it's a waste of a good Hob Nob.

Lovely Granny is probably reading this and dreading the next FaceTime.

P.S. I read this post out to Mr V before I posted it, just in case it would hurt his feelings. Far from it. His delighted response was, 'Do you want a picture of my belly?

19th June 2020

THE DOG'S BOLLOCKS

News just in from Covid Corner. Local residents complained of lewd behaviour last night, when a man was heard repeatedly shouting, 'Show me your bottom.' Those attending the incident found 53 year old Mr V pursuing a speedy Jack Russell around the garden with a set of tweezers. A spokesperson for Mr V has explained that the dog had a tick on his bum and he is not, in fact, a pervert. Counselling has been provided to Old Ivy next door.

And now, the economy. A national emergency was declared last night, following the disappearance of raspberry and dark chocolate ice cream from the shops. Rumours are circulating in the City that there is about to be a sharp rise in Ben and Jerry's share prices, as Mrs V switches back to caramel chew chew. Bottom sizes sadly remain unaffected.

In health news, protests by the canine community have taken place, following the application of antiseptic cream to a raw patch on Vegas' balls and subsequent attempts to make him wear Cherub 1's knickers, so he wouldn't lick it off. Dog owners have explained that this was unrelated to Bum Tick-gate and, in the words of Cherub 1, 'He does spend a lot of time necking his own bits.' A formal pet-ition has been submitted and a spokesdog for Vegas has told Covid Corner News that, despite having a set of cherries like the top prize on a fruit machine, he is still the dog's bollocks when it comes to loudly seeing off potential intruders from behind the safety of the living room window.

Our undercover reporter has observed Cherub 1 going for long walks with a "friend" recently. She has also noted a rise in the number of texts and calls taking place out of earshot of parents. Make up use has increased exponentially and the hair dryer has once more been deployed. Mrs V has taken the precaution of hiding her good perfume lest it be "borrowed" and Mr V has written to the Prime Minister requesting that he delay any easing of social distancing measures. The wee hairy boys have vowed to see off this rival for their affections.

Finally, the weather. Covid Corner will remain sunny with showers of joy this Wineday, as Mrs V knocks off work early. However, an area of high pressure is expected when she reminds Mr V that he still has to fix Cherub 1's bed. There will be storms in the kitchen around 4pm when Cherub 2 eventually gets up and finds there's no milk left for his coco pops, followed by a chill when he flings open the fridge and freezer doors, stares at the 500 things within and declares that 'There is no food in this house!'

Happy Wineday.

*** The part I left out of this post was trying to get Cherub 1's knickers on Vegas. They were far too big. I don't know why we imagined her size 4 knickers were going to fit a miniature Jack Russell! I popped his back legs through the leg holes and thought, 'Well these will never stay on'. So I popped his front legs through as well and hooked the sides over his shoulders. Poor Vegas ended up in a doggy mankini, with his gentleman's bits being strangled by the gusset. ***

21st June 2020

THE DAY THE FOOTBALL CAME BACK

Cherub 1 had her new "friend" over last night. The first words he heard from me, as they passed the open Covid Corner window, were a squealed, 'I told you to warn me if you were bringing anyone over so I could put on a bra!' Anyway, he has now seen me at my lockdown best; stinky old pyjamas, boobs akimbo and nipples pointing due south. What a gorgeous old stick I am.

Confusingly, the new friend has the same name as Cherub 2. This resulted in a weird conversation, where I told Cherub 1 to make sure he walked her home as it would be dark and she told me there was no way she was going anywhere with that little twat.

The football is back on telly and Mr V was in Do Not Disturb mode yesterday. All attempts to talk to him were met with a death stare. The kind of stare he reserves for people who breach social distancing in shops. He is, therefore, going to get a lovely surprise when he finds out I've agreed that Cherub 1 and five friends can pitch tents on his precious lawn and have a socially distanced party. Ground rules are don't come in the house, pee in the trees and if you need help putting up tents, ask Mr V. So, if the BBC reports a mysterious tremor in the North of England, don't worry. It will just be Mr V playing garage jenga to find the tent peg mallet and roaring, 'I told you I didn't want to be involved. Now I'm involved!'

Cherub 2 has a cough, so he booked himself in for a coronavirus test. At 2pm. In the centre of town. He told us about this at 1.30pm. I was delighted that Cherub 2 had taken responsibility for his health and figured out how to book a test. Mr V just looked utterly devastated and said, 'I don't want to sound selfish but the Newcastle game is on at 2.'

I better go and warn Old Ivy next door that if the weather stays fine, there will be drinking and possibly some loud swearing going on in our garden this week. Oh yes, and at some point there will also be a wee party.

Happy More Wineday.

22nd June 2020

DEFINITELY NOT BEING A NUISANCE

Can't believe I thought yesterday was More Wineday instead of Sunday. I was gutted to find out that today is Monday and I have to work.

The good news is that I'm no longer covering for the boss, so the chances of me irretrievably effing something up are greatly reduced. The bad news is that I have to do ten tons of e-learning. I can either feel annoyed about this or look on it as a valuable opportunity to practise falling asleep with my eyes open.

Mr V is back on his man period. You can tell by the volume of clattering when he does the dishes. I asked if there was anything I could do to help and he suggested I 'move to another house…and take the children with you.' So, I'm going to have to make an effort to not be a nuisance. Which is difficult because Being A Nuisance is one of the few things I'm very good at!

Here are five things I thought I could do to not be a nuisance:

1.   Tidy all Mr V's Jaffa cakes into my mouth;

2.   Take the weight off his shoulders by not involving him in the purchase of expensive items that we definitely need. Essential things, like an 8ft elephant statue for the garden;

3.   Only interrupt the football if I have important questions, such as 'you know how you said the measuring tape was in the sacred garage and I should stop being a pain in the arse and

look for it myself? Well, I've moved all the ancient relics, created chaos out of order, knocked over a tin of paint, stepped on a dead mouse, broken your ladder and I still can't find it, so could you look for it please because I really need to do some urgent measuring thank you very much?';

4.   Make room in the freezer. Why do they make ice cream in awkward shaped tubs that slide out when you open the door? I reckon I could solve all our freezer Tetris problems in one delicious sitting;

5.   Stop wearing other people's shoes when I can't find mine. Cherub 2 has actually given me a pair of his shoes that I'm allowed to wear, in order to prevent further shoe thievery. That boy has sucked all the fun out of my little crimewave.

I'm absolutely sure that these things will be a big help and Mr V will be very pleased with me. I've already started on the first one. Cherub 1 texted me yesterday to find out where I was. I told her I was hanging some washing out and I'd be in shortly. I was actually sitting in the garden, having a competition with myself to see how many Jaffa cakes I could fit into my mouth at once. It was three.

23rd June 2020

ROMANCE IS MOSTLY NOT DEAD

I got quite emotional yesterday. When Mr V took Cherub 2 for a coronavirus test the other day, they tested him too. The results all came back negative, so I got to touch my husband for the first time in 3 months. And when I say touch, I mean snog the face off.

I'm not ashamed to say I cried and told Mr V, 'I've been dying for a kiss and a cuddle for months.'

Mr V just looked at me like I had two heads.

'Well have you not been missing a kiss and a cuddle?!' I exclaimed, outraged.

'Yeah, but I'm not dying for it as much as you,' said the love of my life.

Boris has said that in two weeks time I can meet outdoors with five people. It's a bit like choosing your netball team and I honestly don't know who to meet up with. But I think we all know who hasn't made the cut.

Later on we were having a giggle about a friend who had to go to hospital due to the surprise side effects of some medication. To put it politely, his gentleman's area said, 'Well helloooo ladies' then refused to say goodbye. His little soldier stood to attention and was no longer obeying the orders of its commanding officer. The pocket rocket was yelling, 'Houston, we have a problem.' I could go on putting this politely all day.

I commented to Mr V, 'I bet you wish you had that.' Mr V's little face lit up and he got a certain twinkle in his eye, as he realised there was something else we could do in this brief virus-free snogging window.

I thought about my boobs, currently at risk of getting caught in my flies after months of no bras, and my belly, which was looking a tad more rubenesque than it had in March. Then I considered that even though summer is normally lady gardening season, there had been so much neglect this year that we may have to ask the local council if we can borrow one of those machines they use to trim trees back from the side of the road. Then I pondered the inconvenience of shaving off about 3 months worth of leg hair and having a shower.

It took all my willpower not to throw Mr V's own words back at him.

***

I didn't hug Cherub 2, even though I wanted to. He gets all manly about hugging and tells me to 'geroff.' I have to wait until he's feeling upset about something, then pounce when he's at his most vulnerable. Like a big, cuddly lioness. I really am a lioness where my children and parking tickets are concerned. When Cherub 2 applied for something and was unfairly refused, he was quite despondent.

'Never fear,' I growled, 'I will fight your corner!'

'I don't think you can,' he said, glumly.

'Have you not seen me with a parking ticket?   Do you not remember the time they tried to fine you for travelling on the train without a ticket?   Have you no faith in my ability to write fifty zillion emails until they give in just so I'll bugger off and leave them alone?!'

Cherub 2 admitted that, while I may be an awful parent who he hates at least 50% of the time, I am very good at Being A Nuisance.   So I trotted off, filled with determination to fight the good fight, write emails, complete forms and make phone calls.   I came back with the joyous news that I had once more worn down the powers that be and he told me, 'It's okay, I've changed my mind anyway.'

I have a close relationship with Cherub 1 but she's not a hugger.   We are good friends and she is very open with me, sometimes to the point where I have to put my fingers in my ears and shout, 'TMI, la la la not listening.'   I tend to keep our conversations away from her father because the one time I told him something, he looked like I'd just stabbed him in the throat. However, I'm glad that Cherub 1 feels she can tell me things because, growing up, sex was not discussed in my house.   Sex education with my mother consisted of her chucking a packet of sanitary towels into the back of my wardrobe and saying, 'Here, you'll need these one day.'   As a result, when I was attacked by an older lad I didn't tell anyone.   I was walking home and he must have been following me.   He dragged me into an alleyway but that's as far as it went because, as I said, lioness.   I suspect he had a fair few scratches to explain to his own mother the next day.

I had to smile a few years ago when my dad turned to me, his now adult child, and whispered, 'Is dogging a real thing?'

'Yes,' I whispered back, 'I thought that was why you and mum got the heated car seats.'

Here's a post I wrote in 2019 about growing up:

"I'm planning a trip home to Scotland. Lovely, beautiful Aberdeenshire. I wrote a whole post about fancying men in kilts, but deleted it because I didn't want the men of Scotland to feel objectified. I couldn't bear the thought of a big hairy Scotsman going home crying to his wife that some middle-aged pervert looked at his knees funny. So, instead I will tell you about growing up in Scotland.

I spent my teens in a fairly remote village, where the height of cool was having a big perm and hanging out with your friends in the bus shelter. The boys wore short shorts and you never quite knew when something would unexpectedly pop out. A bit like testicle roulette. The girls wore spray on jeans, the tighter the better, and I think it's fair to say there were more camel toes in our village than in the whole of the Middle East. So, with all the sexy bits out there and not much else to do, the bus shelter was hormone central. It was where we got the bus to school in the morning and where we snogged and fumbled our way towards adulthood at night. If you swabbed the walls today, they'd still test positive for slobber and pheromones.

On the cold nights, we'd retreat to the chip shop. It had a big windowsill, a Space Invaders machine and a wee dining area at the side where you could play cards. In these technological times, the kids are aiming for likes and snapchat streaks. In the 1980s, if your name was at the top of the leaderboard in Space Invaders, you were a god. The chip shop is where I met my lifelong best friend - the two of us sat there on the big windowsill, barely 13 years old and tutting like a pair of disapproving little pensioners at the boys throwing fireworks in the street outside. Almost 37 years later nothing has changed - we just pick up where we left off. And he's still in my phone under the daft name that sat at the top of that Space Invaders leaderboard.

School was like survival of the fittest. If a well-meaning parent asked my school about their bullying policy, they'd have probably been taken outside by three teachers and the head boy and had the shit kicked out of them in the staff car park. When the teachers weren't having affairs or disappearing off to the staff room to smoke whatever they'd confiscated off a hapless fourth year, they were terrorising the pupils with leather straps, whipping them out from shoulder holsters like angry, gingery second-rate cops and slapping them down on desks and hands. I emerged, after six years, with a handful of mediocre grades and enough Scottish Country Dancing lessons to get me through most Scottish weddings unscathed.

At this point, I'd like to apologise to my PE teacher (one of the few nice teachers). I didn't appreciate that those hours of being forced, to our collective teenage disgust, to lock sweaty palms with other girls through Gay Gordons and Dashing White Sergeants were actually preparing me for a future of men in kilts. If someone had sat me down at the time and said, 'Listen, some day you're going to need this stuff because you'll fancy all men in kilts,' teenage me would have said, 'Why thank you very much, I'll stop spending the entire lesson arguing with Karen about who has to be the pretend boy and pay attention now.' At the words, 'Today, girls, we'll be doing dancing instead of hiding in the woods smoking cigarettes when you're supposed to be cross-country running,' my heart would have soared, instead of dropping into the soles of my sister's old gym shoes, lovingly painted white by my mum to give them a new lease of life.

And so, after all, we are neatly back at men in kilts. How did that happen? I'm fairly sure I told my subconscious that she was not to mention it again! "

When I look back on my childhood it is with wonder. Mostly wonder at how all the bonkers things seemed perfectly normal at the time. When I was little, I had lots of questions about 'what if we had coloured farts?' Would everyone have the same colour? Would different kinds of farts be different colours? What would it look like if you farted underwater? If three of you ran up the street farting, would it look like the Red Arrows had been? I never actually asked my mum these questions because she was quite tight-laced and I didn't fancy getting my mouth washed out with soap.

My mum wanted nice children, who she could take anywhere. Instead, she got me and spent her life trying to head me off at the pass before I told filthy jokes to my granny. Mum put a lot of effort into making us speak properly rather than sounding like heathen Scots, because, 'You'll appreciate it when you're applying for jobs someday.' 'Aye mum, I'm 9, I lie in bed at night wishing I was either a princess called Araminta or a high flying executive.' In fact, 'aye' was one of the banned words. Mum would hear me speaking to my friends, saying, 'Aye, aye, aye,' and she'd correct me, telling me, 'It's yes, not aye.' Which was very confusing when my granny had her cataracts done and I told my teacher that she was having an operation on her yeses.

I was a child with an imagination. I used to think someone switched on the cats eyes in the road at night and could never figure out how the cats eye man knew when it was dark in different places. I asked my dad and he said that it was just as well the cat hadn't been facing the other way, otherwise the cats eye man would have invented the pencil sharpener. My mum choked on her tea when I told granny.

My granny had lots of old books filled with stories about children at boarding schools, whose mothers packed their trunks full of sweets. I desperately wanted to go to boarding school so I could have a trunk full of sweets. Essentially, I was ready to ditch my family for a few sherbet dib dabs and a bar of chocolate. A lot of fainting went on in my granny's books. All the other children would gather round the fainted girl and look after her, while someone went to get the school nurse. Eventually, a kind Matron would appear with smelling salts and the girl would be packed off to her dormitory with biscuits and lots of fuss. When I pretended to faint, all the other children gathered round me, gave me a sharp poke with a stick, said, 'Nah, she's faking it,' and left. Nary a hob nob.

Cherub 2 used to have weird worries when he was little and once woke me up at 2am to check if we had loft insulation. He also had global warming in his legs and firmly believed he was allergic

216

to Christmas trees. I never told him about cats eyes and rainbow farts because he seemed to have enough on his mind already.

Overall, I had a happy childhood in a house where everyone was welcome, nobody knocked and there was always a pair of wellies in your size by the back door. Even years after I left home, my childhood friend would go round to my parents' house in the evenings and help himself to a cup of tea. My parents fostered children and, often as not, he'd be handed a baby while mum went off to stir a pot of soup. I wanted to create that easy warmth for my own children, hence (in normal times) their friends regularly troop through, clearing my fridge like a plague of locusts on the way. The one saving grace of lockdown was that I didn't have to put up with Mr V roaring, 'Who ate my sausage rolls? That was my lunch for work tomorrow!'

***

24th June 2020

SHORT BUT EN-SUITE

The good thing about hot weather is that I have no appetite. I also have no desire to move off this camping chair, so swings and roundabouts weight-wise.

The camping chairs are still out from the day I declared that we'd pretend we were on a campsite in France. Today we are clearly pretending to be on one of those sites where you have to take your own loo roll. There is none to be found in the bathrooms. Mr V is at work and I'm not allowed to go to the shops, so I'm using his super soft double strength tissues. I checked the box to see if they still said "man sized" but the makers have dragged themselves into the 21st century and now call them "extra large". Which is just as well, because coincidentally that's also the size of my bottom.

26th June 2020

STOP THE PRESSES

Covid Corner has declared a state of emergency. Only three quarters of the shed and the hind leg of a wee hairy helper have thus far been painted a lovely shade of blue. Mr V, minister for the Department of DIY, has released a statement saying that the job will be finished once the collection of useful bits of wood has been moved from the side of the shed...and it's a dry day...and Mr V has a day off...and pigs fly. At a hastily arranged press conference yesterday, the embattled Mr V defended his DIY record, pointing out that, 'The upside down cat flap is still within SLA. It's only been six months.' When asked for further details of the SLA, the Department of DIY mysteriously became unavailable for comment.

In other news, Professor Willie Burns of the Institute of Good Boys has hypothesised that the current state of the dog's testicles may be linked to his insistence on lying on the patio in the sun. There was a brief glimmer of hope for Vegas' cherries yesterday when things got a bit hot and he rolled over. However, full contact with hot stone was soon made again and Mrs V had to put him indoors. As Vegas, aged 13, stared forlornly from behind the Covid Corner window, a spokesdog said, 'This is a load of old bollocks.'

This just in. Our employment correspondent reports that a work meeting next week will be cameras on. Covid Corner resident, Mrs V, has consulted workplace rights experts and was advised that being told you can't wear your pyjamas to a meeting is not grounds for constructive dismissal. The boss is currently ignoring all Mrs V's emails on the subject of bras.

And finally, over to the weather. The recent run of 'two ice cream' days is coming to an end. The prediction of rain today is merely coincidental to the (far more important) fact that Mr V is refusing to go to the shop for supplies of the sweet stuff. This follows hard on the heels of Storm Gin, where an area of high pressure built up because Cherub 1 forgot to buy Mrs V's tonic water. Today's drop in temperatures has been marked by Mr V wearing socks with sandals. A slight frost may develop later when Mrs V informs him that under no circumstances is he to leave the house looking like that.

27th June 2020

THE OLD BOILER

Our hot water isn't working properly. This is a disaster and I texted Mr V to let him know that Something Must Be Done About This. Mr V is in charge of keeping our ageing boiler limping on. The boiler, along with the shed, the garage and the odd sock mountain on the bedroom floor, has been designated man territory.

Does anyone else keep their odd socks in a pile? I seem to keep mine balled up in the corners of freshly laundered duvet covers. Like a normal person.

Anyway, it is just as well that we all have more time at home than usual. There's a queue for the shower on the occasions when the boiler works and a queue for the air freshener when it doesn't.

The wee hairy boys are, of course, quite happy to forego a few baths. I told Old Ivy next door about the hot water situation and nearly ruined neighbourly relations forever this morning, when she overheard me saying, 'Get outside now. I'm fairly sure it's not my bottom that smells like that.' Turns out she thought I was talking to Mr V.

Old Ivy is clearly unaware that I'm a delight.

28th June 2020

FANDANGO IN THE NIGHT

Every day I sort out the throws and cushions on our old armchair. Every day my efforts are ruined. Vegas says he has no idea how this keeps happening,

The brain gremlins were on top form last night. Just as I was falling asleep they said, 'What if you die in your sleep? You have no knickers on and people will see your old fandango.' Then they shouted fandango at me until I got up and raided my underwear drawer. They wouldn't even let me choose a nice, big, comfy pair of period pants because, 'Jeez woman, have you no shame? What will the undertakers think ?!' I pointed out that I'd be past caring, but the gremlins insisted on choosing the fancy, lacy things. Then they spent the rest of the night waking me up to tell me, 'That's them up your bum crack again.' I swear my knickers thought my arsehole was an escape tunnel and I wouldn't have been surprised to cough them up in the morning. Also, I'm never wearing a cami top again. I woke up at 7am and my left boob was downstairs making a cup of tea.

So, I'm tired and in no mood to argue with Vegas today. Which is why I'm sitting writing this in chair that cuts off the circulation to your legs, while Vegas is having the genital snogging session of his life in the comfy old armchair.

JULY

***

July at last. Proper summer. Except I was starting to think we had used up summer in April, May and a tiny bit of June. Boris promised that the shielders could meet up with people in July. He promised we would be freed on the 1st of August. Then Leicester had a second wave and had to go back into full lockdown. We saw the rising rate of infection in America and a second lockdown in Spain. We shook our heads in dismay and anyone planning a Costa Del Holiday watched as the cracks began to appear in the air bridge. In the meantime, the pubs, eateries and hairdressers opened and the press got very excited about any breaches of social distancing they could find. Boris poshly mumbled that everyone must be on their best behaviour, so naturally many ignored him. All the shielding people sagged a little and started to wonder if we would ever get out. I told a friend that I'd intended to finish this book by the time I was released at the end of June, but was weirdly relieved when Boris extended my sentence because it gave me more time. Although I wondered if at this rate, we might all end up shielding until December, in which case...enjoy the next thousand pages.

The newspapers at the end of June/beginning of July were full of wrath about how the government had spent vast amounts of money on a contact tracing app that didn't work. Truth be told, I was a wee bit jealous because nobody has ever offered me millions and I'm absolutely shite at inventing things! I once invented a machine to pick up slow cars and toss them into the side of the road as I was driving along, but when I asked Mr V to make it he said it was impossible. I even bought him a new screwdriver! And I'd thought through how to avoid damaging the road, so I could continue my journey uninterrupted. But, instead of being all impressed and enthusiastic, Mr V just went on about something called The Highway Code and a tiny speed bump called The Law.

By the beginning of July, the newspapers had found new stories that didn't involve coronavirus. The government threw an epic tantrum with China and decided to let millions of people from Hong Kong become British. Tens of thousand of jobs were being lost and somebody came up with the whizzy idea of testing sewage to avoid a second spike. There was general grumbling about a trade deal with the US, which would have us all eating chlorinated chicken and cheese in cans. Okay, maybe it was just me who was worried about the cheese in cans. If the millions did arrive from Hong Kong, then they had unemployment, poo testing and malnutrition to look forward to. Yay! Go us!

I had the whizzy idea of becoming self sufficient. Keeping vegetables, planting chickens, that sort of thing. Mr V said this was a marvellous idea and I should start tilling the soil straight away. I looked at the rain lashing down outside, picked up my iPad and said, 'Why yes, lovely supermarket, I would like to order some broccoli using your free app that actually works.'

***

1st July 2020

MUFFIN TOP

'You see, you have to eat them within a day or two otherwise they'll go stale,' I mumbled through a mouthful of crumbs.

Mr V peered at the empty spaces in the muffin box. 'Yeah, you keep telling yourself that,' he said.

I'm trying to be good, but there's no getting around cake.

Back in March, I had a notion that I'd eventually go back to work and everyone would exclaim, 'Wow you've lost so much weight, you look fabulous!' Four months on, I suspect they'll actually say, 'Bugger me, we'd better get the doors widened.'

I'm worried that if I ever have to travel by train or plane, I'll bisect myself with a flip down tray. When they talked about social distancing on public transport, I'm fairly sure they didn't mean my legs should be two metres apart from my boobs. On the upside, if I carry on snacking then I won't need a scarf this winter, my second chin will do the job nicely.

So, July is the month of Making An Effort. Move more. Snack less. Get rid of a few pounds by shaving the legs. Chins up, head high. Be less flabulous and more fabulous. Get out there and do STUFF. Yeah! Whoop whoop!

I'll finish the muffins first, of course.

2nd July 2020

MR V THE MOVIE

Coming to a cinema near you.

Beneath the surface of this grumpy, middle aged man and his increasingly lurid range of Hawaiian shirts lies a dark secret. A mystery so profound that even a crack team of government scientists are baffled.

The question is simple. What do all the wires behind the telly do? Only Mr V knows and he will take that secret to the grave.

Follow Mr V as he attempts to explain AV and HDMI to his unwitting family. Feel his pain as he has to deal with cretins, who phone him up at work to ask how to turn on the DVD player. Marvel at his towering rage when Mrs V says, 'I've found the Apple TV controller thingy and I'm pressing the button but I'm still on Netflix.'

Yet Mr V is a conundrum within a mystery. Why does this king of telly gadgets object so vociferously to anything which requires the downloading of an app? The answer lies in a tension laden scene, where we see Mr V explode with frustration as he tries to remember a password. No CGI necessary. Later on there is a moment of triumph, as the GCHQ supercomputer finally hacks into the gmail account that Mrs V made him set up to control the heating. We watch with bated breath as the head of cyber security tells the prime minister, 'The password is Ihatef**kingpasswords1.'

In the final scenes, a covert team sent in to find Mr V fails to spot him among the household relics in the sacred garage, where he earlier sought refuge because Mrs V hinted that she fancied going shopping. Mr V finally emerges from the towering piles of ephemera and tells Mrs V, 'There's no more room in the sacred garage. You think that if you leave things by the front door they just magically disappear! Well they don't. I have to find places for them and there are no more places.' Mrs V is confounded by the news that all along it was Mr V and not the sacred garage performing these miracles.

Yet despite the high drama of nobody but Mr V being able to work the telly or put things in the sacred garage, this is a heartwarming tale of a man who is exactly what it says on the tin. In a tender love scene, Mrs V gazes deeply into his eyes and asks, 'What are you thinking right now?' Mr V takes her hand and pulls her close. 'I'm thinking about getting a new watering can.' Then he happily skips off into the sunset to prepare a fresh spreadsheet comparing the prices and qualities of every watering can on the market.

The end.

***

Mr V really does not like apps. He is perfectly capable, he just can't be bothered learning. I have to remind myself that it's genetic - Lovely Grandad gets cash back at the supermarket because he doesn't want to use infernal ATMs. Presumably, somewhere a few generations back, there was an ancestor who starved to death because he preferred to barter rather than use these new-fangled coins.

Pre-lockdown, we often used to go for breakfast on Sundays. One morning, Mr V appeared downstairs at 11:15 in a panic. The pub stopped serving breakfast at 12. Why had I not got him up?! Apparently not being his mother was a poor excuse.

We made the pub with ten minutes to spare. 'I'll use the app to order,' I said.

'Noooo, it'll take too long,' cried Mr V, 'And apps cannot be trusted. I'll queue.'

'It's fine. Look, I've already located the pub and put in our table number,' I reassured him.

He was not reassured. He hovered over my shoulder shouting, 'Traditional breakfast extra mushrooms! What do you mean I can't have extra mushrooms?!' Then he confidently declared that breakfast definitely would NOT arrive.

Seconds after ordering, a server appeared with cups and pointed us towards the nearest coffee machine. Mr V looked at me like I'd just pulled a unicorn out of my backside. Suddenly, the man who phones me at the office to turn the heating up because he can't work the app was nose in phone, searching for the magic pub app that makes breakfast happen.

At some point I'll introduce him to Uber. It'll blow his mind.

3rd July 2020

TOP 1 MOST WANTED

Covid Corner news, special Wineday edition.

A canine crisis was declared in Covid Corner yesterday when Vegas rolled in badger poo. His human, Mr V, went into the garden to find the poo, but readers need not worry, Biggles got there first and ate it. Vegas was denied entry to Covid Corner pending a bath and neighbours reported sightings of a small, surprisingly brown dog standing forlornly at the back door, whining, 'But I smell so delicious!'

A middle aged man's head exploded this morning when his wife tried to explain how to turn supermarket reward vouchers into other vouchers to get free stuff. The man's wife, Mrs V (aged 49 and seven quarters), commented, 'His brains went everywhere, poor man. It's just as well they're doing 2 for 1 on cleaning products or I'd never get the marks out of the carpet.'

In celebrity news, police are hunting a certain well-padded Scotswoman after a series of threats were made against The Legend in Tartan Lounge Pants, sometimes known as Mr V. The threats were issued in response to Mr V's annoying habit of forgetting that it's his turn to do the dishes. A spokesperson for the suspect said that the threats could not be taken seriously and there was no way the washing up liquid bottle would fit in there anyway. Members of the public are advised not to approach the suspect as she may be armed with a washing up brush and scouring pads.

Our special correspondent for Cherubs reports that Cherub 2 broke the world record for being a teenager yesterday when he slept for 20 hours. Cherub 1, on the other hand, skipped sleep in favour of drinking gin with friends and woke up this morning with her pyjamas on back to front. Her mother has issued a statement saying, 'I am proud of Cherub 1 for maintaining the family tradition of being a bit of a twat.'

And finally, the weather. Lashings of rain and wishings of sunshine this weekend. Things will become a bit hazy tonight after Mrs V gets the bottle of Pinot out of the fridge, forgets she's supposed to be cutting out snacks and wolfs down half a tub of Ben & Jerry's. Expect a sharp drop in temperatures later when Mr V gets home from work and says, 'I thought you were supposed to be on a diet?' There is a 90% chance of a hail of swear words. By Sunday evening, the strong wind will die down and become a light breeze, as the effects of Saturday night's curry wear off.

Happy Wineday.

4th July 2020

GINDEPENDENCE DAY

The pubs and eateries are open today. Life is vaguely back to normal for most of the non-shielding folk. We are lucky that we haven't lost anyone to coronavirus, but we did lose other things. Cherub 1 lost her job. Cherub 2 lost his health. Mr V lost his patience. And I lost two pairs of glasses and my waistline. Fortunately we didn't lose our sense of humour, which was important because it's how we got through the ups and downs of the last few months without losing sight of the fact that we love each other. Yes, even you Cherub 2, despite all your assertions that you still don't like me.

I thought Cherub 2 had hit peak teenager when he slept for 20 hours the other day. Then I had to say those three little words that make Mr V's heart melt. The three little, precious words that will carry him through his day. I. Was. Wrong. Cherub 2 was completely alone in the kitchen yesterday when I overheard him drop something and immediately say, 'Wasn't me, not my fault.'

Also...ALSO...I went to get my Wineday bottle of Pinot out of the fridge last night and it was gone. I interrogated the chief suspect and Cherub 1's defence was that Cherub 2 drank half of her wine so she took mine! This was all perfectly reasonable and was absolutely not the fault of either Cherub.

Well somehow, despite my resolve to cut back on snacks, the Cherubs' favourite biscuits have accidentally fallen into my mouth this morning and it's most definitely not my fault.

5th July 2020

THE PEN PUSHER

I have submitted my book to a publisher. One of the questions they asked was, 'Why are you the person to write this book?' I told them 'I'm of an age where I'm considered not sexy enough to warrant anything beyond the odd ad for a funeral plan. I write for ordinary, middle aged people like me. People who forget to put the big dish in to soak and who use the free pen from the funeral plan to push their husbands' piles back where they belong.'

Where the feck did that come from?! I steal pens all the time so I get loads of free pens. I've never once thought of sticking one there! There isn't even a need! Curse you More Wineday and your large glass of Pinot. Curse you brain gremlins, who opened the filing cabinet of Inappropriate Random Nonsense and threw the contents onto my frontal lobe.

Anyway, I think I might have blown it. Who the heck knows. I told Mr V this morning and he said I wasn't getting anywhere near his bum with a pen. He also said people don't find bums as funny as me but I reckon he was just being cheeky, talking out his hole, enjoying the crack, giving me the bums rush...I could go on but I've bottomed out on ideas.

On the upside (or is it the backside? sorry, couldn't resist), if I'm annoyed with him all I need do now is get a pen out and he'll run a mile. And that, folks, is why the pen is mightier than the sword.

***

Yes, sometimes I need to grow up. We're all entitled to a juvenile snicker now and then, though. When someone commented on the Pen Pusher post, 'Good luck to Mr V with his piles,' I panicked. I rang Mr V at work to say that I might have accidentally given thousands of people the impression that he had piles and that if anyone at work offered him a small inflatable ring, this might be why. I swear I heard his eyes roll as he said, 'This is just like the time I had shingles and you told everyone I had scabies.'

By the way, while we're in the juvenile section, did you know that men don't have unexpected poos. I found this out in May last year:

"I quizzed Mr V about men's toilet habits yesterday. It was like pulling teeth because he was very reluctant to discuss this subject, but we eventually got to the bottom of it (pun intended). What I wanted to know is if men need a wee and a poo do they stand up and do the wee first or do they sit down and do the whole lot at once. I had many follow up questions such as, 'Sometimes ladies are sitting having a wee and our bums unexpectedly decide we need a poo, does that ever happen to men when you're standing?' I'm not going to give you the answers because Mr V said, 'I don't want to see what I've said on the blog tomorrow.'

Anyway, once our dinner guests had departed I got rather a ticking off for having an enquiring mind, or "being inappropriate" as Mr V calls it. I've resolved not to make chocolate Swiss roll for pudding ever again."

Of course, every man in the universe rushed to assure me that if they were standing up then they never had the urge to sit down. Every lady in the universe was quite pleased I'd asked because, even if they hadn't thought of the questions before, they really wanted to know the answers.

235

I am a mine of useful information. While I was looking for that old post I came across another one where I'd been planning our new bathroom. All I will say is that if you are ever tempted to swap your silver hardware for gold, do not Google golden showers.

Right, that's my sewer of a mind empty for now. Let's get on with the 6th of July.

***

6th July 2020

THE MATURE BRAIN

Cherub 1 gave me her views on dating last night (apologies for the language - I promised myself that, after yesterday's post, I'd behave today, but that's not working out for me so far). She said, 'I'm not having a serious relationship until I'm 25 because by that time the lad's brain will have fully developed, so if he turns out to be an arsehole then he'll always be an arsehole and I can just dump him straight away.'

It was one of those moments when you could just high five yourself. When you think, 'I've totally cracked parenting, brought my girl up to be a strong woman, role modelled some good stuff. Yay go me! Yay go her!'

Then she said, 'My brain will be fully developed in six months time. Are you excited for it?' I wasn't sure how to answer this, but my own brain immediately started to plan a party for the time when everything is no longer my fault.

I can't really afford a party at the moment. Mr V saw my online shopping bill and queried the purchase of a personalised doormat. Apparently 'I like it dirty' is not an appropriate way to greet callers, although I'm fairly sure that Bobb With Two B's from the courier company would just nod knowingly and make a note to come back once social distancing is over. On second thoughts, maybe the doormat wasn't one of my better ideas.

It is just as well that paying for Cherubs' weddings is years away. There is a lot of novelty nonsense to buy between now and then. Many, many lectures on spending to be ignored.

Having told me off for wasting money on novelty doormats, Mr V said, 'I'm making lunch. Do you want anything putting in the oven?' 'Yes,' I replied, grumpily. 'Your head, so I can collect the life insurance.'

Honestly, if it wasn't for me Mr V's life wouldn't contain things like singing Christmas trees, Halloween costumes for dogs and a wine stopper shaped like a man with an enormous erection. I am doing him a favour! He should be high fiving himself and saying, 'I've totally cracked husbanding, got an empty bank account but a happy wife and a home full of shiny things I don't need, despite all my role modelling of boring fiscal behaviour. Yay go me! Yay go Mrs V!'

9th July 2020

MORE CAKE PLEASE

Honestly, I must stop buying everything I see on Facebook. Sarah Millican (British comedian and brave lady who somehow struggles through her IBS to eat cake anyway) posted that she'd made a chocolate peppermint tray bake from a book called One Tin Bakes. Well, I was straight down memory lane to my mum making tray bakes for church coffee mornings and me being tasked with delivering them to the church hall. Using the simple equation of distance x (mum not duct taping down the lid of the Tupperware box + my love of cake), I reckon approximately 50% made it to the good people of our village.

That was a great equation. If algebra involved more cake I'd have paid attention in class. I'd be saying, 'Move over Einstein, let me plonk my fat bottom here and tell you about relativity. $E=mc2$? Forget about all that gravity nonsense. Eating=munching cake and more cake.'

The upshot is that I've now bought the recipe book. Oh and maybe some other things I've seen advertised. Mr V will be pleased.

*** *The recipe book is One Tin Bakes by Edd Kimber. I later made one of the cakes and none of my family would eat it. It was a struggle, but I reluctantly ate the whole thing myself* ***

10th July 2020

SURVIVING STORM SAUVIGNON

It's Wineday, so it must be time for a round-up of this week's news from Covid Corner.

The Prime Minister of Covid Corner, Mrs V, this week announced the mandatory wearing of masks after 7pm. Covid Corner residents are not worried about coronavirus, but serious concerns have been raised about the noxious emissions from Vegas' rear end of an evening. Pollution levels reached a record high on Thursday night when someone did a poo in the downstairs loo and left the door open afterwards.

A domestic dispute broke out on Tuesday as a 53 year old man attempted to fix a chest of drawers. His wife remained unrepentant about breaking the drawers, merely adopting a glazed look and saying 'uh-huh' a lot when he gave a detailed explanation of how the drawers would be fixed. The drawers are currently in bits in the hallway awaiting specialist treatment. All complaints of them 'being in the bloody way' have been met with the death glare normally reserved for people who leave shopping trolleys in supermarket car park spaces, instead of putting them away.

An investigation was launched on Wednesday, following reports of theft. Cherub 2's favourite jeans were missing and suspicion immediately fell on Mrs V, a notorious local Jaffa Cake thief. Her defence of, 'What would I be doing with them skinny things? Wearing them as giant nipple tassels? Have you even checked your bedroom?' was not accepted by the court. However, an apology was issued the next day, following the discovery of the jeans in Cherub 2's bedroom.

In budget news, a resident of Covid Corner totted up how much she spends on ice cream and decided she wanted an ice cream maker. A business case was put forward to the Treasury but the Chancellor, Mr V, pointed to the bread maker, muffin maker, slow cooker and deep fat fryer, gathering dust on the shelves, and said there would be no rescue package for ladies with a sweet tooth and a large bottom.

After months of neglect, Jimmy, a little car in the North of England, has been taken into the care of mechanical services. A spokesvehicle said, 'Poor Jimmy hasn't been filled up since March, his brakes were sore and his body was covered in bird sh*t.' Brave little Jimmy is now undergoing a full service and will be returned to his owner, Mrs V, with admonishments about oil, tyre pressure and other mysterious things that have been explained to her fifty times and that she still doesn't understand. In an exclusive interview with Covid Corner news, Mrs V said, 'The most important thing is that they always vacuum Jimmy before they hand him back.'

Finally, the weather. After enduring floods this week, when Mrs V knocked over a case of wine, wee hairy boys face a damp weekend as she washes their beds. Storm Sauvignon left a trail of damage in its wake and one survivor, Mr V, is being treated for trauma inflicted when he had the cheek to point out that Mrs V didn't put the broken bottle in the recycling bin. Four bottles retrieved from the wreckage have been safely rehoused in the fridge and sunshine is expected later this Wineday when Mrs V opens one of them.

11th July 2020

SLEEPY HEAD

Mr V was very annoyed with me yesterday morning. I wouldn't let him buy the Radio Times and I told him he smelled. The fact that all of this happened in a dream made no difference. What is the meaning of this dream? We only buy the Radio Times at Christmas to circle all the films we'll forget to watch.

Last Christmas Mr V hit peak curmudgeon when the shop told him they'd run out of copies of the Radio Times and wouldn't be getting any more in. I had to endure days of rants because he went to great lengths to source a copy from elsewhere then the first shop got more in. The irony being that we all looked at the magazine, discovered barely anything we fancied and went back to bingeing Netflix.

This is not the first time Mr V has taken umbrage with a shop. He punishes them by deciding never to shop there again. Or at least until I insist we go because it's 20% off. Then he has to content himself with trying to turn all the shop assistants to stone with the intensity of his glare, while I cheerfully clear the shelves of all the things he never knew he needed.

I think Mr V's dream was just his brain preparing him for the season of 'What day is it and did I have a shower yesterday, this morning or three days ago? More chocolate please.' Or, maybe he's getting over lockdown, because that's been pretty much the same. Except there haven't been nearly enough presents, in my opinion.

Normally Mr V has really interesting dreams involving rescuing people on trains. More than once he has kicked the dog out of bed whilst battling a particularly evil group of baddies. I, on the other hand, have lovely dreams about giant chocolate pillows and all the road markings being pink.

Except when I elbow Mr V in the head for snoring. Then, as far as he's concerned, I was definitely 'just having a bad dream.'

12th July 2020

AN UNEXPECTED RELEASE

Good news! The NHS have written to me again.

Dear Mrs V,

We know you have missed hugs and stealing chips from other people's plates and snogging the face off Mr V, so we decided that you can stop shielding and leave Covid Corner. Your time as an armchair diva is at an end and you can once more vacuum the living room and clean the bathrooms. You can pop to the shops for other people, dust the telly and change Cherub 2's sheets.

Hooray!

All the lovely people at the NHS xx

Naturally I haven't told my family.

You know, a family doesn't turn into a smooth and efficient ice cream delivery service by accident. It takes months of moaning and wheedling. Guilt tripping them with, 'I would go if I could.' All that effort and training will now be wasted, as they gleefully tell me to bugger off and go to the shops myself.

This also means Mr V can move back into my...erm...our bedroom. I hope he's not expecting sexy shenanigans because I've put on a few pounds during my incarceration and I'm not sure the springs can take it. Also, he's going to have to find a new lamp because I accidentally stole his one when I broke mine. Oh and I might have flipped the mattress because my side wasn't comfy. I'm pretty sure he'll be excited that he can once more share my...erm...our bed.

Now that I don't have to self isolate, we can get the dishwasher fixed. That alone is making me think I should perhaps tell my family about my early release.

I'd quite like to see Lovely Granny too. I've missed LG loads. And Lovely Grandad of course. As I don't have to social distance from Mr V any more, he can drive me to see LG and Grandad and I can drink their wine and he can pour me back into the car and I can sing all the way home and he can put the football on the radio to drown me out. If I told Mr V about being released into the wild again, we could do all these lovely things together.

And there's my friends and family in Scotland. I'm not sure if Scotland is accepting incomers yet, but maybe if I offered to pop past Nicola Sturgeon's house with a bottle of Edinburgh gin and a white pudding supper she'd make an exception?

I've been dying to go for a day out with Mr V and the kids. A good yomp through castle grounds or beaches with the dogs, spending ages hanging around while Mr V messes about with camera lenses, arguing about whose turn it is to pick up the dog poo and moaning at everyone to hurry up because I need the loo and my feet are sore (this is Mrs V code for 'take me to the nearest tea room immediately'). I've missed those things.

On balance, maybe I will tell my family. Or maybe I'll leave it until tomorrow. Mr V is on a day off today and there's vacuuming to do.

***

Of course, I told my family.

I had mixed feelings about my freedom. After almost four months (FOUR BLOODY MONTHS) of isolation I had become quite used to having my own little space. I was quite fond of Covid Corner and I'd created a comfortable little nook for myself. All my stuff was there. Except my glasses because I'd lost the flaming things again. I'm going to have to tweet J. K. Rowling to get her personal assurance that house elves aren't real. Because that is the only explanation for how I have been living between four rooms yet things constantly disappear. It definitely isn't my fault!

The day after I got The Important Letter, I told Mr V that I wanted to keep Covid Corner as my personal space, but I realised that this might be inconvenient for everyone else. I mean, I'd remove the barricade of dining room chairs, of course, but, with things getting back to normal, there might come a day when people want to actually eat at the dining room table. At the moment it's covered in computers, phones, Kindle, notebooks and every piece of post I've received since March. Plus quite a few cake crumbs. Despite anything I have said, Mr V is really a lovely, good man. He told me, 'If you want to keep it, keep it. If we need the table then we'll just have to move things around.' Hooray for Mr V! Also, I'm positive he will have read between the lines and understood that I want a new armchair, a standard lamp and a posh rug rather than the one I have now (which is the one we normally use to cover up the burns in the living room carpet from when Mr V got a bit overenthusiastic with the wood burning stove). Hooray for shopping!

The response to my post on 12th July was brilliant. Loads of hurrahs, but also lots of Americans asking about white pudding suppers. To be fair, when I wrote that bit I was aware that it was Scottish humour, which a lot of people wouldn't get. However, the idea of popping round to Nicola's house with a bottle of gin and a bag of chips appealed to me. A lady asked what wine would go with white pudding. I replied Irn Bru. But then I had a moment of guilt about my flippancy and added a link to the Wikipedia page and a winky face. My friend Jack, however, had no qualms and cheerfully tried to convince all the Americans that Gretna Green was deep in the Highlands.

Because Boris had earlier announced that shielding would end on 1st August, I had set myself a goal to finish this book with a final post on that date.   I decided that, despite me no longer shielding, I would carry on.   It seemed a bit odd to say, 'And then I was suddenly free. Goodbye.' 1st August was going to be the big fanfare moment when millions of shielders, myself included, rode off into the sunset.   It still is, really, because around two million people have to carry on shielding until then.

At the time of writing, I'm not sure what that day will bring but, assuming we don't all end up back in lockdown, I will be raising a glass to all the lovely people out there who have kept buggering on.   KBOs all round.

***

13th July 2020

FIRST DAY NERVES

I cracked yesterday and told my family about my early release into the wild.

Mr V said he was going to Costco. Because I hadn't been to any shops for four months, I was a bit worried about the queuing and one way systems, so I decided to go with Mr V. I reckoned he could gently explain things to me. 'Don't worry,' he said, 'There are loads of idiots in the shops. So you won't stand out.' Well, thanks for that...I think.

Before we left, I decided to have a quick shower. Mr V asked, 'Can you do it in ten minutes? I'm leaving in ten minutes.' Knowing how much he hates being kept waiting by other people, I assured him that I'd once got ready for a work video call in seven minutes. Then I took advantage of my new found freedom to give him a cuddle and tell him I loved him. 'You're wasting valuable time,' said the old romantic, pointedly tapping his watch.

When we arrived at the shop I felt quite giddy with excitement. Cherub 1 asked later, 'Did you enjoy your first time out?' 'Yes,' I replied, 'I wanted to buy everything in sight.' Sadly, my pleas for a lamppost, a giant cool box, new towels, a posh barbecue, a gazebo etc. etc. fell on deaf ears. 'But I like towels and gazebos,' I wailed. 'And I like not being in debt,' said the big spoilsport, as he strode off to buy fripperies, such as bread and chicken. He was a man with a list and, by jove, he was going to stick to it. However, now that I know how all the queuing works, I can go back when he's not looking. I just have to figure out a way to convince him we've always had a giant lamppost in our front garden.

***

Here's the bit that never made it into that post.

"Mr V's response to my sudden freedom was to sneak up behind me later, give my boobs a squeeze then wander off, commenting, 'Well that felt unusual.' This, good people, is why it is pointless telling a man you love romantic surprises. You're thinking of stuff like being whisked off for a weekend in Paris. He's thinking that your arse looks jolly inviting when you're bending over filling up the dog's food bowl and, what with him being a total sex god and all, sneaking up behind you and simulating a sex act will be just the ticket."

Because...

Mr V told me, 'Even though I tell everyone at work that you exaggerate things about me, they still believe every bloody word you say. And these are intelligent people who know me! If you put that in the blog, then everyone will think it's about me, even if you say it's not. Don't you remember the post about the piles the other day?'

Fair point, that was not good. 'I may have accidentally given thousands of people the impression you have piles,' is not the sort of awkward conversation I ever imagined having with my husband. Although, moi, exaggerate?!

'Okay,' said I. 'I'll cut it, but it's going in the book and I'll make it clear you have never pretended to shag me when I'm filling the dog's dish.' He hasn't. But I think we already established on the 22nd of April that he likes my boobs and my sense of humour. So, having helpfully provided both in a few short sentences, my understanding about his point was pretty much on a par with his understanding of romantic surprises. And just to be clear, he has never ever given me a romantic surprise.

249

I read all of the above to Mr V, so that I could ensure I had made his lack of pretend shagging sufficiently clear. He looked at me with a hurt expression. 'I have given you a romantic surprise. I bought you a coffee machine.'

Perhaps he thinks it was a romantic surprise because I wrote this about it:

"Once upon a time a handsome, middle aged, slightly curmudgeonly King bought his beautiful, well-padded Queen a barista-style fancy coffee machine.

Armed only with a book of complex instructions and limited patience, the King and Queen set forth on a quest to make a cup of coffee.

The Queen was in charge of vaguely reading out the instructions in whichever random order struck her fancy and the King, being a manly man, was in charge of the machine. The Queen started on section 15. The King could not make the machine work as it appeared that some instructions had been skipped. The Queen swore blind that section 15 was absolutely the right place to start. The King asked to see the instructions. The Queen refused because she was in charge of instructions.

Ten minutes later, the King and Queen stopped arguing and, muttering darkly about pedantic people, the Queen turned to section 1. The complex instructions had clearly been written by someone who was not very politically correct, so it was with great glee that the Queen relayed the instruction that the machine should not be operated by people with mental deficiencies. This, she declared, meant that none of her family should use it. Especially the King.

Ten minutes later, the King and Queen stopped arguing and, muttering darkly about people who make wild accusations just so they can take over the manly task of pressing all the buttons, the

King filled the grinder with magic beans. There followed a heated debate about what the little door inside the grinder was for.

Ten minutes later, the King and Queen stopped arguing and, muttering darkly that a special door for the coffee fairies was a perfectly reasonable explanation, the Queen skipped straight to section 6.

Approximately 100 years (okay, an hour) passed. The King and Queen had figured out what all the buttons did. It was now time to take things to the next level. Using the steamer. The King insisted he could just put coffee and milk in a cup and steam the lot. The Queen insisted that, for once, she had actually read the instructions and he should steam the milk first. The Queen advised him that he should put the nozzle in the liquid then press the steam button. The King reminded the Queen of the number of parking tickets she had received due to not reading instructions properly and declared himself sceptical of her advice. The Queen decided this was not the time to confess that she had received far more parking tickets than the King knew about and was quite surprised that they could even afford the coffee machine!

Ten minutes later, having cleaned the King's coffee off the kitchen ceiling, the palace walls and the King, the Queen sat back and basked in the warm glow of being able to say, 'I told you so.' Then she texted another member of the royal family to get a pint of milk on the way home because the royal parents had used all the milk in their experiments and the little princeling would get most annoyed if he didn't get his Coco Pops in the morning.

By this stage, the King and Queen had made about ten cups of coffee during their experiments. The princess returned to Castle V bearing gifts of milk, to find her royal parents on a jittery caffeine high, bickering about where they were going to put the toaster now they had a coffee machine. The King was muttering darkly that only an idiot would suggest remodelling an entire kitchen so they could relocate an effing toaster and maybe it was the Queen who should not be allowed to operate the coffee machine."

I have no idea how this romantic surprise slipped my mind.

14th July 2020

MRS V.I.P.

Doing an important video conference after you've been shielding for months can be quite exciting because you get to talk to new people. It is, however, a good idea to stop talking at some point. Two minutes of everyone else talking, fifty eight minutes of me bouncing off the walls.

Now I'm out of shielding, I'm zinging with energy and purpose. I feel like I've woken up after a long sleep. I'm not craving comfort food any more (except maybe ice cream) and I've worn non-pyjamas - I believe they're called...clothes? - for three days in a row. Obviously, I only wore a bra on the first day when I went to Costco. Didn't want to turn a sharp corner and take out three pallets of loo roll with the force of the old boobage.

By the time I got to yesterday morning's bout of verbal diarrhoea, I'd already had three cups of coffee and done something which made me shit my pants. I'd proposed an idea. Even worse, someone thought it was a good idea. And now I have to write a very long report without mentioning Wineday, men in kilts or lady gardens even once! I'm going to have to break this to my lovely boss and yet again she is going to wonder why she thought it was safe to take a day off.

Coming out of shielding meant I could use our little study for my important video conference. Unfortunately, I've purloined the good chair for Covid Corner and the crappy old chair in the study is stuck at its lowest setting so, to avoid everyone having to stare at my forehead for an hour, I propped myself up high on a pile of cushions. But not so high that, given the bra situation, we'd have to give the video conference an R rating.

Vegas, of course, completely ignored my warning notice on the door, casually burst in and dug his paws into the carpet when I tried to eject him. He couldn't understand why I wouldn't want him slurping on his balls while I said Very Important Things. The Cherubs and Mr V, however, were well warned that they must not appear in their underpants, asking who had eaten all the ice cream. Because I have absolutely no idea who ate all the ice cream. After all, I am out of shielding and no longer craving comfort food!

*** The manky bit at the top of the notice is eyeshadow off my fingers. The video conference was actually a job interview, hence my attempt to look a tiny bit less lockdowny. Not much I could do about the hair, though. I didn't want to say on the blog that this was a job interview because I couldn't bear the thought of having *to write something a week later saying I didn't get the job. Better to just let things take their course and await the polite feedback - 'Had rather a lot to say for herself.' ****

17th July 2020

A LIFE IN THE DAY OF MRS V

Hello Wineday. Are you here already? I've had a bit of a break from writing this week, although I did write the big boss' work blog for him. Now the whole company believes he enjoys pyjama days and hasn't worn a bra for months.

I'm back in Covid Corner today until we find out whether a friend has coronavirus. Mr V said, 'I'm afraid we're going to have to pop you back into isolation until tomorrow.' I said, 'In that case, here is a list of all the comfort food I need and all the housework that urgently has to be done before tomorrow. Now off to the spare bedroom with you.' I mean, it's hard not being allowed to vacuum the living room and not being woken up every five minutes by loud snoring emanating from the unconscious lump next to you, but somehow I struggle on.

Cherub 1 has been going on dates. Until I meet prospective boyfriends, they will always be serial killers to me. Even if this one did pay for her taxi home. I think I might be Being A Nuisance by asking thousands of questions. Just the usual motherly questions about who he is, where they're going, when can I meet him and has she thoroughly searched him for a sturdy rope and a bag of roofies. I didn't binge watch every series of Criminal Minds for nothing, you know.

Mr V and I have next week off. I told my lovely boss that if she needs me to attend any morning meetings, I don't mind. Mr V was outraged. 'But we will be doing Things!' he cried. 'This will interrupt our doing of Things!' I didn't tell him, but what I said to my lovely boss was, 'Mr V will think we're going to be doing Things, but in actual fact he won't get up before midday.' I love that man but I once set myself the challenge of painting the kitchen wall before he got up. I painted the entire kitchen. Two coats.

Finally, a friend had an operation on her wrist which means her hand won't work properly for a while. I was very kind and caring. She was very nervous about the operation, so I sent her a reassuring text - 'Just focus on the big picture. In a few weeks time masturbation will be back on the cards.' Afterwards, I texted her, 'Have you any idea how hard it is to avoid saying cross fingers?! Something happens to my brain when I'm in a situation where it would be insensitive to say something. The only thing in my head is the thing I'm not supposed to say! I reckon this operation has been harder on me than you.' She hasn't texted back. I can only put this down to her hand not working.

*** *I actually texted my friend just before I posted this, to make sure she was okay with what I'd written. She duly said, 'Ha ha yes,' so I texted her back to say, 'Cheers. I was going to put on the end "or maybe the hand is working and she's otherwise engaged" but I didn't want to make you sound like a total wanker.' Still waiting for a reply...* ***

19th July 2020

STAR JUMPS AND LETTUCE

The weekend got off to a great start yesterday, with me signing up to a fitness app then spending the rest of the day eating chocolate biscuits. Tomorrow is surely a better day for star jumps and lettuce.

Cherub 1 was dating serial killers again and arrived home at 4.30am. Cherub 2 is in the dog house because he'd put the chain on the front door so that Cherub 1 couldn't get in. Then the little fecker waited up all night until she got home so he could revel in the results of his evildoing.

Mr V set his alarm for 9.30am and got up at 2pm sharp when I shouted my entire collection of swear words at him.

I was feeling quite annoyed with everyone until I remembered that I'm the only one who knows how to change the wifi password. I could change it then eff off to a holiday cottage on my own for a week. Preferably somewhere with no phone signal. And next door to a cake shop.

Sod the bloody fitness app. Next week is surely a much better day for star jumps and lettuce.

***

Middle age is not a joke
Don't eat
Don't laugh
Don't drink
Don't smoke
You'll give yourself a massive stroke!
No, fool, not THAT kind of stroke!
The kind that leaves your brain all broke.

Well sod it, if I'm going to go
Pass the cake
And best Bordeaux
Pass the gin and make it sloe
No, fool, I said SLOE not SLOW
Be quick, a vessel's going to blow.

Dancing shoes are on my feet
Vodka
Gin
All iced and neat
I may have years before I'm beat
Lying still beneath a sheet
No, fool, I said SHEET you twit
Now turn your volume up a bit!

I'm 50, not exactly A-list
Pubic hair is on the grey list
80s music fills my playlist
Name is on a Saga mail list
Wrinkles like my face turned facist
School friends who've turned weirdly racist!
Here's an update, Facebook status,
Fingers up to all the haters
All of us are on God's wait list
So let each moment be the greatest.

My farts may now creep up on me
And pop out unexpectedly
My bingo wings are wild and free
And when I cough I do a wee
My boobs may gently graze a knee
But I love all the bits of me
No, fool, I said BITS! You see
I'm growing old disgracefully.

Cheers

Mid July already. Doesn't time fly when you're contemplating your own mortality? I go through exercise and healthy eating fads from time to time. However, now I'm 50 it has been more difficult to shake off the thought that my mum had a stroke at 59 and was gone at 63. I don't want Mr V or the Cherubs to go through that. Even more, I don't want Mr V to be giving me showers and wiping my bum! So, I need to be a less well-padded Scotswoman, someone who can zoom upstairs even when there isn't the incentive of a glass of wine at the top.

I last had a proper exercise fad in 2018/19 when I joined a gym. I love swimming and it's great for my arthritic joints, but I hate the public pool. It's always cold and, because it's for everyone, you can only use it at certain times. On the other hand, the gym is a very expensive way to spend half an hour paddling in other people's pee. Plus, I'm too ordinary for posh gyms. I only embarrass myself. There's nothing like the sound of a middle-aged woman farting in rhythm as she uses the step machine. Here are my gym adventures:

"I decided New Year, new me, so I got my fat backside down to the gym yesterday. A lovely man called Jim showed me how to work some of the machines. I enthusiastically pulled stuff and pushed

stuff. I had a go on the running machine and made a mental note to get an appointment at M&S for a bra fitting.

I don't think Gym Jim appreciated my comment that if I had a cycling machine at home, I would put a little basket on the front for the wee hairy boys. However, on reflection, I didn't explain what the wee hairy boys were and, from the look he gave me, I suspect he imagined that I had a fine collection of men's dangly bits. He was certainly a bit nicer to me after that.

The step machine required enormous amounts of focus. Gym Jim was trying to make me step higher and faster. I was trying to clench my buttocks and hold in a giant fart. I ended up doing this weird thing where my legs were moving but the rest of my body was frozen. Just imagine a large sweaty woman doing a fast Irish Dance up six flights of shallow stairs.

The last machine Gym Jim showed me involved lots of leg opening and closing. I was a bit reluctant to have a go of this one because of...wafting. If you're going to do gym stuff and get all sweaty, you don't really want Gym Jim standing over you telling you to squeeze harder, while your legs unexpectedly spring into a position only your husband and your gynaecologist would appreciate. At least they get the benefit of you having a wash first!

So, I've decided that maybe I should stick to the swimming. Much less sweaty and if I need a fart I can just pop into the jacuzzi to cover it up."

"Yesterday I went for a swim. Well I say swim, I mean snooze in the gym car park.

I could feel myself flagging, so I popped to Lidl to do a bit of a shop and wake myself up. When I got cash back at the till, immediately lost it and five minutes later found it shoved down the side of the bread with the receipts, I knew I was still half asleep.

So, I got the cossie on and drove to the gym intending to go for a swim.

I parked and had a 'quick look' at the news on my phone. Half an hour later, I was woken by a man tapping on the window, checking if I was dead. He was with his mates from Birmingham on a stag do and I suspect I sucked some of the drama out of their visit by being alive. They had visions of ambulances and blue lights, but all they got was a well-padded woman in a red jumper, with a bit of drool on her cheek, sitting up and exclaiming 'WTF!!'

Thinking a coffee might wake me up, I headed off in the direction of the nearest latte. Sadly, the latte machine was broken and the server asked if I'd mind instant. No, I didn't mind. That'll be £3 please, says he. Yes, I do mind, says me! The coffee didn't wake me up, but paying £3 for a spoon of instant and some hot water did. So, I told him it was too weak and I got a free extra spoonful just to get my money's worth.

In the end I did go for a swim. I have one of those swimming costumes with a skirt. I bought it in a sale and, even if it is a bit naff, it removes all worries that I may frighten innocent bystanders with my porridgey thighs and spider's legs popping out of the bikini line. In it I am beach body ready. The body may be that of a beached whale, but the word beach is in there somewhere and that's good enough.

So, there was me, beach (ed whale) body ready and hopped up on caffeine, all set for a swim. Unfortunately, it was only as I was passing the changing room mirror that I realised the skirt bit of my swimming costume was hanging out from under my jumper and had been the whole time. I was a vision in jeans and a red jumper with a big flowery bum.

I just looked at my ridiculous reflection and decided I was quite glad I wasn't dead in my car because the headline would have been 'Knackered Mum with Flowery Bum Found Dead by Brum' "

"As I write, I'm in the swimming pool car park. I only really came to the pool for a shower because we've had no functioning shower all week at home. When I went for my arthritis check-up today, I had a moment of panic that if I had to remove an item of clothing then I'd also have revive the doctor afterwards. I spent most of the journey to the hospital trying to remember CPR. Fortunately, the doctor didn't need me to take clothes off. I just did the arthritis pub quiz (what score would you give your pain level with 1 being great and 100 being the worst? 90 - oh hang on, which way round was it again?) and smugly informed the doctor I was off to the swimming pool. I repeated the word exercise a couple of times, just to make sure I hadn't said cake by accident.

As I was at the pool, I thought I ought to do some swimming. This was a mistake. Every parent and child in the land had decided to go swimming today, all of them in my pool. I spent my swim wondering if the chlorine could cope with this level of urine in the water. As a sticking plaster gently floated past me in the deep end, I decided enough was enough and headed for my locker. Now, what was the code?

Dripping wet and freezing, I plodded to reception and asked them to break into my locker as none of the codes worked. The receptionist duly came and entered the 'master code for idiots who can't retain numbers for more than five minutes' and opened my locker. Hang on a minute, these weren't my clothes? Who had stolen my clothes?! The receptionist kindly asked if I was sure this was my locker.

So, now I'm off home. In about half an hour's time I will probably be standing in the kitchen saying, 'Who's stolen my kitchen?' as a stranger gently points me in the direction of my own house."

Ideally, when I grow up, I'll be fabulously wealthy and have my own swimming pool...in my villa in the Bahamas.

Anyway, mid July. What was going on in the world? Government confusion about wearing masks in shops was in the headlines. Masks had been mandatory on public transport since June but there were lots of exceptions. Did we actually need to wear them in shops too? Nobody knew quite what to think, as government ministers said, 'No need for masks, look at me, I'm not wearing one' and 'Yes need for masks, look at me, I'm definitely wearing one.' Boris put an end to the arguments by sending all the cabinet ministers to bed with no supper and declaring that from 24th July everyone in England should wear a mask in shops - except for all the people who couldn't. Suddenly, a lot of people started shouting, 'Well what about me?' as they put forward reasons as to why they should be an exception. And all the other people shouted back, 'There are doctors who have to wear these things for hours and you're whining about putting one on for an hour to go to the supermarket. FFS just put the damn mask on.' I thought that sounded a tad harsh, until I read an article about people claiming that masks might trigger a fear of feeling enclosed and I too found myself feeling a bit forfucksakey. Scotland had already been through this and Nicola Sturgeon had delivered smacked bums all round.

The good news was that, despite the inclination of a good proportion of the British public to behave like headless chickens, England had somehow managed to avoid a second wave, although Scotland was seeing the beginnings of an increase in cases. Local authorities were given powers to manage local outbreaks and the mayor of Leicester, where a local lockdown was being eased, got very angry with the government for not being clear about things and demanded that the entire cabinet go on the naughty step. In the meantime, the UK government was demanding the same of Vladimir Putin, as it accused Russia of trying to steal coronavirus research. It also very firmly told the Chinese that nobody likes a bully and our dad could beat their dad, so bring it on.

People hacked Twitter, hi-jacking the accounts of the rich and famous and making off with a goodly sum. The newspapers said that not all the accounts sent tweets asking for money. I checked my account because, you never know, it could be just me and the Kardashians. Surprisingly, the hackers must have seen my grand total of six followers and decided to try their luck elsewhere.

There were massive job losses and I despaired of my Cherubs ever finding work in the current climate. Five hundred people applied for two jobs in a pub. As businesses started to open up again, the devastation to the economy was keenly felt on the high street. Coronavirus had done quite a number on us. In fact, many, many numbers and none of them were good. Especially the millions spent on PPE that never arrived.

The overall picture in the news was uproar, confusion and general twittery twattery. I just focused on the good stuff; the barbers cutting the hair of homeless people for free, the fact that lockdown had shown us that homelessness is a problem we can solve if the will is there to do it, a princess had a wedding, care home visits could be resumed and 100 year old Sir Tom Moore was knighted for raising squillions for NHS charities. Watching Sir Tom and the Queen together was lovely. You knew, at their age, they probably both just wanted a comfy sit down, but there they were, all dolled up in their Sunday best for the cameras, both of them praying the Queen's hand didn't slip when she wielded that heavy sword, then Her Majesty doing polite chit chat before she went back to the palace and told Philip to put the kettle on.

The good stuff is what keeps us going. It reminds us that there are more decent people out there than there are twats. We must do all we can to maintain the delicate noble-numpty balance. And cocktail roulette! I can't believe I forgot about cocktail roulette! Scratch everything I said before. We must do all we can to get *back to a state where I can walk into a bar and say, 'Make me a cocktail, any cocktail.'*

***

20th July 2020

THE LEAKY LADY

According to this fitness app, I have to drink 1.6 litres of water a day and do squats. FFS after 1.6 litres I don't dare so much as sneeze! There are settings for goals, calories, exercise, steps etc. No setting for leaky ladies. So, I'm doing pelvic floor exercises and when the app asks, 'Have you done your exercise for today?', I can honestly answer yes.

All this fitness lark had better work out. Workout? Yes, you can groan. I'm full of nonsense today.

Mr V is less than fit this morning. He earlier announced, in his most outraged voice, 'I've been injured by my breakfast.' You'll be disappointed to learn that I didn't lace his cornflakes with arsenic. The life insurance isn't enough to risk the jail time. No, an errant piece of cornflake had stabbed him in the mouth. A sword-wielding cereal had the cheek to pierce Mr V in the...erm...cheek and I am going to suffer for it all day, until I find myself howling, 'Mouthwash,' so loudly that Old Ivy will call the police to report a domestic disturbance and a SWAT team will helicopter in and break all our windows and we will all end up doing life in a federal prison and I will make Mr V share a cell with Old Ivy. As you can see, I thought this through very carefully and I advised Mr V that unless orange was his colour, he may want to say no more about it. Then I went back to binge watching old episodes of Law & Order. I'm one of those lucky people who is not influenced by television at all.

Well, I'd better be off. I have thousands of steps and 1.6 litres of water ahead of me today and I need to plan a route that passes multiple large bushes. Just as well I'm not in an orange jumpsuit. Those things were also not designed with leaky ladies in mind.

***

Mr V's outrage was not helped by the fact that Cherub 2 announced that, at the weekend, he'd been with someone whose friend had coronavirus. So, it was back to the test centre with Cherub 2. Let us cross our fingers that Cherub 2 hasn't got the dreaded lurgy because then we'll all have it and I don't think I can survive that level of curmudgeon from Mr V. Last time Mr V was ill, I put a shortcut in Lovely Granny's phone so that every time she typed 'sorry', it autocorrected to 'sorry, not sorry.' Mr V had leave his sick-sofa to deal with the fall out when LG tried to sympathise with her friend about her budgie dying. He was not best pleased with me. Before I go on, I should mention that there are strict rules for when we are ill:

The 10 Demandments for Mrs V Being Ill

1. *Thou shalt lie down a lot.*
2. *Thou shalt eat Mr V's ice cream when thee have finished thine.*
3. *Thou shalt insist other people get thee things when it requires going up or down stairs.*
4. *Thou shalt nag other people to tidy the kitchen.*
5. *Thou shalt ignore other people when they point out that thee weren't so sick thee couldn't hobble into the kitchen to get thy wine.*
6. *Thou shalt demand that thy family take thee to the shoppes and push thee around in a wheelchair.*
7. *Thou shalt take thy family's advice to 'FFS shut up about shoppes' and watch telly instead.*
8. *Thou shalt make a nest on the sofa containing all the things thee needs. This to include All The Remotes, wine, ice cream, wee hairy boys, snacks and medicine (thou canst*

ignore the instructions on the medicine that say no alcohol - those instructions must be meant for other people).

9.   *Thou shalt limp horribly if there is any suggestion that thou art laying it on a bit thick.*

10.   *Thou shalt wear pyjamas at all times for verily 'tis an excellent excuse for a pyjama day or two.*

The 10 Demandments for Mr V being ill

1.   *Thou shalt malinger for three times longer than necessary.*

2.   *Thou shalt ensure that Mrs V is made aware of how ill thou art, every hour upon the hour.*

3.   *Thou shalt phone thy mother for sympathy when thee senses that Mrs V's well hath run dry.*

4.   *Thou shalt mention any new symptoms at least five times daily to any who will listen.*

5.   *Thou shalt wear thy tartan lounge pants at all times.*

6.   *Thou shalt demand cooked meals then get thy belly out to show all the people how bloated thou art. Even though thine illness is a cold.*

7.   *Thou shalt decide to comfort thyself with thy chocolate thee had saved from Christmas and hidden in thy most secret place. Thou shalt not swear at Mrs V when thee finds it mysteriously gone.*

8.   *Thou shalt be mortally offended when Mrs V suggests that 'it's just a sniffle so get thine arse out of bed.'*

9.   *Thou shalt compare this illness with past illnesses in order to convince thy wife just how seriously ill thou art.*

10.   *Thou shalt ignore all advice to 'see a doctor if thou art so ill', for verily other people do make a fuss.*

The Demandments for Cherub 1 being ill:

1.   *Thou shalt moan at thy mother for months.*

2.   *Thou shalt share thy father's Christmas chocolate with thy mother then get thy belly out of thy tartan lounge pants to show all the people how bloated thou art. For verily thou art thy father's daughter.*

3.   *Thou shalt ignore thy mother when, for the eleventy hundredth time, she says, 'Forsooth, I have no idea what's wrong, make a doctor's appointment.'*

4.   *Thou shalt eventually see a doctor, get prescribed ye olde antibiotics and pay no heed to thy mother when she says thee must definitely follow the instructions that say no alcohol.*

5.   *Thou shalt not let illness affect thy social life.*

The Demandments for Cherub 2 being ill:

1.   *Thou shalt Google all thy symptoms and pronounce thyself at death's door.*

2.   *Thou shalt insist thy mother phones the doctor.*

3.   *Thou shalt refuse to speak to the doctor on the basis that thy mother knows about all thy symptoms.*

4.   *Thou shalt get very annoyed with thy mother when she tells the doctor something thee didn't deem relevant*

5.   *Thou shalt sleep all day and spend thy nights surreptitiously emptying the fridge.*

***

21st July 2020

SHOPPING IS NO FUN ANY MORE

Mr V knows how to treat a girl. Take her out to buy slug pellets. We went to Wee & Poo yesterday. It was my first time dealing with one way systems in shops and I was determined not to break the rules. So, if you were in Wee & Poo and spotted a grumpy, middle-aged man muttering about slugs, being pursued by a well-padded Scotswoman screeching, 'FOLLOW THE ARROWS!', then I apologise. I got slightly over-zealous about arrows, queues, masks, social distancing, touching things and any breathing at all. In some sort of weird role reversal, Mr V was going against the arrows when nobody else was around and I was doing the ranting. Rule bending is normally my job!

Afterwards, we went to the chemist. A notice on the door said only two people at a time were allowed inside. There was already one person in there but Mr V told me we could also go in because, as a couple, we only counted as one person. My brain immediately exploded. After all, I was now a rule follower and there would be three people in the chemist, not two. 'WTF?' I asked. I had many follow up questions for Mr V. How did he know this? Was this some ancient secret handed down through chemist lore? How could three be two? And if three was the new two, could I now have three biscuits at Lovely Granny's house without seeming like a greedy cow? Mr V told me to shut up and asked a somewhat bemused assistant where he could find the ibuprofen.

Then we went to the little village supermarket, where people would suddenly lean over you and expect you to dance out of the way. I overheard someone bumping into an old friend and giving him a hug, while she told him, 'I don't believe in all that coronavirus nonsense.' I was quite annoyed with her. She was even more well-padded than me, so I contented myself with the bitchy thought, 'It's a bit like your feet, dear, just because you can't see it, doesn't mean it isn't there.' Oh Mrs V, you are going straight to hell for that one.

I'm normally a positive and forgiving person, but one trip to the supermarket and I could feel my soul shrivelling. I even had to make Mr V buy some ice cream to plump it back up again!

On the way home Mr V suggested that we go to the shopping centre soon and maybe even get a coffee somewhere. My brain again exploded at the thought of yet more rules and arrows, so I confidently told him that all the coffee shops in the shopping centre are closed. This tiny bending of the truth reassured me that my adherence to the rules had been but a temporary aberration. All is well and I'm still me.

23rd July 2020

OH KNICKERS!

I think I might need a mask with a little flap for the extra chin I've grown during lockdown. We went to buy some dog food yesterday and I noticed that everyone had masks which tucked neatly under the chin. If I tried to do that, my mask just slid off my nose and it looked like I'd been gagged. Mr V told me to stop fiddling with it because it was making him feel like a kidnapper. I agreed, but not before holding up a newspaper to the CCTV camera and saying loudly, 'It's the 22nd of July. I'm okay. The man says to leave the money in the park and don't call the cops."

Ha! And Mr V thought the most exciting thing he was going to do all day was use a different lane in the petrol station.

All the way round the shop my knickers kept falling down. I had one hand on the mask and the other scrabbling at my bottom in a desperate attempt to rescue my drooping drawers. Mr V told me to stop fiddling with my mask and knickers because it looked like I was trying to escape my own farts.

I was wearing trousers, so there was no chance of my undercrackers succeeding in their bid for freedom. However, it's surprising how low your knickers can go, even when suspended across the crotch of your pants. Upon returning to the car park, I gave a grumpy looking old man in a Volkswagen an unexpected treat when I shoved both hands down my trousers and wrangled my errant underwear back onto my bottom. Mr V said he enjoyed the treat, thanks very much, and he was no longer grumpy.

24th July 2020

MRS V TO THE RESCUE

Superheroes don't always come in capes, you know. Sometimes they come in pink fluffy dressing gowns, work shoes and Winnie the Pooh pyjamas.

We had a cat burglar last night. One of Old Ivy next door's feline friends paid us a visit at 4am and frightened the sh*t out of Cherub 2.

Normally Cherub 1 + Cherub 2 = World War 3, so upon being woken by shouting, I leapt out of bed and, pink fluffy dressing gown flying, charged downstairs to break up whatever argument my wee angels deemed necessary at this ungodly hour. However, I was met by Cherub 2 streaking up the stairs, screaming, 'OMG CAT IN COVID CORNER!'

He'd heard noises, investigated, realised it was a cat and ran away. Lord knows what he'd have done if it had been an actual burglar, but I do know that the world could not contain enough washing powder to get his underpants clean.

We debated whether to wake Mr V. I should explain that waking Mr V is almost impossible. Someone once suggested I make him sleep in a cart, so I can wheel him into the garden in the mornings then wheel him back indoors at night. I figured it would take longer to wake him up than it would to catch the cat. Had it been a real burglar, I'd have taken the same approach.

Cherub 2 and I crept quietly into Covid Corner to confront the intruder. Well, I crept. Cherub 2 hung back behind the safety of the door assuring me, 'It's definitely a cat.' Yep. Definitely a cat. It glared at me from amidst the wreckage of all the things it had sent flying in its haste to escape the big, hairy human who had screamed and run away.

'What are you going to do? How will you rid us of this terrifying monster?' asked Cherub 2, peering round the side of the door.

'Never fear, for MrsVWoman will save you. Stand back, puny human, and I will cast the monster out, back to whence it came.'

I tightened my dressing gown cord (I wasn't wearing pyjama bottoms and things were stressful enough without adding a surprise appearance by my bare backside), bravely strolled over to the patio door in Covid Corner and turned the key. The monster cat duly hopped out and buggered off into the dawn. The day was well and truly saved.

In the morning we told Mr V about our adventures. Mr V was very confused as to how the cat got in. When he installed the cat flap upside down, creating the world's first cat shelf, the thing had annoyed everyone so much with its tendency to flop open that he'd taped it shut. I've been nagging him for months to take the bloody thing off and put it back on properly.

I checked the cat shelf. The tape was still intact. The cat had battered its way in, broken the hinges at the bottom, and the cat shelf is once more a cat flap. Albeit dangling off a bit of duct tape. Mr V now considers the matter of the cat shelf closed. It has fixed itself. Job done.

*** *A lady asked what Vegas was doing during all the shenanigans. I told her, "Vegas appeared about ten minutes later because, unlike Mr V, he noticed I was missing from the bed. Disconcerted by the fact that I had broken canine law, which states I must at all times be within three feet of Vegas, he set off on a doggy mission to find me. By this time, I was sitting with a cup of decaf, wondering if I'd ever get back to sleep, so Vegas just settled himself down on his bed in Covid Corner and had a snooze, safe in the knowledge that he'd made his point about canine law and I'd let him know when it was bed time again."* ***

25th July 2020

THE WALKING DEAD

We went for a lovely woodland walk yesterday. Four months of being cooped up has left me very unfit and the hills were what I can only describe as 'a real bugger.'

I tried to pretend to Mr V that I was fine. Not out of breath at all. Nothing to see here. Keep going. But all the time I was carrying on an inner dialogue along the lines of, 'I'm actually dying. Maybe I can pretend I need a wee behind a bush, so I can just stop for a minute without it being embarrassing. But a wee behind a bush is also embarrassing. Oh Lordy, how can I make this stop? I know, I'll suggest we eat our sandwiches.'

'Darling, I'm starving. Shall we eat our sandwiches?'

'Okay, I'm quite hungry too. We'll stop at the next bench.'

Approximately 500 miles later...

My inner dialogue was screaming, 'Where the eff are all the effing benches? Also, I really do need a wee now. How did the Proclaimers do this sh*t? They must have worn their good trainers. Why didn't I wear my good trainers? My feet are killing me. Why is he torturing me like this? I'd Google 'can you divorce your husband for making you walk what feels like the length of Britain?' only there's no phone reception in this godforsaken place. Maybe I could just murder him and bury the body in the woods?'

Approximately 1000 miles later...

'Look, here's a good spot by the river to eat our sandwiches,' Mr V shouted back to me, as I brought up the rear roughly half a mile away.

Is it possible to faint in an upright position with your legs still moving? I stumbled towards a large rock and plonked my bottom down, hoping in vain that it wasn't igneous, so I wouldn't leave a sweaty bottom mark. Nevertheless, a sandwich perked me up and by the time Mr V declared us ready to go and I'd finished shouting at him because I was still picnicking, I had my second wind.

Ten tortuous minutes of walking back uphill later, we met another couple out for a lovely woodland walk. 'Are there any viewpoints or places of interest here?' Mr V asked them. They assured us there weren't. Just a 10,000 mile path through trees. Mr V, gutted that he had lugged his fancy camera all this way for nothing, suggested we turn around and head back.

'Hooray!' said my inner dialogue.

'Oh what a shame,' said my mouth.

Approximately 1 million miles later...

'I need a pee. Sorry, I know this is going in the Red Book, but can you hold my bag while I find a bush?'

Mr V has an imaginary Red Book for all the annoying things I do and a Green Book for all the lovely things. I suspect that the Red Book stretches to several volumes.

My inner dialogue thanked me for the wee and the rest. So did my back, which had been hauling the picnic because Mr V had his backpack full of camera equipment. I emerged from the bushes feeling about ten pounds of water lighter and ready to carry on. However, I realised to my delight that we were nearly back at the car park.

I staggered to the car and flung myself into the front seat, panting with the exhilaration of having made it to the finish line. Triumphant at having done exercise. Victorious in the face of hills. Mr V asked me to check my watch to see how far we'd walked. 3.5 miles!

***

On 25th July the world was in full on soap opera mode. We'd been following Johnny Depp's libel action with interest and the Harry and Meghan book came out. The gossip columnists were having a field day. Some time in the future, when I'm a rich and famous person being chased by the paparazzi (well, not so much chased as stalked slowly because, unless I tuck my boobs into the tops of my trainers, me running is likely to result in two self-inflicted black eyes and a hernia), the Mr and Mrs V story will come out - a romantic tale of two old lovers cast out by their children for thinking they're hilarious when they're just being embarrassing.

Me: *Can you drive faster, I need a poo.*
Mr V: *Well I don't think that would go down very well with the police, 'I'm sorry for speeding officer, my wife needs a poo.'*
Me: *You could say, 'She's nine centimetres dilated and has the urge to push!'*
Mr V: *Ha ha yes, 'She's giving birth to a baby poo!' Maybe we'd get a police escort home.*
Cherub 2 *in the back seat: Will you two shut up, you're not funny.*

Oh yes we are.

The UK government suddenly imposed a two week quarantine on people returning from Spain (then later other countries). Cue chaos. Cancelled holidays and tourism jobs back on the line, never mind all the inconvenience for the returning holiday makers. It was a shame as many of them would have had a difficult choice about going on their holidays because, once everything opened back up, they wouldn't be able to cancel and get refunds. The press had a little snicker about the Transport Minister, whose department had imposed the new rules and who was currently in Spain on his holidays. The number of Covid cases across the world was rising and several European countries were worried about a second wave.

I suggested to Mr V that we save up our leave and go away in the camper van for six weeks next year. He said, 'I don't mean to be depressing, but we might not even get away next year.' Well, can we at least do something then? Facebook has been dredging up all these memories of 'here's what you did in 2013, 14, 15, 16 etc' and they all involve spectacular mountains and lakes. If 2021 is a stay at home year then something amazing had better happen or I will surely have to put my foot down with a firm hand. I'm not sure who I'm threatening here, but I feel much better for it and it's my book, so there. Harumph.

I wrote this poem on 31st December 2019 and came across it the other day. Oh what a naive fool I was!

2020 Vision

Last year I swore by now I'd be
A slim and healthy, yummy me
So full of hope and wine and beer
I danced into another year

Now here I am still round and stout
Seeing 2019 out
Still sure that I will drop a size,
Despite my ever-growing thighs
(And my fondness for mince pies)
The evidence somewhat belies
That chances of success will rise
If I continue eating fries!

Well sod the old goals, aim for fun

278

To see us through to '21
Fly a plane or join a club
See a band or buy a pub
Climb a hill or climb a tree
As long as there is twattery
So make some noise and raise your glass
Let's kick some 2020 ass.

We can take it as read that all of the above no longer applies and scoot forward in time to 25th July again. England's rules on wearing masks came into force the day before and suddenly we had anti-maskers. We didn't think we had those! But we didn't think we had racism and white supremacists either. Most of us had watched videos of daft people in other countries and felt smugly complacent that this couldn't possibly happen here. People are sensible in the UK. Okay, we all went a bit weird over Brexit but then it was back to cups of tea, flying the Union Jack and God Save the Queen. Wasn't it? Nope. Turns out we're just as bonkers as everyone else. And not necessarily in a quaint, charming way!

I am hoping that things will calm down now that the Great British Bake Off is set to hit our screens. Remember the national scandal when it moved from the BBC to Channel 4? That's the sort of normal we need to get back to.

Last year Mr V took a liking to what he called 'boob cakes.' All the way round Waitrose it was effing boob cakes this and effing boob cakes that. We eventually got to the bottom of it. He'd been watching patisserie week on the Great British Bake Off and they did dome tarts. 'Jeez', I thought, 'He's only one small step away from dying himself orange and trading me in for a younger model.' When I asked him about the sudden interest in boob cakes he said, 'A man has to have a hobby!'

For all the non-Brits, Bake Off is a baking competition judged by an orange man called Paul and a nice lady called Prue, who seems like the sort of person who carries an emergency cardigan at all times. Waitrose is a posh supermarket for stout middle-class *ladies and older men who wear knickerbockers tucked into tartan socks and who consider themselves endearingly eccentric. If those men shopped anywhere else, they'd be called cockwombles.*

We were just passing Waitrose and popped in for some dog food. We passed the quinoa test (you have to know how to say it properly or you're not coming in), but I think the fact that one of us was going on about boob cakes and the other dropped the eff bomb when she saw the price of wine meant that, in this hallowed ground of the semi-trousered, we were the cockwombles. I was tempted to give everyone a rousing chorus of Jerusalem on the way out, but I didn't know the words. I'm Scottish and somehow 'England's green and pleasant lands' never came up in the Church of Scotland's répertoire.

Anyway, I was very pleased to come away with a Waitrose plastic bag. I told Mr V, 'It'll replace the Co-op bag for life that is my gym bag. With this Waitrose carrier bag, all the folk at the gym will think I'm dead posh.'

Yes, that's definitely the sort of normal we need to get back to.

***

26th July 2020

LG SAYS THIS IS A BIT MUSHY

I am loving this weekend. We went to see Lovely Granny and Grandad yesterday for the first time since March. Mr V has been, but I couldn't go until now because I was shielding. My heart soared because I've missed them so much. I know you're looking for hilarity, it's coming (I hope), but let me have my moment of joy first.

Nothing has changed. LG is still battling technology and determined to crack it. Right down the middle with a big hammer some days. Grandad's book club is now on Zoom, so they've been figuring out how to do Zooming on LG's iPad. I told them that at their age they might need a Zoomer Frame. I'm not sure they got the joke and I'm slightly worried that at this moment LG is planning a trip to the Apple Store to ask a nice, young hipster if he could kindly point her to the Zoomer Frame section.

I'd arrived bearing a packet of Jaffa Cakes. I should explain that Mr V hit the mother lode of Jaffa Cakes in Costco the other day. A massive box of 180 Jaffa Cakes. I haven't seen him this happy since I let him have first go of the new vacuum cleaner and he got to parade around the living room, pressing buttons and stopping every square foot to exclaim in wonder at how much it had picked up. The big box of Jaffa Cakes is currently in the laundry room with a 'Hands Off Mrs V' note attached. I kid you not. So, Mr V was most careful to remind LG at least fifty times that she may have the Jaffa Cakes, but I was not allowed any. Of course, LG duly appeared with the Jaffa Cakes and other, inferior biscuits on a plate. 'Oh goody,' I delightedly cried, 'Biscuits on a plate. Now I feel like a proper visitor!' Then I proceeded to slowly eat a Jaffa Cake, all the while staring Mr V down. Where chocolate is concerned, his mother will always be on my side.

Later on, Mr V signed his own death (or at least emergency phone call) warrant by connecting LG's telly to a TV streaming service and teaching her how to work it. He kept stopping to point out all the useful features, none of which LG will remember. He then made her write down all the steps and declared, 'If you phone me because you're stuck, there will be one simple answer.'

'Bugger off,' I said, helpfully.

'No!' exclaimed Mr V, once LG had picked her jaw up off the floor, 'Are you using the correct remote control?!'

We all decided to have fish and chips for dinner, so Mr V and I were duly packed off to the chip shop. The area was teeming with Saturday night pub goers. Ladies in little dresses and lads trying to impress them with how little they gave a toss for social distancing. We walked all the way down the street, trying to avoid the drunks like a game of reverse pinball, but we couldn't find an open chip shop. Then we weaved our way back up the street and found one we'd failed to spot earlier, what with it being right next to where we'd parked the car.

I have to say, it felt so good to be doing something normal like going to the chip shop. They were only letting one person in at a time, so I stood outside and bellowed my order at Mr V and anyone else in a five mile radius. 'DON'T FORGET THE SALT AND VINEGAR. HAS HE PUT THE SALT AND VINEGAR ON? TELL HIM TO PUT SALT AND VINEGAR ON.' The chip shop server man behind the counter bellowed back that he'd put the salt and vinegar on. I have no idea why he felt the need to butt in. He wasn't even involved in the conversation!

We made it back to LG and G's with boxes of lovely food and proceeded to tuck in. Just like old times. LG offered to pay for the fish and chips. How much were they? 'A hundred thousand pounds,' I confidently told her. I have no idea why she didn't believe me.

I really wanted to give LG and G a big hug when we left but obviously couldn't. Nevertheless, it was the best day for months. As I said to LG, 'You're the first real people I've talked to!' Mr V strode off muttering something about did I think he was a pretend person. There might also have been a mention of people helping themselves to bloody Jaffa Cakes. But I wasn't listening. I was too happy about seeing two of my favourite people in the whole world.

27th July 2020

COVID CORNER NEWS - THE FINAL EDITION?

Covid Corner News - proper reporting on stuff that really matters.

An 18 year old was rushed to a coronavirus testing centre this weekend when he developed a fever. His kind, caring mother told Covid Corner News, 'This is the third time! I've tried to find him a new family but eBay say it's "against their policy".'

A search party was sent out last night to rescue two bars of chocolate which had become stranded. Slightly hormonal Covid Corner resident, Mrs V, told reporters that she recalled buying the chocolate and hiding it from herself and if someone didn't find it immediately she was going to be very very angry. Mrs V's family are currently sheltering in a secure location until the chocolate can be found.

Residents of Covid Corner are returning to work this week after some time off. This has led to a 90% reduction in Footling, Fannying On and General Buggering About. The Covid Corner Prime Minister, Mrs V, put together a rescue plan to create more pottering opportunities, but sadly the Finance Minister, Mr V, has blocked all her moves to retire at 50. At a hastily arranged press conference, the Finance Minister announced, 'The rescue plan failed take into account that any increase in pottering opportunities was likely to cause a sharp decrease in shiny things or posh presents. And posh presents are apparently a top priority for the Prime Minister.'

There were angry scenes in Covid Corner this morning when a large bottom descended upon a small dog, who had just settled down for a comfy snooze in an armchair. Yelps of protest caused the immediate removal of the bottom but the dog in question, Vegas, has demanded compensation for the trauma. An out of court settlement of three treats and a big belly rub was agreed.

(Limb) Breaking news. The Finance Minister was almost hospitalised this afternoon when he failed to stop going through the bank statement and querying the Prime Minister's essential purchases. The Finance Minister argued unsuccessfully that personalised knickers for each day of the week, including Almost Wineday, Wineday and More Wineday, were outwith budgetary restrictions. The Prime Minister asked how else was she to know it was Wineday, and proposed knickers as a new method of time keeping for the nation. Threats escalated and the Finance Minister demanded compensation for the trauma. An out of court settlement of three treats and a big belly rub was agreed.

And finally, the weather. Mild with an outbreak of swearing when Mr V finds out that Cherub 1 got a new tattoo today. Followed by a brief storm later when he asks why Mrs V knew about this and didn't tell him. The storm may become slightly worse when Mrs V replies that she did tell him, he just happened to be sleeping at the time, but it still counts as telling. The sun will shine on Mr V about 7pm when Mrs V takes the lasagne out of the oven, but strong gales will arrive around midnight when he discovers that she used wholewheat pasta.

***

I'm going to have to dismantle Covid Corner, or at least start calling it the dining room again at some point. It might be next year before I get back to the office and I have another book planned, so I will be working in Covid Corner for some time. Perhaps I'll ask my blog readers to suggest a new name. Mr V asked me what I was planning next. He has suggested more than once that I should collate all my other posts into an anthology but

I've refused. I told him I'm writing a novel. 'Ooh a noooovel! You mean a book,' he said, implying I was being slightly up myself. It is just as well he was driving when he said this because I spotted a map book, which was very large with sharp corners, in the back seat. Maybe if I ever do an anthology of my posts I will insist that it is very big and very hardback - a dual purpose book/weapon, if you like.

The bits that didn't get included in today's post:

A rather off colour joke about me being fed up with taking Cherub 2 to the coronavirus testing centre and half wishing he'd get an STD like a normal teenager because the clap clinic is much closer. I changed it to the eBay thing at the last minute because I didn't want him to get a hard time from his friends. However, because they are teenagers, I'm fairly confident that his friends won't read this book. I'm slightly outside their demographic. And if they do read it? Well, those are the intelligent ones who know a joke when they see it, and they're welcome to raid our fridge any time. By the way, as I write, the Covid test has come back negative - woop woop and well done to the NHS - the results were back in 12 hours!

I once made the mistake of asking my Cherubs if it's cool to have a mum who blogs on social media. Turns out it's not. Neither is it cool to say cool. Although their friends do get excited when they witness twattery and I say, 'Well, that's going in the blog tomorrow.' She really doesn't make all this shit up!

The other bit that didn't make it in is about a blog post I wrote for work being published today. It was a celebration of all the people who will come out of shielding on 1st August. And we should definitely celebrate! These people have self-isolated since March. All of a sudden they'll be able to touch their own family members, visit people, go to the shops. It's liberating and scary at the same time. I thought that shielding hadn't affected my mental health, but all of a sudden I was scared to go to shops, crying when I kissed Mr V and I couldn't stop bloody talking. I didn't get the job I applied for, by the way. Looking at the feedback, I suspect that verbal diarrhoea played its part. You know, diarrhoea is very difficult to spell. I feel I should be awarded all the jobs for my excellent spelling alone. 'And why do you think you should get the job, Mrs V?' 'Prepare to be amazed. D-I-A-R-R-H-O-E-A.' Although, after that, I should probably avoid assuring them that I can hit the ground running.

***

28th July 2020

I'D LIKE TO SPEAK TO THE PERSON IN CHARGE

Mr V came back from taking Cherub 2 to the covid testing centre yesterday, full of curmudgeon. They had changed the staff. The army were no longer helping out, so he didn't get to talk to any soldiers about manly stuff then come home and wistfully say, 'If I could have a do-over I'd join the army.' And I didn't get to wistfully say, 'But you'd be away for months and there would be nobody to snore me awake fifty times a night.' Instead, Mr V came home grumbling about being asked the same question three times, there being no manager there and how if he was in charge then everything would be perfect. Let's mull that one over for a moment.

Mr V is in charge of fixing some drawers. I was in charge of breaking the drawers and did a sterling job. The drawers have spent the last four weeks on the floor crying, 'Wood glue please.' I did my bit, Mr V should do his!

Also, Mr V is in charge of making one phone call to arrange for the dishwasher to be fixed. He has been in charge of this for several weeks now. It's his turn to do the dishes tonight and I heard him earlier bribing Cherub 1 to do them for him.

You might think, 'Well why don't you sort it out, Mrs V, instead of moaning?' I did! I put myself in charge of phoning the dishwasher repairman but it turns out that dishwasher repairmen ask lots of difficult questions. Things like, 'Can you switch it on and tell me the error code.' 'Nope, the thing is dead.' 'Okay, it'll be switched off at the wall, can you find the switch on the wall?' 'Hang on a minute. Nope, that's the toaster...' We agreed that Mr V would phone him back. I did my bit, it's time for Mr V to step up to the plate. Ha! Plate. You see what I did there?

Anyway, in the face of all the evidence, I have decided that things are much better when I'm in charge. Which is why I've applied for a job as a covid testing centre manager. Never let it be said that I don't put 100% effort into annoying my husband.

P.S. Despite Cherub 2's best efforts at being a teenager, his covid test results came back negative.

29th July 2020

SUPER POOPER SCOOPER

Biggles pooped on Cherub 2's bedroom carpet twice yesterday. Cherub 2 was raging. 'A dog has pooped on my carpet again!' he bellowed. 'It was definitely Biggles.'

'How do you know? Did you ask him? Did you give him the turd degree?' I wondered.

'I know it was him. If he ever does that again then he's banned from my bedroom!'

'Turd strike and he's out!' I cried, delighted to have struck such a rich vein of juvenile puns.

Cherub 2 just rolled his eyes and asked if I'd clean it up for him. Do you remember that Kirsty MacColl song from years ago - There's a Guy Works Down the Chip Shop Swears He's Elvis? Turns out the lyrics fit 'there's a skid mark on the carpet left by Biggles.' I sang my way through the clean up operation and came downstairs to tell Cherub 2 it was all done. 'I think he must have got shut in your room by accident,' I said. 'Keep your bedroom door closed because you don't want this happening a turd time.'

Then I thought I should perhaps be kinder because I felt a bit sorry for Cherub 2. He hasn't been well and, after the cat in the night incident the other day, he's had to put up with Mr V screaming, 'OMG CAT!' each time a cat comes on the telly. I gave Cherub 2 a loving, motherly hug and said sympathetically, 'You've had a hard week. And it's only Poosday. I hope you're feline better soon.'

'Okay, you can stop now,' he said.

'This will never stop,' I assured him. 'It's what families are for.'

30th July 2020

NOT JAFFA CAKES AGAIN!

I've lost my mojo this week. The most mischief I could get up to was hiding all Mr V's Jaffa Cakes, then sitting back and enjoying the fireworks as he stomped around accusing everyone of stealing them. Cherub 2 approached me this morning to ask if I knew anything about the Jaffa Cakes. I denied all knowledge, of course. Because Cherub 2 is getting quite some heat from Mr V, I knew he'd crack under the pressure and grass me up. I just joined him in blaming Cherub 1 and having a good moan about his unreasonable father.

Mr V finally gave up on his wild accusations this afternoon and bought another stash of Jaffa Cakes. So I've hidden those as well. Admittedly, I may have inadvertently hidden some of them in my mouth.

The only problem with hiding seven boxes of Jaffa Cakes is remembering where you put them. I'm good at losing things and terrible at finding them. Now, if I could just work out where the heck I put my mojo...

P.S. if you hear on the news that there was a major explosion in the north of England, don't worry. It will just be Mr V when he reads this post.

*** Poor Mr V. He spent two days looking for his Jaffa Cakes. He takes them very seriously. He appeared with his phone in Covid Corner, where I was typing away, trying to finish this book. 'What are you doing?' I asked, as he loomed over me. He pointed to an empty Jaffa Cake box and took a photograph. 'Gathering evidence,' he replied, giving me a stern look. ***

31st July 2020

WINEDAY RUINED

Happy Wineday. Or it would be if some little fecker hadn't helped himself to my last bottle.

This morning started with a bang. The bang of me slamming the fridge door and storming through to the living room.

'Have you pinched my wine?' I asked Cherub 2.

'I drank a bit of a bottle that was in there,' he replied.

'A bit of a bottle! A bit of a bottle! There was a bottle and a half! It's Wineday!' I ranted, like 'it's Wineday' explained both the seriousness of Cherub 2's crime and the depth of my outrage. 'Now I'm going to have to be nice to your father so he'll go to the shop for more. He might even make me tell him where I hid his Jaffa Cakes and I'll have to admit to how many I ate. Do you even realise just how far reaching the consequences are?!'

Cherub 2 was unrepentant. Cherub 2 did not care about his parents' ongoing War of the Jaffa Cake. Cherub 2 had no regard for the hours his father had spent snooping around the house, taking covert photos of Mrs V with an empty Jaffa Cake box so he could later shout, 'Aha! Evidence!' in the Jaffa Cake court, like the Perry Mason of the baked goods world. He gave not a fig for his mother's ingenuity in finding the best Jaffa Cake hiding places. He was completely oblivious to the fact that he had totally ruined Wineday.

Now, I don't know how it works in your house, but in mine I find that revenge is best served steaming hot with a good sprinkling of Tabasco and a few chilli peppers. When you're a teenager who knows everything, it is very easy to forget that the idiots you live with have quite a bit of power. However, the idiots do not forget. They are very, very sneaky idiots. They plot ways to use this power, yet give themselves complete deniability.

'I'm going out tonight. Can you wash my white t-shirt?' Cherub 2 asked, a couple of hours later. This would normally prompt a rant that he's old enough to do his own washing. However, today I said nothing. I just popped his t-shirt into the washing machine, along with his undies and a pair of white shorts. Then I eyed a red sock and wondered what would happen if it accidentally fell in.

Parents are always suspicious about what their children are up to when they're too quiet. Children really should learn to be the same about their parents.

AUGUST – HOORAY!

1st August 2020

SHIELDS DOWN

Hello shielding people of the UK. Welcome back to the world. How are you feeling?

I'm going to write one of my usual posts later but I wanted to write something just for all you lovely people who have been self-isolating for months on end.

It has sometimes felt like the shielding people were forgotten in all the kerfuffle over how the rest of the country was getting back to "normal". Unless you've been through it, I think it's difficult for other people to appreciate just how disruptive, lonely and bloody boring shielding can be. So, we need to make a fuss. Have a little celebration of the fact that you've made it through and can finally get in a car with your nearest and dearest, go visiting and eat someone else's biscuits for a change.

You might have all sorts of worries right now or you might be cracking open the champagne. Or you may not be in the least bit bothered. However you're feeling about coming out of shielding, I hope today you finally get all the hugs you deserve for enduring these months of isolation. And if there's nobody there to give you one, then I'm sending a nice, big, digital hug your way.

*** *I had to add a little edit onto this post because someone kindly pointed out that Wales wasn't out of shielding until 16th August. I rather shamefacedly replied, 'Well, I cocked that one up, didn't I?' Some local lockdowns and a pause in the easing of lockdown measures in England had been suddenly announced the day before, which meant that, even though some people were technically out of* *shielding, they couldn't go anywhere or have anyone to visit. The comments on this post reflected a sense of worry and frustration about the rising number of infections and the irresponsible behaviour of others. There was also excitement, relief and a feeling of strangeness.* ***

Here's my second post of the day:

Slowly coming to terms with the fact that I am probably the biggest twat in the village right now.

I went to the shop on my own for the first time yesterday. After Cherub 2 put a pause on Wineday with his pilfering of the Pinot, I was forced to go out in search of a replacement bottle.

I parked outside the little supermarket in the village, gave myself a quick high five for remembering to take a mask then confidently strode in, determined to follow All The Rules. Unfortunately, my brain gremlins got so excited by the thought that Mr V wasn't with me (so I could buy anything I wanted), that I instantly forgot about All The Rules. It's just as well it wasn't very busy. Half way through, arms full of pizza, wine and chocolate, I suddenly remembered that there was something about arrows and one way systems in supermarkets. I quickly scanned the floor. Phew! No arrows.

I made my way to the ice cream section and gazed at all the lovely tubs, waving at me through the freezer window. 'Come here,' purred a sexy salted caramel, beguilingly, 'You know you want me.' A large tub of mint choc chip shouldered its way to the front and bellowed, 'No, pick me!' I looked at the forlorn, plain little vanilla, sitting quietly by itself in a corner, and wished I could lick it better. 'I'm sorry,' I told all the delicious ice creams, 'I only came in for wine and now my arms are full of all the other junk food, plus some bananas to make me feel less guilty. I'll come back for you another day, I promise.' With that, I turned my back on the freezer of dreams and made my way to the checkout.

I have a new mask. The last one kept sliding down and made a smashing gag. The new one slides up and pokes me in the eyes. It seems there is no happy medium with masks and I felt the need to tell the checkout lady that, even though I couldn't have any ice cream, I wasn't crying. It was just the mask making a desperate bid to become a blindfold and making my eyes water. (Jeez, there's an idea, if I ever truly want to embarrass Mr V in a shop then I could wear both masks and pretend to be a hostage).

With everything tucked away in my bag, I left the shop and drove home. On the way, I spotted Cherub 2 cycling up the street, headphones on, one hand on the handlebars and the other snapchatting away on his phone, completely oblivious to the world around him. It is just as well he was cycling on the pavement because I briefly wondered if 'He ruined Wineday' was sufficient defence for inadvertently losing control of the vehicle and accidentally running the thieving little bugger over.

When I got home, I dutifully wiped all the shopping down and put it away in my mouth (except the bananas). Mr V asked how I managed, what with it being my first time out on my own.

'Absolutely fine,' I assured him, 'I stuck to All The Rules, got what I came for and came straight home.'

'Did you have to queue to get into the shop? There's always a queue there, it's sometimes quicker to go to the big supermarket down the road.'

'Erm...there wasn't a queue,' I said, picturing myself striding confidently past a few people, who inexplicably seemed to be hanging around the shop entrance. 'As I said, I stuck to All The Rules and everything was absolutely fine, no problems. Tell you what though, this new mask keeps poking me in the eyes. Couldn't see a thing for my eyes watering!'

***

Before I go, I will offer some words of wisdom to carry with you as and when the world slowly returns to normal:

Life Hacks and Top Tips, Mrs V stylee

1. *Always tidy up Jaffa cakes using your mouth. People who inadvertently leave them in cupboards and biscuit tins will be very pleased you made the effort.*

2. *Ladies, never drop biscuit crumbs down your top if you're wearing skinny jeans. They fall down your trouser legs when you go to the loo and torture you for the rest of the day.*

3. *Working from home feels like an attractive sunny day option, but is ultimately pointless because you will still end up doing a teleconference in the dining room in your pyjamas at 1pm.*

4. *Cut your toenails when they start curling over the edges of your flip-flops. It's not an attractive look.*

5. *Posh hotels are a great source of free stuff. Always take a screwdriver in case they've accidentally bolted the fancy hand cream to the wall.*

6. *Gin and tonic is an effective antidote to the urge to do housework.*

7. *If you're worried about people stealing your chair at work, make sure everyone knows you have a dodgy pelvic floor and a very bad cough.*

8. *Unless you enjoy wandering around the shops looking like you've been punched in the face, leave your eyebrow wax until the end of your shopping trip.*

9.   *If you need to tell your partner something you know they'll be annoyed about, tell them when they're asleep. That way you can honestly say that you told them, you don't get shouted at and they get a grand surprise later. Many birds, one stone.*

10.   *Smelly feet, very useful distraction technique if you're at the gynaecologist.*

Follow these tips and you will never go wrong. Mostly.

THE ENDING

....

All good things come to an end. We began this story with God creating Woman and Man, so I am ending it with a little revelation.

Once upon a time three friends, let's call them War, Famine and Death, were having a group chat and decided that what they really needed was a lads weekend away. After some initial excitement, where they exchanged 'beer' emojis and reminisced about the last lads weekend (Famine polished off the entire contents of an all-you-can-eat buffet and the other diners mysteriously came down with salmonella when Pestilence showed up an hour late), the friends got down to some planning.

'Should we invite Pestilence?' asked Death.

'I'm not sharing a room with him. He has six showers a day and he still stinks!' said War.

'Okay, we'll get him his own room,' said Famine. 'Where does everyone want to go?'

The group went silent while everyone thought about it.

'I've done a lot of travelling this year,' said Death, gloomily. 'I'm trying to think of somewhere I haven't been.'

'We could do one of those holidays where you learn to cook,' suggested Famine. 'Or get a cottage by the beach and have picnics every day. Or stay in a fancy hotel with a posh menu or...'

'FFS Famine, this is a lads weekend! We want to drink beer and snog women and do lad stuff, not ponce about making fucking scones,' cried War. The others didn't disagree. They were a little

bit intimidated by War. As War's mum never tired of saying, 'He'd start a fight in an empty room, that one.'

There was a ping and Pestilence joined the group chat.

'Alright lads, where are we going? (beer emoji, beer emoji, eggplant, water drops, taco)'

'Jeez, Pestilence. How did you know we were going away?' asked Death.

'Ah, there's no flies on me, mate,' laughed Pestilence. 'I'd just popped out to do a bit of work in a crowded area when the messages started pinging on my phone. Saw what you said there, War. It's fine. I wouldn't want to share a room with me either. I'm actually grateful for all this social distancing and hand washing - the complaints have halved.'

'How about Newcastle upon Tyne?' suggested War. 'Canny night out, I hear. We can do a trip to Hadrian's Wall. It'll be just like old times.'

War's eyes misted over, as he remembered the glory days of battling the Scots. My, they bred them tough up there. And the weather was shocking! His mum had been forever darning his cloak and warning him, 'You'll catch a chill, you know.' It was almost a relief when Antoninus Pius took over. Once the Antonine Wall was up, War went back to Rome and spent a few lazy years hanging around the Colosseum. His mum stopped going on about chills and started sending him heavenly messengers bearing sun tan oil and notes reminding him to cover up in the afternoons. Ah, good times.

'We're not starting any fights with Scotland,' warned Pestilence. 'But you can buy a replica Roman sword in the gift shop, provided you promise to keep it in the hotel room. If I see that sword appear on any nights out then I'll hide my dirty socks in your bed.'

'What about a nice scythe?' suggested Death. 'It's a bit less stabby and you can cut your mum's grass with it.'

There was general agreement that Newcastle would be a great place for a lads weekend. Famine immediately went onto Trip Advisor to check out the places to eat and Pestilence googled 'best hospitals newcastle 2020 uk'. Death annoyed everyone by repeatedly saying, 'Scythe,' in a Geordie accent. The friends were excited because they'd never managed to get all four of them out and about together at the same time before. They were absolutely sure that this was a good omen - a sign of great times to come.

'Right, that's the hotel booked, lads,' said Famine. 'Nice place near the river. Good restaurants for me, bar fights for War, creepy room in the basement for Death and a short canter to the nearest hospital for Pestilence. Perfect.'

'What about the horses?' asked Death.

'What about them? Ah, right...' War was usually the one charging ahead with the plans, but he paused for a moment as it dawned on him that they'd need someone to look after the horses.

He texted his mum. 'Hi mum. Missing you loads. You are the best mum ever. Any chance you could look after the horses next weekend? (smiley face with love heart eyes emoji)'

Mrs War immediately texted back. 'Sorry. Your dad and I are going to the Famines for dinner on Friday then we have a spa break booked in the Cotswolds.'

'Bad news, lads,' said War, miserably. 'Mum can't have the horses. Does anyone else know someone who could have them?'

'I'd ask my dad but he said they were having another couple over for dinner on Friday and would have to spend the rest of the weekend repairing the house and calming down the local community,' said Famine.

'What about your sister Disease?' War asked Pestilence.

'Nah, mate. She's filling in for me so I can get the weekend off. Bit of a cheek to ask her to do the horses as well.'

'How about you lads go and I'll stay behind with the horses?' offered Death. 'If you see any nice cloaks, maybe you could bring one back? I'm still wearing the one I got during the French Revolution and, quite frankly, it's seen better days. Look for one with a zip. Every time I try to do the buttons up on my old one, I drop my bloody scythe and it's carnage.'

'Awww, maaaate,' sighed Famine, disappointed that yet again they hadn't managed to get the four of them out together. 'You're normally the life and soul of the party. We can't go without you! Why don't we have a lads night in instead? I could do us some snacks. If War's mum and dad are away then we could stay there. Maybe Disease could get her friend Sicknessa to come over. Make a party of it. Pestilence, do you remember those demons we met during the Spanish Inquisition?'

'Mortina and Demise? Yeah, they'd be up for it.'

'Sounds like a plan,' said War, only a little disappointed not to get his replica Roman sword.

The group chat went silent for a moment while they thought about it.

Then...

'Partay! Girls! (beer emoji, face in party hat blowing party tooter emoji).'

And that, ladies and gentlemen, is why the apocalypse didn't happen.

Now we reach the end of five of the weirdest months that many of us have ever experienced. Some of you may still be in the throes of lockdown when you read this. Who knows what the months ahead have in store for us all. Another wave? An effective vaccine? A second book of posts from Covid Corner? Whatever happens, we do know that somehow, despite the removal of statues, we still have history. It is clinging on. Even better, some of us know a bit more history because recent events made us listen and learn. I suspect that 2020 will also go down in the history books. It has been a time where we have seen the best that humanity has to offer and the worst. The best being the incredible selflessness of our medical staff, carers and key workers and the worst being…I was going to give an example of the worst but I will leave you to decide. We each have our personal experiences or opinions and really, when all is said and done, it is the best of us who matter.

I am so thankful to have Mr V and the Cherubs. I am incredibly grateful to the people who checked in on me now and then, just to make sure I hadn't gone stir-crazy. I am truly inspired by all the lovely blog readers who made me laugh with their comments every day. I am extremely proud of my work colleagues, who kept on trucking no matter what. We are blessed by the people around us.

I have deliberately avoided mentioning all the deaths because the numbers are so huge and so sad. It seemed disrespectful, amidst my fluffy ramblings, to speak about the people who are no longer with us. My heart truly goes out to those who lost their lives, to the families who couldn't visit their loved ones in care homes and hospitals, and to the people who couldn't attend funerals. So many small comforts were stolen from you at the end.

Lessons will no doubt be learned. Already we are looking back and asking what we could have done differently. Ultimately, I hope that in the future humanity will reflect on our little slice of history and say that it changed things for the better.

THE END

Made in the USA
Monee, IL
06 June 2022

97563172R00180